There was noth

Nothing disturbed t[...]
Her relief lasted onl[...]
begin to beat again. [...] her to
draw another wheezing breath.

Directly behind her, the water exploded with the
sound of something big breaking the surface. Two
arms, their muscles like cables, wrapped around
her body, locking hers to her sides.

'Stop it, damn it,' a voice grated in her ear.

Her head, the only part of her upper body she
could freely move, thrashed from side to side, as
she twisted her torso. Neither had an effect on
the man holding her captive. Desperate, she
kicked backwards, trying to drive her heels into
his shins. The water defeated her, making those
frantic blows puny.

'Stop it,' he demanded again, shaking her hard
enough that her head snapped back against the
wall of his chest.

'You're going to drown us both.'

Dear Reader,

Welcome to Intrigue!

Starting us off is a new suspense-filled mini-series called MORIAH'S LANDING, a place where evil lurks but love conquers all. Amanda Stevens brings us *Secret Sanctuary* and look out for *Howling in the Darkness* by BJ Daniels in December 2002.

Bestselling author Gayle Wilson is on top form with *Secrets in Silence,* when an old murder case is re-opened with devastating consequences, and do look out for more from Gayle later next year.

Debra Webb continues her COLBY AGENCY stories with a dangerous investigation in *Solitary Soldier*, and there'll be more from the COLBY AGENCY next year, too.

Of course, we have our regular LAWMAN LOVERS story as well, *In His Safekeeping*, which is brought to us by Shawna Delacorte.

Have a great, safe Bonfire Night!

The Editors

Secrets in Silence

GAYLE WILSON

SILHOUETTE®
INTRIGUE™

First published in Great Britain 2002
Silhouette Books, Eton House, 18-24 Paradise Road,
Richmond, Surrey TW9 1SR

© Mona Gay Thomas 2001

ISBN 0 373 04891 2

46-1102

Printed and bound in Spain
by Litografia Rosés S.A., Barcelona

GAYLE WILSON

RITA Award winner for Romantic Suspense and five-time RITA Award finalist Gayle Wilson has written twenty-six novels for Silhouette. A former English and world history teacher to gifted students, she writes contemporary romantic suspense and historical fiction. She has won numerous awards.

Gayle lives in Alabama, where she was born, with her husband of thirty-three years and an ever-growing menagerie of beloved pets. She has one son, who is also a teacher of gifted students. Gayle loves to hear from readers. Write to her at PO Box 3277, Hueytown, AL 35023, USA.

For the faculty, staff, students and alumni
of The Altamont School,
a model for excellence in education

PROLOGUE

SHE ALMOST MISSED IT. Her eyes had begun to burn, her vision blurring with exhaustion. Her fingers had already found the edge of the photograph, ready to assign it to the stack of those she had examined, when something caught her eye. Something seemed slightly out of place. Something...

Her gaze never leaving the photograph, she reached out, groping on her desk for the magnifying glass. She held it above the image, leaning over for a closer look. As she did, her hair fell forward. Impatiently, using the spread fingers of her left hand, she combed through it, lifting it out of her eyes as she focused the glass over the section that had attracted her attention.

She held it there, transfixed, until her hand began to tremble. She laid the magnifier down carefully, afraid she might drop it. Her pulse thundered in her ears, beating loudly enough that everything else faded away. Everything except the photograph and the small, curving red line that disappeared under the fall of blond hair.

She lifted her head, closing her eyes and massaging them with the tips of her fingers. This was too important to be mistaken about. She had to be absolutely certain that what she was seeing was truly what she had been looking for all these months. As she did, she realized with a jolt of nausea how close a thing this had been. If she hadn't stretched her budget to hire the researcher who had sent her the material lying before her, she would never have seen it.

She took a breath, concentrating on slowing her heart rate and steadying her hands. She was almost afraid to look at the photograph again in case she had been wrong, but of course, there was only one way to be sure.

She removed her fingers and slowly opened her eyes. They fell again to the picture in front of her. The round eye of the magnifying glass was resting on the exact spot she had studied before. Exactly over the curving stem of a small red rose a murderer had drawn on the nape of his victim's neck almost ten years ago.

She took another breath, fighting a surge of elation this time. *The beginning of the end,* she thought. No matter the outcome of the quest she had begun more than eight months ago, at least one of the questions that had haunted her life had now been answered.

Even in the midst of this victory, she realized there was no one she could share it with. No one who would feel this same sharp rush of vindication. They were all gone. All the people to whom this might once have made a difference.

She was the only one left. *The only survivor.* It was up to her to speak for all of them.

Her eyes fell again to the photograph. Another child. Another little girl, her hair so blond it was almost white.

Her fingers turned the pages, going back to the front of the file to find the name. The letters were bold, printed with a thick black marker, and they were very clear.

Katherine Delacroix.

Katherine. She had had a name. And she had had a life. Until he had taken it from her. Taken everything.

She opened the folder again, looking carefully at each of the photographs it contained. And this time, she really saw them. She saw the child they portrayed. At least what he had left of her. The broken, empty shell of another child he had destroyed.

Her eyes filled with tears. They were unexpected, because she never cried. She couldn't remember the last time she had been moved to tears. Or to an emotion strong enough to evoke them.

Katherine. And Mary.

For you, she promised them, her lips moving silently as in prayer. And the image in the photograph before her blurred again. *For you. And for all of us.*

CHAPTER ONE

HEAT WAVE. Callie Evers had heard the words all her life, of course. She wasn't sure she had ever really understood their significance until now. Until here.

When she had driven her car into Point Hope late this afternoon, heat had roiled upward from sun-stoked sidewalks and lain heavily beneath the branches of moss-draped oaks. Humidity thickened the air, so that drawing breath became a conscious act, and moisture gathered in body creases, dampening clothing and occasionally breaking free to slide slowly downward.

Just as the bead of sweat rolling between her breasts was now. Ensconced in a cushioned wicker chair on the back porch of the bed-and-breakfast where she had rented a room, however, she was decidedly cooler now than when she had first arrived.

The reality of the house where she was staying was a little less picturesque than the photographs on the Chamber of Commerce Web site, but it was near enough to the center of town for her purposes. And the screened-in porch did, as promised, overlook the tranquil waters of Mobile Bay.

Startled at the sudden bang of the screen door amid all this peacefulness, Callie looked up to find her hostess coming toward her across the porch. The old woman was juggling two glasses of iced tea and a couple of white linen napkins in her palsied hands.

Callie smiled her thanks, reaching up to take one of the glasses, its sides slick with condensation, before the contents ended up in her lap. She laid the napkin she was handed across her knees. Her hostess wrapped the other around the bottom of her own glass as she sank into the cushions of another chair.

"Land sakes," Phoebe Robinson said, "this late in the day, and it's *still* hot."

She lifted the tea to her lips, her hand trembling slightly. She took a long, greedy draught, ice tinkling in the near darkness of the screened-in porch. Then she pressed the glass against her cheek before she turned to smile at her guest.

"I expect you aren't used to this kind of heat. Or are you? I'm never too sure about my geography. Too many years since I was in school, I guess. Is Charlotte near the water?"

"No," Callie said, considering the panorama before her.

The dark bay had become a mirror of the twilight sky, the dying sun's crimsoned golds and yellows spread across it as if someone had spilled paint over the surface of the water. The eastern shore was famous for its sunsets, and this one lived up to the advance billing.

It was already night, however, under the trees that lined the shore, their black branches eerily silhouetted against the spectacle. And for the first time since she'd arrived in Point Hope, it seemed possible that something as brutal as Katherine Delacroix's murder might really have happened here.

"I expect it'll take you a few days to get acclimated," Phoebe said. "Give yourself plenty of time, dear. It's the humidity and not the heat that takes the toll, you know."

Callie lifted her own glass, using it to hide the smile provoked by that oft-repeated Southernism. The coolness of the sweetened tea was welcome against her tongue. She resisted the urge to mimic her hostess and press the glass against her face, allowing her eyes to focus again on the water instead.

The light was fading, and the colors that had dazzled only seconds before were disappearing from the darkening surface. There were already a few stars visible, and soon it would be impossible to determine where sky ended and the bay began.

In the stillness, she could hear the rhythmic lap of the

water. The comforting sound would make sleep easier to-night, despite her excitement. When she had made the deci-sion to come here, she had felt as if she were at the culmi-nation of a long journey rather than at the beginning of one. Now that she had arrived, however, her anticipation had be-gun to grow.

"Vacation?"

Lost in the relaxing, shore-lapped quietness and her own thoughts, she had almost forgotten her hostess. And the ques-tion seemed an intrusion. "I beg your pardon?"

"I asked if you're here on vacation?" Phoebe repeated. "We don't get many visitors this time of year. Fall's really the time for Point Hope. Fall's glorious," Phoebe said, the sound of the ice in her glass again whispering between them.

"Not a vacation, I'm afraid." Callie hesitated, but it would have to be said. "I'm here to work on a book."

"You're a writer? Anybody I've heard of?" Phoebe asked.

"Probably not," Callie admitted, amused by the bluntness. Phoebe wouldn't be familiar with her name. Not unless by some strange accident she had stumbled across the small weekly for which Callie wrote her column. Or unless she subscribed to one of the regional magazines to which Callie sold the local color pieces that kept her solvent.

"Is it a romance?" Phoebe asked hopefully. "Sally Tibbs at the library always saves the new ones for me. They do make me miss Hobart, though. And him dead more than twenty years."

Phoebe's laugh was surprisingly deep, considering her bird-like frame. Callie turned toward the sound, intending to share in the laughter with her own answering smile. Night had descended so rapidly with the setting of the sun that she could no longer see the old woman's features, only the move-ment of a pale arm lifting the glass of iced tea.

Maybe it was that companionable darkness. Or the interest she had heard in Phoebe's voice. Or maybe it was simply that she had to start somewhere, and so she said, "Actually, I'm writing a book about Katherine Delacroix's murder."

The words lay between them for several long heartbeats before Phoebe's voice, flattened, no longer filled with any hint of friendliness, came out of the darkness.

"Kay-Kay? You're here about Kay-Kay?"

"Did you know her, Mrs. Robinson?"

"Everybody knows everybody in Point Hope," the old woman said scornfully, as if that were something Callie should have realized. "I taught Kay-Kay in Sunday school. First Baptist Church. She was there that very Sunday. The one before…"

The words trailed, but Callie knew those that would have completed the thought. *The Sunday before someone murdered her.* The Sunday before someone took the life of a little girl who would never feel the humidity of a summer night gather between her breasts. Who would never read a novel. Who would never make love to a man.

"Would you tell me about her?" Callie asked. Despite her resolve, emotion had gathered in her throat, making her voice husky. And it seemed a long time before Phoebe answered.

"We don't like to talk about Kay-Kay. Or about the murder. There was enough talk when it happened to last us a lifetime."

"I know it's painful for those of you who knew her, but… She was one of you. Somebody who—"

The wicker chair creaked as the old lady stood, the abruptness of her movement cutting off Callie's argument.

"We don't like to talk about it," Phoebe said again.

"Believe me, I understand," Callie assured her. "But a little girl died. And people have a right to know why."

"A right to know *who,*" Phoebe said, the words an accusation. "That's all you're interested in. You and everybody else are only interested in the who."

"Of course," Callie said. *Of course* that's what people were interested in. The identity of Katherine Delacroix's murderer was what they had been interested in for over ten years.

It was a question that had never been answered. Not fully

enough to lead to an indictment, much less a conviction. And it looked now as if it never would be, not unless someone outside this small, elite Southern conclave took a hand.

"Tom Delacroix's dead. Best to let it alone," Phoebe said.

"Do *you* think he did it?"

"It doesn't matter what I think. It doesn't matter what anyone *thinks*," Phoebe said. Her voice rose sharply on the last.

"It matters if he didn't," Callie reminded her. Because if Delacroix *hadn't* killed his daughter, if he hadn't been the one who had strangled that little girl—

"Ben Stanton," the old woman said.

Her voice came from across the width of the porch, and Callie realized only then that Phoebe had already moved to the door that led into the house. She was standing beside it, an indistinct, almost ghostly shape in the darkness.

"Ben Stanton?" Callie questioned, although it was a name she was familiar with. Anyone with even a modicum of knowledge about the Delacroix case knew Stanton.

"If anybody knows…" The old woman's voice stopped, and Callie waited through the silence. "He knows *everything*," Phoebe said finally. "You talk to Ben Stanton if you want to know what all they found that day. Talk to Ben to get the straight of it."

Callie opened her mouth to ask for an introduction to the man who had been at the center of the decade-old investigation. The bang of the screen door put an end to that intent.

She could ask in the morning, she comforted herself. That would give Phoebe time to become accustomed to the idea that she was here about the Delacroix murder. And to the idea that no matter what the people of Point Hope wanted, the outside world wasn't ready to forget the little girl who had died that night.

A quiet, hot August night, which, from everything she had read, would have been very much like this one. Callie turned her eyes again to the water that stretched in front of her.

Ask Ben Stanton, Phoebe had advised. And after all, that was exactly what she had come all this way to do.

"GOING OUT, DEAR?"

As soon as Callie stepped off the last carpeted tread of the staircase and onto the polished hardwood of the front hall, Phoebe's voice floated out from the front parlor. Smiling at her hostess's timing, Callie walked over to its double doorway.

Phoebe and three other people were seated at a card table that had been set up in the center of the room. The drapes had been pulled across the windows to keep out heat generated by the morning sun, making the room unnaturally dim. It took a moment for Callie's eyes to adjust, and when they had, she realized the people at the table were Phoebe's contemporaries. And all of them were looking at her rather than at their cards.

"Come on in, dear, and let me introduce you," Phoebe urged.

Apparently the unease her hostess had felt over Callie's project had dissipated during the days she had lived in this house. Or perhaps Phoebe's innate good manners prevented her from treating a guest with anything other than that much-touted Southern hospitality. Obediently, Callie stepped out of the doorway and into the dimness of the room, smiling at the others gathered around the table.

The old woman seated opposite her hostess shared Phoebe's magnolia-petal complexion. Unlike Phoebe's, her hair had not been allowed to silver. It was almost henna, with one streak of white sweeping back from her forehead. Her drooping earlobes sported multicarat diamonds, and the long, patrician fingers of her hands, as pale as her face, were covered with rings. Green eyes studied Callie from behind bottle-thick glasses.

"Virginia Wilton," Phoebe said, gesturing toward her partner with the hand that didn't hold her cards.

"Tommy Burge," she continued, indicating the small, thin

man to her right. Burge was in shirtsleeves as a concession to the heat, his seersucker suit coat draped over the back of his chair.

"And this is Buck Dolan," Phoebe finished.

Dolan, obviously several years younger than the others, wore a knit golf shirt, open at the throat. His complexion bore evidence of years-long exposure to the Gulf Coast sun, the age spots on his forehead and cheeks marring what must once have been a classically handsome face. His hair was thick and dark enough to make Callie wonder if it were his own.

"This is Callie Evers, everyone. She's going to be staying with me for a couple of weeks."

It seemed Phoebe didn't intend to share the distressing news about *why* Callie was staying with her. Of course, since Callie had spent the last three days becoming familiar with the town and its landmarks, especially those involved in the murder, and given the efficiency of small town grapevines, she imagined these three already knew exactly why she was here.

"Nice to meet you," Virginia Wilton said. "Phoebe says you're from Charlotte. I went to school with an Evers girl from the Carolinas. Belinda Evers. You any kin?"

"I don't think so."

"Her daddy was a doctor. Or a lawyer, maybe. Professional man in any case. *Very* good family. If I remember correctly, and I think I do, his given name was Robert."

"I don't believe I know them," Callie said, fighting another smile at the blatant attempt to trace her antecedents. It was such an accepted form of interrogation here that Virginia's questions couldn't possibly be construed by any Southerner as rude. This was simply the way one greeted new acquaintances—by trying to fit them into the convenient framework of one's old.

"Vacationing?" Tommy Burge asked.

Burge's expression seemed interested. He didn't look as if he were preparing to pretend to be horrified by her answer.

"No such luck," Callie said. "Actually, I'm working."

She was aware peripherally that Phoebe's thin body had straightened in her chair, almost as if she were trying to send her a signal. If these people were Phoebe's friends, however, they might have as long and as intimate an acquaintance with this area and its inhabitants as her hostess. Their insights about the people involved in the Delacroix case would be invaluable.

"Don't let us keep you, dear," Phoebe said.

"Working on what?"

There were all shades and gradations of accents in the South, but the cadence of Buck Dolan's speech was subtly different from the others at the table.

"The Katherine Delacroix case," she said.

At the words, there was a visible change in their postures. Almost a physical shrinking away, as if she had uttered a profanity in church.

"Callie's doing research for a book on Kay-Kay," Phoebe said too brightly.

Despite the danger of revealing the contents of her hand, she was fanning herself with her cards. Her other fist was pressed against her breastbone, the skin on the back stretched so tightly over the misshapen knuckles that it had whitened.

"Really?" Burge said. "I thought people had finally lost interest in that."

"I don't think they'll lose interest until the case is solved," Callie said.

"So you anticipate we shall be forced to endure unpleasant media attention in perpetuity."

Callie's eyes considered Dolan, whose tone had been far less polite than the others. "Does that mean you don't believe it *will* be solved, Mr. Dolan?"

"Not in our lifetimes. They made too big a mess of the thing from the start."

"They?"

"Don't mind Buck," Virginia said. "He never liked Ben

Stanton. He thinks Ben should have been able to prove his case, and instead…'' She shrugged.

"You think the police mishandled the investigation," Callie said.

"I think the police never should have *attempted* to investigate. What kind of credentials did Stanton have that made him think he was qualified to investigate a homicide? A stint in the CID doesn't prepare one to deal with a murder. It was all right for him to play cop when all he had to do was write the occasional speeding ticket, but solving a homicide was beyond his skills. Way beyond.''

"He called in the F-B-I." The initials were separate, precisely pronounced, Phoebe's accent making at least one of them multisyllabic. "You know that, Buck.''

"After it was too late," Dolan retorted.

"I always liked Ben," Virginia offered. "Nicest young man you'd ever want to meet. Leastways up until the murder.''

The murder. This was one of the few places in modern civilization where you could refer to a ten-year-old homicide as "the murder" and be certain everyone understood what you meant.

None of what they had said was new to Callie. Nor did it offer any substantive information about the crime. At least they were talking, and their initial hostility to what she was doing seemed to be fading.

She had known that the region's inherent interest in all things past would work to her advantage. As would its focus on people, that unfailing Southern emphasis on family and neighbors. The Delacroix had been "neighbors" to everybody in this town and probably related to half of them.

Besides, when you got right down to it, their daughter's death had been the most exciting thing that had ever happened in Point Hope, Alabama. These people could disavow interest in that murder all they wanted. It was still there, clearly revealed in their faces and their arguments.

And that, too, was to her advantage. *Everybody knows ev-*

erybody, Phoebe had said. Secrets and human failings were common knowledge. Who was sleeping with whom. Whose child wasn't really his child. And whose behavior on Sunday morning was in direct contrast to his or her behavior on Saturday night.

"Stupid," Buck said dismissively. "Stanton should never have put himself in that position. He should have had sense enough to realize he was in over his head from the start."

"Didn't nobody *know* what was going on at the start," Tommy Burge said reasonably. "You wouldn't have either, Buck. You can't expect the police to be mind readers."

"Not mind readers," Virginia said. "You mean those people that can see into the future. Prognosticators. That's what you mean, Tommy. He couldn't be a prognosticator."

"He could have been a cop," Buck said. "A good cop looks at a scene like that and smells the wrongness of it. He didn't."

Ben Stanton had been called out that morning to find a child who had supposedly wandered out of her home while her father slept. According to most accounts, he had had no reason at the beginning to doubt what he'd been told. The back door was unlocked—from the inside—and there was no sign in the house itself of foul play.

"Were you in law enforcement, Mr. Dolan?" Callie asked. "You sound as if you might have some expertise."

Phoebe's laugh, the full, unexpected one, rang out. Dolan's eyes reacted by narrowing as they moved to her face. He doesn't like her, Callie thought, but the intensity of the look lasted only a second or two. When he shifted the focus of his still-narrowed gaze to her, she wasn't sure which of them he disliked.

"I was never a cop, Ms. Evers, but I'm also not a fool. I read a lot of true crime. I know what the police are supposed to do. And in this case, they did everything *but.*"

"You go talk to Ben," Virginia advised her. "None of us were in Ben Stanton's shoes that morning, so we don't know what we would have done. You don't either, Buck, so hush."

"Hindsight's always twenty-twenty," Tommy Burge agreed.

"Bullshit," Dolan said. "Any good cop—"

"You watch your mouth, Buck Dolan," Phoebe scolded. "You know I don't allow that kind of language in my house. Especially not with a young lady present."

Callie again controlled the urge to smile, thinking about the vocabulary used in the newsroom and by most of her friends.

"She's heard worse," Buck said, echoing her own thoughts.

"Not in my front parlor she hasn't. And she won't," Phoebe said firmly. "Now you hush about Ben. You'll have her thinking we're a bunch of ignorant rednecks. That isn't the way you want Point Hope portrayed in that book she's writing, is it?"

That had obviously been a warning, and Callie could only hope it wouldn't cut off the flow of information.

"It wouldn't be the first time," Burge said. "Didn't any of us come out smelling like roses from that thing."

"I'm sure that Callie—it was Callie, wasn't it?—doesn't have that agenda," Virginia said, without waiting for an answer.

"Just exactly what is your *agenda?*" Buck asked sarcastically, those faded blue eyes again locked on her face.

"To expose a murderer," Callie said. "I would think that would be what everybody here wants."

There was no response. The silence stretched, becoming uncomfortable enough that finally she broke it by adding, "Maybe we can all talk more later on. I'd really like to interview as many people as I can who were living here at the time."

"We play Rook every Tuesday and Friday," Virginia said, seeming relieved that the conversation had moved away from the word *murderer.* "We play at Phoebe's 'cause she doesn't drive anymore. Most days Doc stops by. Just for the company. Doc doesn't play cards. Never did, that I can remember.''

"Doc?" Callie questioned.

"Doctor Everett Cooley. I expect you'll want to talk to him, too. He was the coroner back then. He'd have been here today except he had to go into Mobile.''

"Driving Ida Sullivan to her ophthalmologist appointment.'' Phoebe supplied the information with a tinge of censure in her voice. "I told Everett when he called last night that he was letting that woman take advantage of him.''

Callie wondered, given her tone, if Phoebe might be jealous.

"Doc lets *everybody* take advantage of him," Virginia said. "Lord knows he's done enough for you and me, Phoebe, that we shouldn't complain about him helping poor Ida out.''

"I'm not complaining about *that*," Phoebe said indignantly. "I just hate to see folks run him ragged," Phoebe said, turning back to Callie to explain. "Everett's supposed to be retired.''

"I can't tell he's cut back on his hours much," Burge added. "Only doctor you'll find who still makes house calls.''

"Thank goodness," Virginia said emphatically, moving one of the cards in her hand into another position.

There was another small, almost awkward silence.

"Well, don't let us keep you any longer, dear," Phoebe urged finally. "I'm sure that whatever you write, you'll be fair. After all, the people here didn't have anything to do with…what happened. We all got tarred with it just the same. You go talk to Ben. He can tell you more than any of us can. More than anyone else in town, for that matter.''

"I intended to see Chief Stanton," Callie said. "This morning, as a matter of fact. Could someone give me directions?''

Dolan's vulgarity was muttered under his breath this time. Still, it was enough to draw another chiding look from his hostess. And it was Tommy Burge who answered Callie's question.

"Get back on the main road and follow the signs that lead toward Mullet Inlet. Stanton's got a place down on the water. Anybody can direct you once you get there. Or stop at Galloway's Grocery and ask directions. Less chance of getting lost."

"Thanks," she said, allowing her gaze to move around the small table and touch on each of them individually.

The collective attention, however, had clearly shifted back to the game. She had been handled, neatly and efficiently, and sent off to interview the man who had borne the burden of that unsolved murder for the past ten years. And judging by the reaction of these Point Hope inhabitants to her questions, she could imagine how excited Ben Stanton was going to be to have her show up on his doorstep.

CHAPTER TWO

WHEN SHE REACHED the end of the dirt road, overhung with more of the drooping Spanish moss that attached itself to almost every tree in the area, Callie realized Stanton's "place on the water" was nothing like she'd been imagining. And nothing like the old-moneyed, shabby-genteel atmosphere the rest of this community exuded.

The first thing that drew her eye was the pickup parked next to the house. Its color was so faded from years of exposure to sun and salt air that it was almost indistinguishable, especially under the layer of grime that overlay the finish. The house itself, built of cedar which had weathered to a muted silver, was little more than a cabin.

Behind it, the requisite pier projected far out into the water. At its end was a wooden boat shed, open on three sides and equally weathered. The boat inside had, at least in her uninformed estimation, probably cost more than the rest put together. And in contrast to everything else, it appeared to be both new and well maintained.

Callie took a breath, gathering control—or courage—before she opened the door of her car. As soon as she did, the heat, temporarily forgotten in the cocoon of the vehicle's efficient air-conditioning, assaulted her with a nearly physical force.

She stepped out, easing the door closed rather than slamming it. She didn't intend to give Stanton more warning than was necessary. She stood beside the car a moment, listening. There was a low background hum of insects from the surrounding vegetation. And nothing else. No sound of a tele-

vision or radio drifting out from inside the cabin. No sign of
its inhabitant.

If not for the presence of the boat and the truck, she might
have gotten back into her car, willing to talk herself into
believing Stanton wasn't home. Unless he had walked somewhere in this heat, however, it was obvious he must be inside.

She slung the strap of her purse over her shoulder, feeling
the reassuring weight of her tape recorder inside. She resisted
the impulse to turn it on. Honor among thieves, perhaps, but
she wanted to play fair. If he refused to talk to her...

Suddenly, the hair on the back of her neck began to lift.
She couldn't remember having experienced that sensation before, but she had read enough about it to know what was
happening. The feeling that she was being watched was so
intense that she looked up, her gaze fastening on the dark
rectangle of the cabin's screen door. She could see nothing
beyond it, certainly not enough to tell if someone were standing there.

Given the thickness of the palmetto and other scrub growing around the clearing in which the house was centered, the
eyes she felt might be hidden anywhere. They might not even
be human.

At that thought, there was a discernible check in her forward progress. She had to force herself to walk on toward
the cabin, despite the strength of those physiological responses.

Never let them see you sweat. She gave in to the smile the
phrase provoked, relieved to have something else to think
about. Besides, whatever Stanton's response to her visit
might be—

"That's far enough."

Again her eyes focused on the screen door. There was no
question the voice had come from behind it. Because of his
position, the advantage was all his. He could see her clearly,
yet he was as effectively hidden as if he really had been
standing somewhere in those thick woods.

"Mr. Stanton?"

"Who are you and what do you want?"

"My name is Callie Evers. I'd like to talk to you."

There was a silence, long enough that she was again aware of the buzz of the insects. "About what?" he asked finally.

There was something in the tone, a habitual wariness perhaps, that said he knew why she was here. She wouldn't be the first stranger to have approached Ben Stanton in the last decade. His radar was probably well tuned to curiosity seekers by now.

"About Katherine Delacroix."

As she answered, she crossed the remaining few feet until she was standing at the bottom of the low steps that led up to the porch. Unlike most of its counterparts in the region, this one didn't display a stick of furniture or anything green and flowering. Obviously, it wasn't intended to be welcoming.

"Then you're wasting your time," Stanton said.

"I have plenty to waste."

"I don't."

Deliberately, she allowed her gaze to move around the clearing, over the pickup that looked like it hadn't been washed in months and the encroaching vegetation. When her eyes returned to the screen door, she was smiling openly.

"I can see how *busy* the upkeep on your place keeps you, Mr. Stanton," she said, infusing that same feigned amusement into her tone, "so I promise I won't take up much of your valuable time."

"You won't take up any of it," he said, his voice colder than before. "Whatever you're looking for about the Delacroix case, you won't find any answers here."

"I thought you were the expert."

"You thought wrong."

"You handled the investigation."

"Don't you mean 'botched' the investigation?" There was a hint of mockery in the question.

"Did you?" she asked, wishing now that she had ignored her scruples and turned on the recorder.

"Get off my property."

Anger had replaced the mockery she had heard before.

"If it *wasn't* botched, then why won't you talk to me about it? Wouldn't you like to set the record straight?"

"I won't talk to you because you're a ghoul, Ms. Evers. And I don't like ghouls."

"You don't know anything about me. *Or* about my reasons for being here."

"If you want to talk about Katherine Delacroix, then you're a ghoul. She's been dead and buried for ten years. I'm not about to help you dig her up."

"Would you help me find her murderer?" The silence stretched, broken only by the low hum from the woods around them.

"Get off my property," Stanton said again, his voice flat, all emotion, certainly all humor, gone.

"Because I've read everything about this case I could get my hands on," Callie went on, ignoring the repeated demand.

"That only reinforces my original opinion of you."

"And I've come to the conclusion that Tom Delacroix couldn't have had anything to do with his daughter's death," Callie continued doggedly. If she couldn't charm Stanton into it, maybe she could shock him into talking to her. "What I think is that in your single-minded determination to convict somebody—*anybody*—for that murder, you ruined the life of an innocent man. And because you were so sure Delacroix was guilty, you let the real murderer get away with that… atrocity."

The screen door exploded outward so suddenly her throat closed in surprise, causing her to swallow the last syllable of the word she had settled on to describe the murder of Katherine Delacroix. And just as Stanton's "place on the water" had been nothing like her expectations, the man himself was totally different from the mental image she had brought to this meeting.

There had been plenty of photographs of Ben Stanton in the material she'd studied. She had studied them with an attention to detail which, she had finally admitted to herself, couldn't be credited solely to her interest in the case.

In most of them, he'd been wearing that neatly creased uniform, black utility belt fastened around narrow hips. Blue eyes had squinted into the strong coastal sun or were hidden behind mirrored sunglasses. Hair ruffled by the perpetual breeze off the bay, Stanton had appeared to be the picture of efficiency and dedication to duty. And none of those impressions fit with the reality of the man who had just stormed out of that door.

He wore nothing now but a pair of jeans, faded until they were almost gray. The waistband rode low on his hips, which were as lean as she remembered them. His chest, so brown it looked as if it had been carved from mahogany, was broader and more muscled that it had appeared under those crisply laundered uniform shirts. His feet were bare and they were as darkly tanned as the rest of his body. Even his hair was different. Longer than he had worn then, its ebony was streaked at the temples with silver.

And his eyes were no longer hidden. When hers lifted to meet them after that unthinking inventory, they were filled with fury, piercingly blue and incredibly cold.

"What the hell gives you the right—" he began, his voice taut with the force of his contempt.

"He signed his work," she said.

The angry rush of Stanton's words halted. His eyes, which had been narrowed in anger, widened. Even the pupils dilated, nearly destroying the rim of blue that surrounded them. Her heart leaped in response.

"Maybe you didn't know what that mark was or what it meant," she went on, forcing her voice to remain steady, her sentences measured and sure. "But you saw it. You *had* to have seen it. *Somebody* had to have seen it."

She hadn't intended to play her trump card so soon, but then she hadn't expected to be afraid of him, either. The force of Stanton's hostility had been palpable. And maybe this was better than drawing it out. Better than slowly revealing what

she knew, bit by bit, as she'd planned. After all, the strength
of his reaction had already confirmed that she was right.

And now she had his full and complete attention. Ben
Stanton was literally hanging on her every word, the fury in
that ice-blue glare stunned into something very different.

"He drew a rose," she said, laying out for him what had
brought her here. "It was on the back of her neck, hidden
under her hairline."

Stanton said nothing, but his eyes had narrowed again.
And they were locked on her face.

"It was there, wasn't it?" she demanded.

Just as she had known from the initial shock in his eyes,
she also knew from his silence that she was right. And the
power of that affirmation roared through her body.

"It was drawn with a marker." Her excitement made the
words flow faster now, tumbling over one another. "Or
maybe just in ink. Red ink. But it *was* there, wasn't it, Chief
Stanton."

"Get off my property," Stanton said. He hadn't moved.
He stood on the edge of the porch, his eyes still too revealing.

"I know it was. It had to be. Because whoever killed Kay-
Kay did the same thing at least once before," Callie said,
and watched in satisfaction as his face changed again, the
tight, hard line of his jaw softening in shock. "Sixteen years
before he put that mark on Katherine Delacroix, he did exactly the same thing to another little girl. Or don't you want
to hear about her?" she taunted. "Are you afraid that if you
do, you'll finally have to admit you were wrong?"

THANK GOD he had recovered enough to convince Callie
Evers he wasn't going to talk to her, Ben thought, wielding
a mop over decking that had been spotless before he'd begun.

Physical activity always cleared his head, allowing him to
think more clearly, maybe by rushing blood to his brain. God
knows he had needed that rush when Evers mentioned the
rose. He had literally been light-headed with shock. And then

he had been furious he'd let her catch him off guard. He still was.

That she knew about the drawing on the back of Katherine Delacroix's neck had stunned him, leaving him groping for some response other than "Get off my property."

Eventually he had said that often enough that it had had the desired effect. She'd gone, giving him a chance to fight in private the ghosts she'd revived. Ghosts he had, up until this morning, believed he'd exorcised.

"Damn you," he breathed. Struggling for calmness, he walked over to the bucket he was using to wring out his mop.

There was no way around it. She had done a number on him. At the remembrance of how well she'd succeeded, his hands twisted the cotton strands viciously, using them as a substitute target for his fury, most of it self-directed.

While he worked, he'd finally been able to fit what she'd said into some plausible scenario. Callie Evers, whoever the hell she was, had to have been given that highly privileged information. And she had tried to use it to get him to spill his guts, breaking his decade-long silence about Katherine Delacroix's death. It was the only explanation that made sense.

And he was going to have the hide of the person who had been responsible for that leak, Ben decided, shoving the head of the mop back into the bucket.

THE CURRENT CHIEF of Point Hope's two-man police department was leaning back, booted feet up on his desk, when Ben slammed through the door of his office. That relaxed atmosphere quickly dissipated as Ben launched into his tirade.

"What the hell were you thinking telling the Evers woman about that drawing?"

Doak Withers' feet had come off the desk as Ben came through the door. As he listened to the accusation, his body straightened in his chair. Finally he stood and, leaning across the desk, pushed his nose within millimeters of Ben's, close enough that there had been a momentary danger they might collide.

"Screw you, Ben," he said.

"That *doesn't* answer my question," Ben said, ignoring the display of anger.

His own fury had continued to build on the way into town. He couldn't see any other way that woman could have found out about the rose, except from his former deputy.

"You *know* I wouldn't give out information like that," Doak said. "I ain't told nobody about the mark on that kid's neck, and I'm not likely to at this late date. If I did, it sure as hell wouldn't be some frigging female reporter.

"She'd already been out to your place when she came by here. She told me she'd talked to you. Told me she was writing a book about Kay-Kay. Not that that was a surprise. I've had half the town on the phone the last couple of days complaining about it."

"So what *did* you tell her?"

"Not a damn thing. I figured whatever you wanted her to know, *you'd* have told her. I didn't tell her anything, and that's the God's truth. I sure as hell didn't say nothing about the rose."

"Then who did?" Ben demanded.

He straightened, lifting the heels of his hands from the scarred top of the desk that had once been his, while allowing the tips of his fingers to maintain contact with its surface.

"How would I know?" Doak asked, his beefy face still flushed in spite of the fact that he, too, had straightened, mimicking Ben's action and putting them in a less adversarial position. "What makes you think *anybody* told her?"

"Because—" Ben stopped, his mind supplying an answer he didn't want to think about. If no one in this office had leaked the secret they had kept for more than ten years, then...

Then he would have to face the possibility that the other thing Callie Evers had said might be true. And that was something he wasn't ready to consider.

"Because there's no way she could have known about it otherwise," he finished, his logic pointing out the way, even as he mouthed those empty words.

He heard the huff of breath Doak released, his lips and cheeks fluttering slightly as he expelled it. "All I'm telling you is it didn't come from me," Withers said, his voice calmer.

"Simmons?"

"You think I'd tell Billy something confidential?" Doak asked scornfully. "You know better than that, too."

"There isn't anybody else."

"You put it into VICAP," Doak reminded him.

The national database maintained by the FBI held information about violent, unsolved crimes. Despite what Ben had believed about the identity of the murderer from the beginning of his investigation, he had checked the rose, as well as the other bizarre elements of Katherine Delacroix's murder, against what was already on file there. It had been done simply as a matter of course. A matter of doing his job.

According to the Bureau, there had been no match. There was no other murder on file with the same components as the Delacroix case. So whatever Callie Evers was claiming, Ben knew there hadn't been another unsolved child murder like this one.

That didn't explain how she had learned about that rose. And in order to put all this behind him again, if he ever could, that was something he needed to know.

"It's a closed system," he said, working his way through the possibilities, even as he explained why VICAP wasn't one. "No one gets in to see what's already there. We just provided the info on Kay-Kay's murder. It was checked against other unsolved cases. And in order for Evers to have someone do that..." He hesitated, trying to think if there were another way.

Doak filled in the pause. "To have someone do that, she'd have to already know about the drawing."

The silence grew, as Ben again rejected the other possibility—the one Callie Evers had suggested—as unthinkable.

"You want me to check the case file?" Doak asked, introducing a spark of hope into Ben's growing despair. "Make sure everything's still there. Verify it's not been tampered with?"

"You got some reason to think it might have been?"

The Delacroix file had always been kept locked in the office safe. In the beginning there had been too much media frenzy to chance anyone from outside the department getting their hands on what it contained—especially after the autopsy photographs had been stolen. That was something else that had been blamed on Ben Stanton's inexperience with a high-profile case.

And rightly so, he acknowledged bitterly. He had had no idea then the depths to which the tabloid scum-suckers would stoop. The theft of those pictures had been a wake-up call. One that had come too late.

"Nothing but what you're saying," Doak said, moving toward the old-fashioned safe, its gold script faded with age.

Ben watched as Withers worked the combination, which, he noted, hadn't changed in the years since he'd been gone. Nor had the brown accordion file in which the investigative reports were kept. Just the sight of it, even after all this time, made him sick at his stomach.

All the feelings from those endless days of frustration and resentment came flooding back. Frustration that he couldn't prove what he knew in his heart. Resentment that, despite the fact he had done everything he knew to do, despite the long, sleepless days and nights he had spent on this investigation, it was always going to be his failure. His shame.

A little girl had died, and her murderer walked free. And it had happened in his town. On his watch.

"Seal's intact," Doak said, bringing his attention back to the folder.

"Break it," Ben ordered.

Withers' eyes held on his, perhaps questioning the authority behind that order. They had worked together too long and too intimately, however, to let the fact that their positions were now reversed interfere with the natural chain of command.

Doak's thumbnail slid along the seal, splitting the gummed paper into two parts. He made no move to open the folder, simply holding it in his oversized hands. Surprised, Ben looked up in time to watch his former deputy swallow, the movement visible all along the thick, sun-browned column of his throat.

"Opening this seems like... Hell, I don't know. Like some kind of desecration," Doak said, his eyes still on the file.

Exactly what he had accused Callie Evers of, Ben thought. Of digging up a child's murder to satisfy the unnatural hunger of the same people who had snapped up every copy of the tabloids that had carried those grisly photographs.

Was he any different? He had placed a seal on the contents of this folder eight years ago because he hadn't been able to do anything else with what it contained.

This was material he knew by heart. Every picture. Every comment. Every shred of evidence. None of it had gotten him anywhere. And he had always known that no matter what was in there, it could never bring Kay-Kay back to life.

"The desecration's going to be if anybody gets wind that we held that information back," he said. "We're going to be front and center again in every tabloid in this country."

Doak's eyes lifted, holding on his a long moment. Then his ex-deputy walked over to the desk. Tilting the accordion file so that the open edge of it slanted downward, he allowed the contents to spill out onto its surface.

"Help yourself," Point Hope's current police chief said. Then Withers laid the empty folder on top of his in-box and crossed the room to stand before the window that looked out on the main street of town.

Ben's gaze followed, briefly considering, as Doak seemed to be, the scene that lay beyond the tinted glass. There was no traffic. And no pedestrians. Everyone would be inside, either to avoid the heat or to eat their midday meal.

There was literally nothing out there to watch, so it was obvious what Withers was doing. If Ben wanted to paw through this stuff again, Doak felt he had the right. But he wasn't going to hand Ben a shovel and point him toward the grave.

Reluctantly he began to sift through the stack. When he came to the autopsy photographs, bound by a rubber band, bile crawled upward, burning his throat. He didn't look at them. If he ever wanted to view those images again, they would all be there, perfectly intact and terrifyingly vivid, in his subconscious. And in his nightmares.

He swallowed, forcing the nausea down, as he continued to methodically plow through the rest. He forced himself to compare what was here to the original list of the folder's contents, which he himself had composed.

This would all be on computer nowadays. They hadn't been that sophisticated back then, at least not in Point Hope, so he had kept hard copies of every report that had been generated by the Delacroix investigation. And he had kept his own notes, which were here as well. Just where they should be.

They included the drawing he'd made of that small red rose. He could still remember pushing aside the strands of hair that had been plastered against the fragile nape of Kay-Kay's neck that morning, exposing the tiny red bud.

There wasn't a shot of it among the autopsy photographs. Doc Cooley, who had been acting coroner at the time of the murder, had never seen it. The soft blond hair had dried by the time Doc made his examination, obscuring the flower.

And that had been another mistake. Ben had assumed Doc would see it. By the time he'd opened the folder containing the autopsy photographs and realized there wasn't one of the rose, the Delacroix had buried their daughter. At that point, they weren't about to allow the authorities, and especially not the Point Hope Police Department, to exhume her body.

So there was no way, Ben thought again, his fingers tracing slowly over the faded drawing. No way Callie Evers could have known about this. Not unless she was telling the truth. He moved his head in slow negation, swallowing to force down his building nausea.

''Something missing?'' Doak asked.

He turned and found his former deputy watching him. The light from the window behind Withers provided a halo effect around his bulk.

''Not a thing,'' Ben admitted.

Nothing he had put into this envelope eight years ago was missing. Nothing except the absolute certainty he'd had when he sealed it that he knew who had killed Kay-Kay Delacroix. And that was the only thing he couldn't afford to have lost.

CHAPTER THREE

"I THINK I'LL SIT out here a few minutes longer," Callie said to her hostess. "If that's all right with you."

The peace of Phoebe's screened porch had been more than welcome. As had the glass of homemade scuppernong wine she'd been given. The lap of the water and the alcohol soothed nerves left raw by her encounters with Ben Stanton and Doak Withers.

She was already dreading the same song, second verse aspect of tomorrow's interviews. There were others she needed to talk to who had been as intimately involved in the murder as Stanton. And if they all reacted with the same hostility—

"You do just exactly as you please, dear," Phoebe said. "You don't have to get permission from me. You treat this like you would your mother's house. Or your grandmother's. I imagine I might be *almost* old enough to be that."

Apparently Phoebe had forgiven Callie's reasons for coming here. Or if she hadn't been forgiven, she had at least been accepted. Maybe that was nothing more than the usual Southern tolerance for an eccentric, granted routinely to writers.

"I thought I might walk down to the water. If you think it's safe."

"Safe?" Phoebe repeated, sounding amused. "Honey, you can walk anywhere you want to in this town. Any time of the day or night. We haven't had a crime since—"

Since someone murdered a little girl.

"In a long time," Phoebe finished, producing words quickly to fill in that telltale hesitation. "Point Hope isn't like New Orleans or Birmingham or those other places you read about.''

"I didn't want to bother your neighbors," Callie explained.

A row of more than a dozen houses, including Phoebe's, all built very close together, backed up to the bay. Between them and the narrow beach ran a dirt path, shaded with oaks and overgrown magnolias, which gave the neighbors easy access to one another's backdoors.

"I was afraid I might disturb someone's dogs or something. Cause an uproar," Callie added.

"We're all too old to have dogs. Outlived them. I wouldn't mind having a good watchdog, mind you. Let me know when somebody's coming. Give me a little warning so I can hide my clutter from my friends and the booze from the preacher," Phoebe said, her deep laugh ringing out in the nighttime stillness.

"You walk anywhere down there you want," she continued. "Along the path or down any of the piers. You can even walk on the beach. Just don't go too far out into the water. It's dangerous to swim alone, especially at night."

"Don't have to worry about that," Callie assured her. She wasn't that good a swimmer, and because of that, she had never been overly confident about the water.

"Well, good night, then," Phoebe said. "Sleep tight and don't let the bedbugs bite."

"You better not have any bedbugs, Phoebe. If you do, they'll take away your license," Callie teased.

"You know, I don't even know what bedbugs are," the old woman said. "That's just something I said when I put my boys to bed. I guess 'cause Daddy always said it to all of us."

"I didn't know you had children."

Callie couldn't remember seeing any family photographs around. Perhaps since Phoebe had opened her home to paying guests, those had been moved into her private rooms.

"Two boys. One of them was killed in Vietnam. Just

twenty-one. Had his whole life ahead of him.'' The voice in the darkness had lost all trace of its customary good humor.

''I'm so sorry, Phoebe. I didn't mean to stir up—''

''Oh, honey, that was a long time ago,'' the old woman said, dismissing her attempt to apologize.

''And your other son?''

The bang of the screen door drowned the last word of her question. Even in the short time she had spent as Phoebe's guest, Callie had discovered her hostess was a little hard of hearing. Or maybe, she thought, Phoebe's hearing was selective. Maybe she just avoided subjects that were apt to be painful, as her son's death obviously was.

Ghosts, she thought. So many ghosts.

Maybe that was simply the ambiance from the mysterious moss-draped oaks and old houses. Or the proximity to that dark water. The long history of the area, which stretched back to the Spanish exploration of the New World.

There was no doubt that Katherine Delacroix's small spirit was by far the most famous. And the image of Ben Stanton's face when she had told him about Mary's murder played over and over in her head as she finished her wine.

The last strands of color from the sunset had long ago faded from the sky, and with the overhanging rain roof, the porch had grown very dark. The night was clear and inviting, despite the fact that there was only a sliver of the new moon.

Phoebe's soft-soled lace-ups had made no sound on the wooden boards of the porch, but as Callie crossed them, the heels of her sandals echoed. The hinges of the screen door squealed when she pushed it open, evidence of the corrosiveness of the salt air.

The walk leading to the path was distinct, stretching between the overgrown foliage of what had obviously been, at one time, a well-kept back garden. Judging by the potted impatiens and geraniums on all her porches, Phoebe had a green thumb. The lawn and the shrubs were undoubtedly too much for her now. And the cost of having someone else tend to them probably a factor in her inability to keep their rampant growth controlled.

The breeze off the bay brushed Callie's face as she neared the water, carrying a tinge of brine and fish. Then suddenly, overriding those smells, was the stench of decay.

Something must have washed up on the narrow strip of sand between the bulkhead and the water. In this heat, it wouldn't take long for any organic flotsam to become unpleasant. Unpleasant enough to force her to turn back? she wondered.

As soon as the thought formed, the stench disappeared, replaced again by the not unpleasant smell of the water. She raised her face, nostrils distended, to breathe it in. The wind dislodged a strand of hair, which fluttered over her eyes.

She lifted her hand to push it away, but before she could complete the motion, her wrist was encircled by hard, masculine fingers. She jerked her forearm forward, pulling against their grip. She half turned, the movement stopped by the unnatural position in which Ben Stanton was holding her arm, behind and above her head.

"Aren't you afraid to be out here with a murderer running loose?"

"Let me go," she said evenly.

Obediently, those callused fingers unfurled, freeing her. She turned to face him, resisting the urge to rub at the place they'd gripped. It wasn't painful, but there was a lingering echo of their controlling force, which she didn't like. She felt like one of those gothic heroines who scrubbed at their lips after having been kissed by the villain.

Except this wasn't a villain, despite the fact that he had been accused of being that and almost everything else. And he hadn't kissed her. Judging by the coldness of his tone, that would be the last thing on Ben Stanton's mind right now.

At the realization of what must have brought him here, her heart began to race, beating so strongly it crowded her chest. She worked at mastering her breathing, determined not to let it be audible in the stillness.

"If I were afraid, I would never have come here." After all, if he followed the pattern, the man who had killed Kay-Kay was long gone from Point Hope. "Besides," she added, "I'm sure Chief Withers and his deputy are out on patrol. Making the world safe for democracy." The chief of police's refusal to talk to her still rankled.

"You like easy targets," Stanton said.

She shook her head, the movement small. She didn't understand what he meant, although his remark was obviously in response to hers. *Easy targets.* Withers? Southerners?

"The 'boys' in blue," he said. "The butt of all the jokes."

"Tan."

She was relieved to find her voice was steady, despite her excitement. Ben Stanton had come to talk to her, as unbelievable as that seemed after their confrontation this morning.

At her one-word response, his eyes narrowed. In this light she couldn't distinguish their color. Nor could she tell whether they were as cold as they had been earlier.

At least he was wearing clothes. She had discovered there are few things more intimidating than an angry, half-naked man.

"You wore tan, not blue," she said, wondering even as she did why she was explaining. What could it possibly matter?

"Am I supposed to be flattered you noticed?"

"I told you. I know everything there is to know about this case." *Including what you found on the back of Katherine Delacroix's neck.*

She didn't say that, but it was implied. And maybe the impact was stronger because she hadn't said it again.

"If you're going to make an accusation like the one you made this morning," Stanton said, "you damn well better have some evidence to back it up."

She was relieved they weren't going to play cat and mouse. She suspected Stanton was better at that than she could ever be.

"I can show you," she offered.

She held her breath as she waited for his response. This was all she had hoped for. A chance to find out what Stanton knew. To combine it with what she knew. And maybe then—

"Show me what?"

"My material's inside. In my room. I think Phoebe's already gone to bed, so maybe we shouldn't—"

"Your virtue's safe with me, Ms. Evers." He sounded amused.

"I didn't mean that," she said stiffly.

His comment hadn't been sexually charged, but for some reason she felt her throat flush. Embarrassed that Stanton might think she was playing at that particular kind of coyness?

It doesn't matter what he thinks, she told herself, praying the darkness would hide that rush of color. *Nothing* mattered, not as long as he told her what she needed to know. And so she turned, leading the way back up the path.

"THAT COULD BE anything," Ben said, pleased with the tone. Dismissive, despite the nausea in the bottom of his stomach.

"Except you and I *know* what it is," Callie Evers said. "It's part of the stem of a rose. Just like the one he drew on his other victim."

At that quiet certainty, he looked up from the autopsy photograph she'd laid on the walnut secretary in her bedroom and straight into her eyes. They were gray-green, like the sea when you're far enough out to escape the shoals and bars. The color fit with her skin, which was almost Celtic in its fairness, heightened now by a subtle bloom of color along her cheekbones.

Nervousness or conviction? he wondered.

"I don't *know* anything, Ms. Evers, except what I hear you saying. So far you haven't shown me any proof. Not even that this other crime you keep talking about happened."

"Hawkins Bluff, North Carolina," she said.

The words were low, but her voice had been filled with

expectation, as if that was supposed to mean something to him. And it didn't. It didn't mean a damn thing.

"You're telling me a child was killed in North Carolina twenty-six years ago *exactly* like this?" he demanded, tapping his index finger on the photograph.

He didn't look at it again. He didn't need to. It was one he had examined a couple of hundred times—just as he had all the others—searching them for something he might have missed. Something that would allow him to put an end to the nightmares that had haunted his sleep for almost an entire year after he'd discovered Kay-Kay's body.

That was something he had never found. Something he wasn't going to find here tonight.

"Not…exactly like this," she admitted. "Maybe that's why no one ever made the connection before. That and the fact that you didn't reveal everything about the Delacroix murder."

"Any cop who reveals everything he knows about an unsolved homicide is a fool. Whatever else you think about me, Ms. Evers, I'm *not* a fool. Tell Lorena this isn't going to work. Tell her it's time to quit wasting her money."

There was a small silence.

"You think…*Mrs. Delacroix* sent me here?"

The touch of incredulity was nicely played, Ben acknowledged. Of course, Lorena had the money to hire the best. That had always been part of the problem.

"Or maybe I'm supposed to believe you just enjoy examining autopsy pictures of dead children with a magnifying glass."

He could tell by her eyes that he was right. She'd never have been able to see that small curved line if she *hadn't* been studying the photo under magnification. Only the tail end of the stem was exposed, the line barely visible to the naked eye, even if you were looking for it. It couldn't have been identified as part of a drawing without the use of a glass.

Which was moot, he supposed, since he had never admit-

ted there had been a drawing on Kay-Kay's neck. He wasn't
going to. Not to her.

"I told you," she said. "I was looking for something like
that. And I found it, just where the other one was."

"The other one?"

"The other rose. The other murder."

"In…North Carolina, was it?" The sarcasm was deliberate. If it had any impact, she hid it well.

"That's right."

"Give me year and day."

"In exchange for what?"

"In exchange for jack shit. You're the one who's trying
to sell this cock-and-bull story."

"And *you're* the one who's trying to convince himself he
couldn't possibly have been wrong," she countered, matching his mockery. "If you want that information, you're going
to have to reciprocate with some of your own. Like a public
admission that you found the drawing of a rose on Katherine
Delacroix's neck."

He straightened, pushing his weight off the small secretary
with enough force to rock it. She took an involuntary step
back, her lips parting in surprise or in fear.

He had read that emotion in her eyes when he'd thrown
open the screen door this morning and headed toward her
across the porch. He had sensed it again tonight when he had
grabbed her arm in the darkness. Of course, that had been
deliberate, calculated to shock. He had wanted to throw her
off balance to see how she'd react, and up until this moment
she hadn't let him rattle her. He'd been impressed by how
well she'd handled herself. Now, however, her anxiety was
clear.

*Way to go, Stanton. You're doing a great job scaring the
bejesus out of a woman,* he jeered silently, still watching her
eyes. Reading in them the ongoing struggle to reassert control
and to hide that telltale surge of anxiety.

"I'm not providing you with *anything*," he reiterated.
"Whatever you think you've found in that picture, I wasn't

wrong about Tom Delacroix. And you can tell Lorena that as long as there's breath in my body, I'll continue to say her husband was a murdering son of a bitch who strangled his own daughter to keep her from crying out while he raped her.''

The impact of that brutal description was reflected briefly in Callie Evers' eyes. This time she didn't shrink away. Not from them or from his anger. Instead, she took the single step that would bring her back to the desk and touched the picture she had placed there.

''Then how do you explain the similarity between the two murders?'' she asked. ''How do you explain that other rose?''

''As far as I know, it doesn't exist. Unless, of course, you have some *proof.*''

If she had, she would have put the two pictures on the table together. That's the way you did something like this. You laid everything out at the beginning if you wanted to force the person you were questioning to examine it and admit the implications. She hadn't. She had shown him only what he had already known.

''I can assure you the case is well-documented.''

The flush of color had increased along her cheekbones. And he didn't think it was conviction this time.

''We're through here, Ms. Evers. I might have listened to you if you could have shown me—''

''July 9th, 1975. And in case you don't know where Tom Delacroix was on that date, I'll tell you. He was in the middle of a court-ordered alcohol abuse rehab. Under lock and key.''

There had been one of those, Ben knew, although he wasn't sure of the dates. A six-month sentence, which should have been much longer considering the multiple D.U.I.'s, the last of which had involved leaving the scene of an accident. It would have been longer if it hadn't been for his father's money and position.

''*Proof,*'' Ben said, the word very soft and yet demanding.

''The courthouse burned. The records of the murder—''

He reached out and shoved the photograph that lay be-tween them toward her. The picture sailed over the edge of the fold-down desktop. He didn't even watch it. He watched her instead.

Her eyes followed the photo as it floated to the floor. Only when it landed did they come back up to his.

"It *was* in the papers," she said calmly.

"Police reports, autopsy report, autopsy photographs," Ben enumerated. "You have *any* of those?"

"I told you. The courthouse where those records were stored burned in the early eighties."

"That's too bad," he said. "Or it's *really* convenient. I guess that depends on your point of view, doesn't it?"

"I have the clippings."

"Affidavits?"

She nodded. "From the reporter. He says the sheriff—"

"You have an affidavit from him? From the sheriff?"

The pause was too long, so that again he knew what her answer would be before she gave it.

"He's dead. I talked to his widow, who remembered him mentioning the rose. And the reporter—"

"Either one of those people claim to have seen this rose you're so excited about?"

"No," she said, her voice low.

"And that's your case?" he mocked. He hardened his voice. "You got *nothing,* Ms. Evers. Believe me, I wish you did."

She laughed, the sound harsh enough that its bitterness surprised him. "No, you don't. That's your worst nightmare. The thought that somebody might prove you were wrong. You hung your reputation on Tom Delacroix's guilt. You blamed the Delacroix's money and influence for your failure to solve a little girl's murder. You can't stand to even *con-sider* the possibility that you might have screwed up."

Maybe it wasn't his worst nightmare, but it was damned close. *Too damned close.*

He held her eyes, saying nothing. They weren't nose-to-nose as he had been with Doak, but they were close enough that he could see flecks of brown in the gray-green irises of her eyes.

And just as he had characterized the nature of the police chief's anger as mostly bluster, he acknowledged that hers was not. Whatever she had come here for, whether Lorena had anything to do with it or not, Callie Evers believed what she had just said.

"You don't know anything about my worst nightmare, Ms. Evers. For your sake, I'll pray you never have to find out."

Without another word, he turned and left the room, walking through Phoebe Robinson's darkened house as if he had lived here all his life. He didn't remember to take another breath until he was outside, in the familiar heat of a summer night.

He closed the front door behind him and allowed his body to sag against it. Then he closed his eyes, which were burning. He rubbed at them with the heels of both hands. When he realized what he was doing, he forced his hands away, pressing his palms flat on the door behind him. Finally, pushing against it he straightened, moving upright in stages like an old man.

As he started up the path to his truck, the smell of something foul drifted up to him from the water. His steps didn't slow, the odor slipping virtually unnoticed into the unwanted images that were bombarding his consciousness.

They would linger there all night, tormenting him. Just as they had ten years before.

CHAPTER FOUR

"CALLIE? WAKE UP, DEAR."

Her name, accompanied by Phoebe's genteel pounding on the door, pulled her out of the pit of exhausted, dreamless sleep she had finally fallen into. She opened her eyes, expecting to find daylight seeping in from behind the curtains she'd pulled over the windows of her room after Ben Stanton had left last night.

It was pitch dark instead. Her eyes sought the lighted numerals of the bedside clock, as her hostess knocked again.

"Wake up, dear," the disembodied voice from behind the door called. "You don't want to miss this."

Since she had just discovered it was 3:20 a.m., Callie decided that whatever Phoebe was talking about, she was perfectly willing to miss it. She closed her eyes, trying unsuccessfully to slip back into sleep. Lying in the darkness, she slowly became aware of a dull throbbing at her temples.

And she knew why it was there. Not only had she examined the photograph after Stanton left, even pulling out her maligned magnifying glass to do so, she had spent the following hours tossing and turning. Endlessly analyzing what she thought she had seen in that picture, as well as every word the ex-chief of police had said. Desperately trying to convince herself that, despite Stanton's denial, she hadn't been wrong.

"Callie, honey?"

She opened her eyes, focusing them on the ceiling above her head. She didn't answer, hoping that if she ignored Phoebe long enough, she'd give up and go away.

"You really need to get up, Callie. It's a jubilee."

Jubilee? The only meaning her sleep-deprived brain could assign to the term came from a hymn her grandmother had sung to her when she was a little girl. Something about Judgment Day.

The half-remembered reference to the end of the world and Phoebe's urgency were spur enough that she pushed up, propping on her elbow to consider the bedroom door. She felt disoriented, both from the lack of sleep and the too-abrupt awakening.

Her lips had parted, her mind trying to formulate an answer to a summons she didn't understand, when the door opened a crack. As she watched, the old woman's face, topped by its stock of disordered white hair, appeared within it.

"Oh, good," Phoebe said. "You're awake."

"What's wrong?" She considered possible disasters, ranging from fire to an approaching hurricane, that might require her hostess to wake her at this time of the morning.

"Nothing's wrong. It's a jubilee. Tommy called to tell me, and I didn't want you to miss it. I'll go get you my waders."

The face in the crack disappeared, although light from the hall continued to pour through it. Callie closed her mouth, feeling as if she must have come in on the middle of something.

She glanced again at the clock, just to make sure it really said what she'd thought. There was no mistake, and by now she was awake enough to know that she wasn't dreaming, as much as she might wish she were. Obviously, something was happening Phoebe felt she should see. Or that she would *want* to see. Something that involved water, if "waders" meant what she thought they did.

And suddenly, emerging from some dark recess in the back of her mind, an item she had run across while doing research on this area swam upward in her consciousness. Her writer's instincts had apparently filed it away for future reference. *Jubilee.*

"Here you go," Phoebe said, pushing the door open.

Despite the heat, the old lady was wearing a chenille wrapper over her nightgown, and she was carrying a pair of long rubber boots, one in each hand. Callie identified them immediately. *Waders.* At least she hadn't been wrong about that.

"What are those for?" she asked, although she was afraid she knew. She sat up, running her fingers through her hair.

"I'd just feel better if you wear them. Some don't, but Hobart always did. He made the boys wear them, too."

"Phoebe, I really don't think—"

"Anything out in that ocean can come ashore during a jubilee," Phoebe went on, ignoring her aborted protest. "The good *and* the bad. This way," she said, holding the boots up shoulder high, "you got some protection from rays and such."

Rays? As in stingrays? If so…

"Come on, now," Phoebe urged again. "You don't want to take a chance on missing this. No guarantee there'll be another one while you're here."

As soon as Callie had figured out exactly what rays Phoebe was talking about, her mind began formulating a couple of very *good* reasons for missing it. Before she could voice them, another, more practical thought intruded.

She earned a major portion of her income by writing local color stories for publications that specialized in exactly this kind of regional phenomena. She was sure there had been articles about jubilees through the years, but she couldn't remember any recent ones. Not in the magazine that was the primary market for her features *and* which represented her biggest paychecks.

She had always intended to produce a few freelance pieces while she was in the area. This one was being handed to her on a silver platter. And she literally couldn't afford to pass it up.

She threw the sheet off her bare legs and stepped onto the floor. The worn hardwood was cool under her feet. Phoebe's eyes considered the length of thigh exposed by her little boy-leg pajamas before she pulled her gaze back up to Callie's face.

"And wear long pants," she advised, laying the waders across the footboard of the bed. "No telling what you'll run into. I'll be out on the back porch waiting for you."

No telling what you'll run into. Not the most enticing prospect she'd ever been offered. Money was money, however. She didn't have enough that she could pass up the opportunity.

As she pulled clothes out of the drawers of the old-fashioned highboy, she became aware of the sound of distant voices, their excitement clear. Despite Phoebe's unintentionally dire warnings, she could feel her own anticipation building.

As she dressed, she tried to dredge up what she could remember from the article she'd stumbled across. Not much, she realized, as she struggled into her jeans, sucking in her stomach to get the zipper up.

Jubilees were unique to the eastern shore of Mobile Bay. In spite of Phoebe's warning about "everything out there" rushing to the shore, they weren't fish kills. And that, she decided as she pulled a knit top over her head, was the extent of her knowledge.

There would be plenty of people willing to enlighten her about whatever was happening on the beach tonight. A lot more than would be willing to talk to her about the Delacroix case. Maybe she could use that to her advantage. Make some kind of inroads within the closemouthed local population.

She rummaged in the bottom of her closet, debating the best kind of footwear. She settled for a pair of worn sneakers. If they got ruined, it would be no great loss.

On her way to the door, she picked up the waders her hostess had draped over the footrail of the bed, holding them out to evaluate their size. They looked as if they would fit, which meant they hadn't been bought for Phoebe. They had probably been handed down, maybe from the father Phoebe was always talking about or from Hobart. Maybe even from one of her sons.

Callie slung the waders over her arm, their rubber feet bouncing against her thigh as she crossed the room to grab her camera off the table by the door.

Slipping its strap over her head, she took one last look around the bedroom. It felt as if she were forgetting something. Despite the nagging sensation, she couldn't think of anything else she could possibly need.

And since she wasn't planning on getting into the water, she realized she could leave the rubber boots here. Her arm had already begun the motion that would drop them on the table when she remembered she wasn't going out there to sightsee. It was possible she would need to become physically involved in the clamor she could hear in the distance.

Better safe than sorry, she decided. She'd take the waders and decide what to do with them when she got down to the bay.

IF THE POPULATION of Point Hope was almost a thousand, as she'd been told, at least a tenth of them were gathered on the strip of beach when she arrived. Someone had set portable lights up on the bulkhead and pointed them at the water. They illuminated the scene like a movie set.

She expected to find the bay churning with fish, fighting their way inland like whales trying to beach themselves. The shallows were filled with people instead, some in bathing suits and others in what appeared to be street clothes.

The containers they were using were as diverse as their attire, everything from nets to metal buckets to Styrofoam ice chests. Well beyond the area illuminated by the lights, a couple of skiffs patrolled, shadowy figures on board pulling up seine nets heavy enough that they were awkward to handle.

"First jubilee?"

Callie turned to find Tommy Burge, dressed in a dark polo-style shirt and khaki walking shorts, coming toward the beach from between the two houses behind her. He was carrying a long pole with a spike on the end in one hand and an open willow basket in the other.

She nodded, grateful to see a familiar face. "And I'm not sure what I'm supposed to do."

"Got a bucket of some kind?" he asked.

"I think I'd rather just take pictures of everyone else."

"Get out in the water beyond the lights and shoot back at them," Tommy advised, his eyes skating over the crowd.

She considered the people in the shallows, each of them intent on scooping up whatever was in the water. No one was paying attention to anyone else around them, which provided a great opportunity for some candid shots.

"Well, got to go," Tommy said taking a step toward the bay. "They never last long in August."

"Of course," she said. "You go on. I'll be fine. I may just watch from here."

Her eyes followed Burge as he jogged across the strip of coarse grass that separated the row of oaks from the water. She framed a couple of shots of the beach, realizing with the second that she couldn't manage the camera effectively and hold onto Phoebe's waders. She debated whether or not to put them on, but she was beginning to perspire. She could imagine how much hotter it would be with a layer of rubber covering her jeans.

She laid the boots on the ground, looking around at the surrounding landmarks to make sure she could find them again. Hands free except for the camera, she walked toward the bay.

Burge had been right, she realized when she reached the bulkhead. Since the beach was so narrow, she would have to be *in* the water to get the shots she needed. Not looking into those powerful lamps, as he had suggested, but taking advantage of them to light the scene. Maybe…to the side of the area that was the center of activity? she wondered, glancing in that direction.

Buck Dolan was sitting on the wall of pilings that formed the boundary between the land and the beach. He was smok-

ing a cigarette, holding it affectedly between his thumb and
finger. As she watched, he tilted his head, blowing a cloud
of smoke upward. Illuminated by the lights, it drifted toward
her.

"They're called floundering lights. Appropriate."

"Why appropriate?" she asked.

His profile, as classic as those on old Greek coins, was
silhouetted against the lights he was describing. She thought
again what a striking man he must have been, especially now
that darkness hid the effects of age and climate she'd noticed
before.

"Most of what's out there will be flounder. Plenty of crabs
and shrimp. Some cats. Eels. The occasional mullet or spec,
although the shrimpers have taken care of most of those."

The last part of that explanation meant nothing to her, but
she assumed from its context that he was still talking about
different species of fish. "Are they safe to eat?" she asked.

It was obvious they were, or these people wouldn't be out
here. She needed to ask him something, however, to keep
the conversation going. Dolan was a local resident, and he
seemed willing to tell her whatever she wanted to know about
this, even if he hadn't been willing to talk about the murder.

"They aren't sick. The oxygen in the water just gets too
low. Nobody knows why. Maybe rain or the heat or an influx
of fresh water from the rivers that empty into the bay. Whatever it is, it mostly affects the bottom dwellers. I've seen
flounder going for pennies a pound after a good jubilee."

"Fishermen can't be too happy with that," she said.

He turned his head, looking directly at her for the first
time. She wondered how clearly he could see her, considering
the placement of the lights.

"They'll take whatever they catch to the markets in Mobile, Gulf Shores, and Pensacola, and they'll make a *very*
good profit from just a couple of hours worth of work. You
won't hear any fishermen complaining about a jubilee."
Turning back to face the water, he took another drag, blowing
the smoke into the air.

"Are they shrimping out there?" she asked, nodding toward the distant boats. When she remembered that he probably couldn't see the gesture, she added. "The men in the boats, I mean."

"Shrimp and a little bit of everything else, I expect. Beggars can't be choosers."

There was a thread of amusement in the comment. As she watched, he threw the stub of his cigarette in a glowing arc toward the water. Her eyes followed it automatically, and she wondered for a second or two if it might hit one of the milling people. When no one reacted, it was apparent it hadn't, but the unthinking, or uncaring, gesture bothered her.

"You're not fishing?" she asked, bringing her eyes back to Dolan and trying to keep that reaction out of her voice.

"I'm an observer, Miss Evers. It is miss, isn't it?"

"It is," she agreed. "An observer?"

"Of my fellow man. It's a fascinating study."

"I can imagine," she said noncommittally.

She couldn't decide if Dolan were hinting that he could give her information about his fellow citizens. For some reason, despite her need for that, the suggestion made her uneasy, as encountering a tattletale in school might once have.

"Having any luck?" Dolan asked.

Despite what she'd been thinking, she wasn't sure if he were referring to her camera, the fish or her interest in the murder.

"With your book, I mean," he clarified.

"Some."

"I'm surprised. I thought people around here had just as soon forget that murder ever occurred."

"Why do you suppose that is?" she asked, injecting interest into her voice. Tattletale or not, this was why she was here. She might not like Buck Dolan, and she wasn't sure why she didn't, but he was a potential source of information.

"Fear," he said.

Fear? "Of what?" The interest this time was genuine.

"That all their dirty little secrets might get exposed."

"Are there dirty little secrets?"

"Dozens."

His voice was again amused, slightly cynical. Of course, what he said could only be the truth. Even in a town this small, there were bound to be things people didn't want exposed to the relentless glare of more publicity.

"Would any of those secrets make good stories?" she asked, wondering where he was going with this. Was there something he wanted to tell her? Was this his rather cryptic way of revealing information he thought she should know? Or was it something more personal. Something vindictive.

"A few. Isn't that what you're here for? To figure out which ones will and which ones won't?"

"I'm here because a little girl was murdered and the murderer was never punished," she said fighting to hide her distaste for what he was doing.

"Then I take it you don't buy into Stanton's theory?"

"Even if Delacroix did it, he was never punished," she said.

"Do you think he did?"

"That's what I'm here to find out," she evaded.

"Ever think about the consequences if he didn't?"

"I'm not sure I understand."

"The consequences of you stirring this all up again. Stanton let it drop years ago because he was convinced he knew who the murderer was and couldn't get him. However, if you succeed in proving that Delacroix didn't do it..."

He left the sentence hanging, but by now, she had figured out what he was doing. "Are you trying to warn me this could be dangerous?"

"I'm sure you were aware of that when you came. After all, there's no statute of limitations on murder."

"Then you believe the murderer is still alive?"

"I guess I'll have to read your book to find out, won't I?"

The amusement was back, along with a strong dose of sarcasm. Dolan stood, brushing sand off the back of his trousers.

"Well, this has been very pleasant," he said. "You have fun down there, you hear? Don't let the crabs get your toes."

Or the bedbugs bite. Everybody wanted to warn her against something.

"I won't," she said. "Maybe we can talk more later?"

"Of course. We'll all be at Phoebe's again next Tuesday."

The last was thrown over his shoulder as he headed up the slight rise toward the path that connected the old houses. Whatever message Buck Dolan had wanted to convey when he had spoken to her had been delivered.

She watched until she could no longer distinguish his shape in the shadows under the moss-draped oaks. And when she turned back toward the water, she realized that the people, still scooping fish into their containers, had drifted a few hundred feet further along the beach. A couple of men were moving the lights to that location.

Put up or shut up time, Callie thought, walking reluctantly down to the water. It looked as black as the night sky, and she could see nothing alive in it. The jubilee had moved past this stretch of beach, and if she were going to get any usable pictures, she would have to follow it.

A wave lapped over her shoes, soaking them and a couple of inches of the bottom of her jeans. The water wasn't cold, but it was cooler than the air around her. Surprisingly pleasant.

She glanced to her right, watching the crowd while Tommy Burge's words echoed in her mind. *They never last long in August.* She tried to pick him out, but she couldn't. Maybe he had already filled his basket and left.

His advice had been sound. The best shots would *be* from the water. And she was now off to the side of the activity, just where she'd decided she needed to be for her pictures.

Another wave washed over her feet, and steeling herself, she stepped into the bay, walking into the water as it retreated. She had anticipated that it might get deep fairly quickly, since everyone was staying close to shore. Instead, even though she waded farther out than any of the townspeople, it was only slightly above her knees. And still pleasant.

Maybe if there had been any of the things Phoebe had warned her about visible in the water, she might not have been so brave. Once she was away from that line of cream that formed when the waves touched the narrow beach, the water seemed as calm as a lake. As warm as bathwater.

She lifted her camera, sighting through it. She touched the button to activate the zoom. It was so quiet she could hear the small mechanical purr as the motor sent the lens out. She framed a shot and squeezed. And then another, this one of a mother helping her little boy scoop fish into a plastic sand bucket, its fluorescent yellow vivid in the glare of the lights.

Smiling, she moved back a couple of steps, trying for a wider angle. Someone shouted, and several of the people she had been focusing on straightened, pointing down the beach.

Curious, she lifted her head, looking up at them over the top of the camera. At that moment something hit the back of her knees hard enough that she staggered forward.

Ray? Or, my God, a shark. Could that have been a shark?

The thoughts flew through her brain as she floundered, arms windmilling to maintain her balance. She knew she had to stay out of the water where whatever had hit her was swimming.

By the time she had remembered there were people on the beach and that she could scream to attract their attention, a hand had closed over her mouth. It pulled her backward, trying to topple her into the dark water. She fought to escape, clawing at the fingers that were clamped over her mouth, even as she staggered back. She had time for one terrified breath before something swept her legs from under her and she was pulled down into the brackish darkness of the bay.

CHAPTER FIVE

FRANTIC, no longer a sentient creature, but something primitive and unthinking, she struggled against the hand which inexorably held her under. Fighting to get her face above the surface. Fighting to draw another breath.

She was propelled relentlessly backward, pulled into deeper water as her fingers tore at the forearm that was wrapped under her chin. Her assailant had obviously been prepared for her initial reaction because he had placed his other hand, palm down, on her forehead to make sure she couldn't get her head above the surface. No matter how much she fought, she couldn't escape that implacable hold.

Her world had shrunk to a formless void of black water. There was nothing but its airless environment and those controlling hands. Sheer animal terror and a will to survive she hadn't known she possessed made her keep struggling. She twisted and turned, clawing futilely at his arm as she was towed farther and farther away from shore.

Finally, deprived too long of oxygen, she felt her strength and resolve begin to fail. She couldn't hold her breath any longer. The instinct to fill her lungs with something, even if it were the deadly water that surrounded her, was too strong.

There was one last cogent second when she knew with absolute clarity she going to die. Even in the midst of the terrifying realization, she understood, on some level at least, that only a few hundred yards away people moved along the beach, heads down, eyes locked on the teeming waters of this same bay. Not one of them aware of the life-and-death struggle occurring in the moonless darkness behind them.

As the powerful hand on her brow held her under, consciousness began to fade. The mist formed first at the edges of her ability to think, blurring it. And then, moving with appalling suddenness, it spiraled inward, as if someone were turning a lens, closing the shutter of a camera.

Her body went limp. Her arms and legs, no longer capable of fighting, floated weightless in the water. She was no longer aware of its womb-like warmth. No longer capable of sensation.

Just before the last particle of light blinked out at the center of that collapsing vortex, the hand on her forehead and the arm around her throat suddenly released. His palms slipped beneath her shoulders, pushing upward with such force that her face broke the surface violently.

Either the shock of the blow or the abrupt change in position jerked her out of that apathetic surrender. Her first response was to draw breath, to pull life-giving oxygen into her starving lungs, which could then feed her dying brain. The second instinct, following within less than a heartbeat, was to expel the water she had inhaled. And those two vitally necessary acts were mutually exclusive.

Blind and deaf, she alternately gasped and choked and coughed. Water poured from her nose and gushed from her mouth in between the whooping, gagging breaths she drew. She flailed at the surface to keep afloat until she could reestablish the seemingly forgotten pattern of drawing air into her lungs.

Through the eternity that took, she never thought about where her attacker might be. All she was capable of at that moment was trying to restore an automatic, physiological process with which she had never before in her life had to be concerned. One which now seemed impossible.

Gradually—so gradually that she was almost unaware it was happening—she spewed forth the vileness she had swallowed and replaced it with gulps of air. The sound of them was so loud they echoed in her ears as her senses began to return.

She was alive. *She was alive.*

Then, just as that realization formed, hands grasped her shoulders again. Despite the numbing exhaustion which had, only seconds before, seemed overwhelming, panic gave her renewed strength. And a boundless determination. He would not pull her under again. She couldn't let him, because this time, weakened as she was, she knew she would die.

Screaming with rage, she raised her fists, beating at a face she couldn't see, flailing at it as wildly as she had at the water that had almost taken her life. In response the hands tightened painfully, digging into her flesh, even through the water-logged fabric of her knit shirt. Her assailant held her at arm's length, and still she struck out at him. And then suddenly, unexpectedly, the hard fingers released her.

Attempting to clear the water out of streaming, salt-seared eyes, she bobbed on the surface like a cork. Squinting first to the right, toward the blur of lights she knew represented the shore. Then to the left, blinking blindly at the void of sea and night sky. And then behind her.

There was nothing there. Nothing disturbed the tranquil water around her. Her relief lasted only long enough for her heart to begin to beat again. Long enough to allow her to draw another wheezing breath.

Directly behind her, the water exploded with the sound of something big breaking the surface. Two arms, their muscles like cables, wrapped around her body, locking hers to her sides.

"Stop it, damn it," a voice grated in her ear.

Her head, the only part of her upper body she could freely move, thrashed from side to side, as she twisted her torso. Neither had an effect on the man holding her captive. Desperate, she kicked backward, trying to drive her heels into his shins. The water defeated her, making those frantic blows puny.

"Stop it," he demanded again, shaking her hard enough that her head snapped back against the wall of his chest. "You're going to drown us both."

You're going to drown us both... The words were so illogical, given he was trying to kill her, that despite her terror, they reverberated in her brain. You're going to drown us both...

Stunned by the thought that he could believe she might not want to drown him or that he might not want to drown her, she stopped struggling. It was not a conscious decision so much as an admission that her reserves of strength were at an end. And if he really didn't intend to kill her...

"It's Stanton. I've got you. Now stop it," he ordered again. Unnecessarily, this time.

As soon as she ceased writhing, his arms loosened minutely, allowing her room to draw a breath. And another. They began to come faster, the harsh, jerking sound of them audible. Telling.

Not attempts to draw air into her lungs. She was sobbing because she had just realized she wasn't dead. And because she had finally decided that the man who was holding her from behind wasn't the one who had been trying to kill her.

Not a villain. She had thought that before, when he had grabbed her arm last night. She had known it on some instinctive level that was as primitive as the one which had forced her to struggle against whoever held her head under water.

She turned her body within Ben Stanton's embrace and wrapped her arms around his neck, clinging to him as if doing that were the most natural thing in the world. Her reaction caught him unprepared. For a fraction of a second, the powerful motion of his feet, kicking in the darkness below them, faltered.

They began to sink, slipping far enough into the water that its saline warmth trickled into her nostrils. Terrified again, she clutched Stanton tighter, attempting to climb him. Her legs wrapped around his and using the strong muscles of her thighs, she surged upward until her chin was above his shoulder.

He began to kick again, propelling them both above the

surface. His arms tightened around her once more. Not in anger this time, but in comfort. To offer reassurance.

"I've got you," he said, his deep voice infinitely soothing. "It's okay. Everything's going to be okay."

She nodded, her chin rubbing against the cotton shirt he wore. Her sobs had lessened, sounding now like the snubbing noises a baby makes when it has cried too long and too hard.

"You got her?" a voice called from behind them.

She refused to turn her head. She rested her cheek against Stanton's shoulder, feeling the rise and fall of his breathing. She could feel his heart, beating beneath her own. It was racing, not from fear as was hers, but because of his exertions.

"Get in closer," he called, "and I'll hand her up."

His hands fitted under her armpits, preparing to lift her up to the owner of the other voice. A man, she realized, in one of the boats she had noticed earlier. It was right beside them, swaying gently in the low swells.

Her face buried against Stanton's neck, she could hear the slap of the water against its side. She could also hear the questioning shouts from the people on the shore, probably in response to her screams. She ignored both, clinging like a limpet to the man holding her.

"You're going to have to help," Stanton said. There was a thread of impatience in his voice now, but it was still calm, still reassuring. "I'll lift you up as much as I can, but you're going to have to pull yourself over the side."

She wanted to refuse. She didn't want him to stop holding her. She didn't want to have to take her arms from around his neck. She didn't want to move, not even to get out of the water, which she now abhorred.

There was something about the authority in that demand, however, that reached the innermost part of her. The part that was still a child, terrified by the darkness.

You're going to have to go back to your own bed, her mother would say, taking her by the hand. No matter how much she cried and begged, each night it was the same. *You're going to have to go back to your own bed.*

This was that same reasonable tone. And despite her fear, it evoked the learned response. She turned her head to look over her shoulder. A man she had never seen before was leaning over the side of the skiff. She turned back, searching Stanton's face for reassurance.

In the darkness, his features were indistinct, but she could distinguish his eyes from the surrounding skin. She couldn't read the expression in them, but like her mother's voice, coming to her in the middle of a nightmare, she knew they would be determined. A determination too strong for her present weakness.

She nodded, and then she released her death-grip on his neck, turning toward the skiff that was as close to them as the moving water would allow.

There was nothing graceful or athletic about the process she employed to get out of the water and into the boat. Once she had made the decision to do what Stanton had told her she must, she moved with an eagerness that belied her physical exhaustion.

She scrambled upward, Stanton pushing her from behind, his hands impersonally under her buttocks. The man in the boat pulled her up, his hands underneath her arms.

In a matter of seconds, she was sitting on one of the boat's flat metal seats. Her feet rested on top of a mass of tangled nets, which still contained whatever they had borne out of the sea. Dragged from it, just as she had been.

The hull rocked violently as Stanton pulled himself onboard. She clutched the sides of the boat, knuckles whitened, frightened it would overturn and throw them back into the bay. The skiff gradually steadied, and by the time it had, Stanton was kneeling beside her, wrapping the dry warmth of the other man's shirt around her trembling shoulders. It was only then she realized that she had lost the camera during that desperate struggle.

"Get out too far?" he asked, trying to pull the edges of

the garment together, despite the fact that her fingers were still locked around the sides of the boat.

Stanton's gaze was level with hers, examining her face in the light of the flashlight the fisherman held. She couldn't imagine what he saw, but his eyes were both compassionate and concerned.

Relishing her safety, she didn't understand at first what he had asked her. *Get out too far?* Which implied...

"He tried to kill me," she said.

The blue eyes narrowed. "Tried to *kill* you?" The inflection had jumped at the end. "*Who* tried to kill you?"

Her teeth had begun to chatter. "A man," she managed through lips gone numb.

She wasn't sure how she could be so certain it had been a man, since she hadn't seen his face. The impression of his hands, their fingers incredibly powerful, was indelibly imprinted on her senses. It *had* been a man. Another woman wouldn't have been strong enough to control her frenzy.

"Who?" Stanton asked, as if he really expected she would be able to tell him.

He glanced up at his companion, who was still holding the flashlight. Her eyes followed automatically, and then she blinked, ducking her head against the intensity of its beam. She could see nothing of the face behind its glare.

"I don't know," she said. By now she was shaking so badly that the words came out as a stutter. "I couldn't see him. He held my head under."

Stanton's eyes had returned to hers, and he nodded as if that made sense. As if, thank God, he accepted the explanation. His next question ruined that surge of gratitude.

"You sure you didn't get tangled up with something?" he asked. "A lot of flotsam gets washed in with the tide."

Flotsam. The word brought back the stench of decay that had drifted up from the water's edge earlier tonight. Then it had been Stanton's hand, coming unexpectedly out of a similar darkness, that held her.

With that memory came the first splinter of suspicion. Ben

Stanton had been out in the water with her. And apparently neither he nor the other man in this boat was going to admit to seeing anyone else out there.

"He put his hand over my face," she said, the words coming in spurts. "He held my head under. It wasn't flotsam, damn it. Somebody tried to drown me."

She could hear the edge of hysteria in her tone. What had happened to her was bad enough, but not to be believed—

"I didn't see anybody else," Stanton said.

Maybe it wasn't meant to be the accusation it seemed, but she was beyond trying to read nuances.

"Murderers usually don't want to be *seen*," she said.

It didn't come off quite as she'd intended, but it was difficult to be sarcastic when you were shaking hard enough to make the words quaver. The gratitude she had felt when she'd realized Stanton wasn't her attacker, but her rescuer, had faded, replaced by anger and resentment.

"Okay," he said, his voice still calm and as authoritative as it had been in the water. "That makes sense. Charlie, let's go take a look," he suggested to the man holding the light.

Whoever Charlie was, he moved quickly to obey, heading toward the seat beside the outboard motor at the back of the boat. He took the flashlight with him.

No longer pinned by its light, Callie lowered her eyes, and forced her fingers to loosen their grip on the sides of the boat. She brought them together, entwining them in her lap instead. The blood rushed back into their flattened tips, stinging, but she welcomed the pain. Something to feel besides fear.

She was breathing in jerky, too-audible inhalations. She worked on deepening them, determined to control the sounds they made. Stanton hadn't moved, still crouching on the balls of his bare feet in front of her.

She jumped when Charlie started the engine, and he reached out, putting his hand over hers. It was big enough to cover both of them, and it was warm and hard, the palm and the fingers callused. *Unmistakably masculine.* Just as those that had touched her face had been.

"He had big hands," she said. "As big as yours."

"Okay," he said again.

He sounded interested. And still calm, despite what she was telling him. *Professional,* she realized. This was probably a tone he had perfected through countless interrogations. And then, perversely, she wondered how many suspects Stanton could possibly have interrogated in a place like this.

A place where someone just tried to kill me.

"I'm not making this up," she said defensively.

"I never said you were. That's why we're going back to take a look." His eyes considered the water as Charlie slowly guided the boat in circles, his flashlight moving in all directions.

In the stillness, Callie realized that the sound of the motor, loud enough to block the voices that had been coming from the beach, was familiar. She had been aware of its vibration before. While she was under water? Or while she had been absorbed by that paroxysm of coughing? Recently, in any case.

Which meant that Stanton couldn't possibly have been the one holding her under. She felt guilty, as well as stupid, for having allowed herself even to consider that it *could* have been him. Ben Stanton might despise the media, but he wasn't the kind of man who would try to kill to keep the story of Kay-Kay's death from coming under public scrutiny again. No one—

No one? The thought was unbelievable and then unbelievably logical. *No one but the real murderer could possibly care enough about that to commit murder. Another murder.*

"It was him," she said, the words only a breath.

Despite their softness, Stanton turned, his eyes questioning. She replayed in her head the chain of logic that had led her to that conclusion and found no fault in it. There was no one else who would feel anything more than annoyance and aggravation if she produced the book she claimed she was here to write. No one except the person who had the most to lose by having the investigation of the Delacroix murder reopened.

"Don't you see?" she asked Stanton. "This *proves* it."

Her teeth were no longer chattering as the heat of excitement raced through her veins. She wasn't dead, thanks to Stanton, and now she knew she was right. She had been right all along. She had just had it confirmed in a way that not even he could deny.

"Proves what?"

"That was Kay-Kay's murderer in the water," she said. "It had to be. And now you'll have to admit I was right. Because whoever that was out there tonight, it wasn't Tom Delacroix."

"WHY DON'T WE go through the sequence again."

"Land sakes, Doak," Phoebe said, her accent stronger for her exasperation. "Even *you* ought to have it letter-perfect by now."

Callie glanced up at that, but there was no reaction in the broad brown face of the police chief. Either he hadn't realized he'd just been insulted, or he was honoring another longstanding regional tradition. The elderly were allowed to speak their minds, no matter how rude or insulting their thoughts might be.

Callie was grateful for Phoebe's intervention. They were sitting in the front parlor of her house, and they had been over everything that had happened out in the bay at least a half dozen times.

After they had finished searching the water, Charlie had guided the skiff to the shore. Then, in front of all those gape-mouthed people, Ben Stanton had picked her up, without asking permission or announcing his intent, and waded through the shallows with her in his arms. As embarrassing as that had been, she had been infinitely grateful he hadn't suggested she step out of the boat and back into that black water.

As soon as they reached the house, Phoebe had taken charge, helping her strip off her wet clothing and bundling her, still shivering, back into her pajamas. Withers' arrival, announced by the doorbell, had interrupted them as Phoebe was rubbing Callie's hair dry between the ends of a thick towel.

The old woman had gone to answer it, leaving Callie to finish the task. When Phoebe returned, she had belted her own chenille bathrobe around Callie and then led her down to the room where the two men had been waiting.

Stanton hadn't changed clothes. The whole time Doak was asking his questions, he leaned against the wall of Phoebe's front parlor, the water that dripped from the bottom of his jeans forming small, gleaming puddles on the hardwood floor.

During the course of the interview, he hadn't said much, but Callie had been aware of his eyes intently focused on her face. Maybe because she hadn't made the accusation she had blurted out in the boat.

It wasn't that she doubted the conclusion she'd reached. She had finally realized, however, that broadcasting something like that might make whoever had tried to kill her tonight more determined to succeed the next time.

"...Ms. Evers, so I'm not sure what you want from me."

Jarred from her internal reverie by the sound of her name, Callie looked up. Three pairs of eyes were on her face. And the expression within each of them was subtly different.

"I'm sorry," she said. "I'm afraid...I didn't get all of that." She *was* sorry. Not paying attention to Withers was only going to prolong this. And she needed it to be over.

She needed time to think about what had happened. More important, she needed time to decide what to do about it.

"Nobody sees nothing," Doak said patiently, looking at the notebook where he had written down what she'd told him. "Ben says there was nobody else in the water when him and Charlie got to you. At least they couldn't see anybody. So..."

"So... What?" she asked. "So you think it didn't happen? Is that what you're implying? That I'm making this up?"

"Of course, he doesn't think that," Phoebe said loyally. "Tell her you don't think that, Doak."

There was a revealing delay in the affirmation she had demanded from Withers. He said instead, "I'm just wondering if you could maybe have been a little bit *mistaken* about what happened out there. About what you thought happened." He sounded almost apologetic, although it had been fairly obvious for a while this was the direction he was going to take.

"Flotsam," she said bitterly.

"Ma'am?"

"I suggested Ms. Evers might have gotten tangled up with some flotsam and panicked." Stanton's voice didn't seem apologetic, although it was impossible to tell from the inflection what he was thinking.

"Is that possible, ma'am?"

"No," Callie said, her eyes on Stanton's.

The moisture made his hair blue-black in the lamplight. The shirt she had laid her cheek against was a gray T-shirt that, because of its dampness, clung to his chest like a second skin.

"No," she said again, forcing her eyes back to Withers' earnest face. "It wasn't flotsam or jetsam or seaweed. Or anything else the two of you are going to suggest. It was a man's hands. He put one of them over my mouth so I couldn't scream, and he pulled me under. Then he shifted that same arm under my chin, so he could tow me out into deeper water. Classic lifeguard carry, except he also put his other hand on my forehead to keep my face under the water. Not flotsam. A man's hands. Believe me, I *know* what a man's hands feel like."

Again there was a small, awkward silence. She hadn't realized the sexual connotation of that unfortunate construction until it came out of her mouth. Ignoring it, she stood, still concentrating on the current chief of police. For some reason that was easier than having to face Ben Stanton.

"If we're through here…" she said.

That's what Stanton had said to her, she realized. And it sounded like dialogue from one of the lawyer shows on TV.

"Folks are pretty stirred up about this book you're writing. I'd guess somebody's emotions just got a little out of hand," Doak said. "I'd like to apologize to you on behalf of this community, Ms. Evers. This isn't typical of Point Hope. I can tell you that."

"Just somebody having a little fun at my expense? Is that what you're suggesting?"

"Somebody trying to discourage you from what you came here to do," Withers acknowledged.

Someone out to discourage her? Maybe it was comforting to him to believe that.

"If you think of anything else," he continued, sounding almost as professional as Stanton had on the boat, "anything that might help us get a handle on who could have done this—"

Withers had risen as well. She had told her story and answered his questions. And she had heard the theory he was probably going to use tomorrow to explain what had happened to those people who had watched her being pulled from the water and then carried ashore. She couldn't see any point in either of them beating this particular dead horse any longer.

"If I do, I'll call you," she finished for him.

She walked past him, heading for the hallway that led to the stairs. Behind her, she heard Phoebe's voice, her tone querulous, though the words were indistinguishable.

Maybe that was just as well. She really wasn't up to listening to anybody's theories about anything. Not even if Phoebe's were about the police chief's stupidity. It seemed there had been more than enough stupidity to go around tonight. Including hers.

She had come here to discover a murderer, someone who

had, to her certain knowledge, killed at least twice. And she had announced her intentions to the world. Then she had walked out into that water, never thinking about the possibility of danger.

Something important had come from tonight's fiasco, she told herself as she climbed the stairs. Because now she knew he was willing to kill again to keep a secret that was more than twenty-six years old.

CHAPTER SIX

"WHEN I HEARD what happened, I just had to come over and make sure you were all right."

Coffee mug suspended in midair, Callie turned her head and found Virginia Wilton standing outside Phoebe's back porch. Her hand was cupped along her forehead, and she was peering in through the screen, her glasses almost touching it.

By now, the whole town had probably heard what happened last night. She was surprised Virginia had been their only visitor. Of course, it was still early, a little after seven. *Give them time,* she thought, remembering the throng that had lined the beach, watching Ben Stanton carry her to shore.

"I'm fine," she said, completing the motion to bring the mug to her mouth.

Neither she nor Phoebe had tried to go back to bed after Stanton and the chief of police had left. Callie had known she wouldn't sleep. Even if she had, she would have dreamed about that endless struggle to breathe and the sensation of dark water rushing over her face as she was dragged farther and farther out.

The screen door creaked, announcing that her answer, not surprisingly, hadn't satisfied Virginia. Callie again turned her gaze away from the sunlight dancing on the surface of the bay and toward the door. Phoebe's friend walked across the porch to lower herself into one of the wicker chairs.

Once seated, she dabbed at her forehead with a lace-edged handkerchief before she asked, "Phoebe inside?"

Callie nodded, feeling no compunction to help the conversation along. Judging by their first meeting, Virginia would be more than willing to do most of the talking.

"So what does Doak think?" her visitor asked, right on cue.

Virginia lifted her hair off the back of her neck to dab the cloth along her nape. Her eyes were still on Callie, who hesitated, unsure how much of what she'd told Withers would be common knowledge. However, knowing small towns...

"He suggested I must have been mistaken about what I thought happened."

"Were you?" Virginia asked, the damp handkerchief balled in her unmoving hand. Her eyes, magnified by the thick lenses, made her look perpetually surprised.

"No."

"You think somebody was really trying to drown you?"

"Somebody held her head under water," Phoebe said from the doorway. "Doak thinks they were trying to scare her. To keep her from writing her book. You want some coffee?"

"Only if you got decaf," Virginia said. "That other stuff gives me palpitations."

Phoebe disappeared back inside the house.

"Doak thinks somebody held your head under the water to scare you?" Virginia asked, picking up where she'd left off.

"The other version is that I must have gotten tangled up in some seaweed and just *thought* someone was holding me."

Virginia's hoot of laughter was welcome, Callie decided, taking another sip of coffee.

"Seaweed," the old woman repeated after the cawing sound of it had died away. "That's what this town gets for driving Ben Stanton out of office. I swear Doak don't have sense enough to get in out of the rain."

"The seaweed was Stanton's idea." No need not to share the blame, Callie decided. There was enough to go around.

And she was finding that recounting the highlights of last night's interrogation before an appreciative audience was balm for her anger.

"You're kidding? Or maybe he was," Virginia said. "Because Ben *isn't* a fool. He'd know you aren't one either. Wonder what made him say something that."

"Well, it *is* hard to believe somebody would grab Callie and try to drown her with half the town watching," Phoebe said.

She was carrying a cup and saucer, which tinkled alarmingly in her trembling hand, as well as the glass carafe from the coffeemaker. She set the cup down on the table by Virginia's chair and began to fill it. Although the stream of coffee was wavering, its landing was fairly accurate. From the pocket of her slacks, Phoebe produced a spoon and a packet of artificial sweetener, which she handed over to her guest.

"You ready for a refill?" she asked, turning to Callie as Virginia began to doctor her coffee.

"I'm fine. Sit down and drink yours before it gets cold."

"If I drink any more, I won't sleep for a week. Callie and I been drinking coffee since the police left," Phoebe said, the last directed to her friend. "Beats all I've ever heard."

"I heard Ben made him turn you loose," Virginia said, her magnified eyes studying Callie over the rim of her cup.

"He heard the boat, I think."

"Ben's boat?"

"Stanton and another man, somebody called Charlie, had a skiff out there. I think he must have heard the motor."

In the hours since the incident, she had thought a lot about what had happened, reliving the sequence over and over in her head. Since she remembered hearing the approaching engine, subconsciously at least, she had to assume that her assailant, whose head was above water at all times, had heard it as well.

"He knew it was time to get gone," Phoebe said in agreement. "Good thing for you Ben was out there."

That was something else Callie had been forced to acknowledge. It hadn't been an easy admission to make, but it was nothing less than the truth. Stanton had saved her life, even if he hadn't believed it was in danger.

"I wonder why he was," Callie said. "Out there, I mean. Considering how far away he lives." The comment didn't come out as she'd intended, sounding ungrateful if nothing else.

"That's the way jubilees run," Virginia said, as if that explained everything.

Seeing Callie's blank look, Phoebe explained, "They move south to north like the tide. Ben was probably following it along the shore from the inlet. He'd know where it was headed. Ben knows these waters like the back of his hand."

"Stanton's a fisherman?" As she asked, Callie remembered the boat out at his place. Not the one he was in last night, but the larger, more expensive craft sheltered in the boathouse.

"Charters mostly. That's about the only way to make a living down here anymore," Phoebe said. "There's shrimping, but mostly Ben takes people out in the Gulf. 'Course, he knows all the bays and rivers, too, if they want to do that."

"You think he was bitter being forced to leave office after the murder?" Callie asked.

She should feel guilty about picking their brains. Despite Stanton's reluctance to talk to her, however, he was still one of the people at the very heart of this case. And neither Phoebe nor Virginia seemed averse to discussing him this morning. Distracted by what had happened last night, or sympathetic about her experience, they seemed to have forgotten Callie was an outsider as well as a member of the despised media.

"Bitter?" Phoebe asked, her puzzlement clear. "About what?"

"Well, he does seem to be struggling."

"Struggling? To make a living? That kind of struggling?" Virginia asked. "What in the world makes you think that?"

"His house," Callie said. "How he lives."

"Oh, the Stantons are just land poor," Phoebe said, seeming relieved. "No need to worry about Ben and money."

"Land poor?"

"You know how those houses out on Mullet Inlet are all built right up next to each other? At least until you get to Ben's?"

They had been, Callie realized. Then there had been a long stretch of pine forest before she had come to the dirt driveway she'd been directed to at the grocery.

"And you saw how isolated Ben's place is?" Phoebe went on. "Sitting all by itself out in the middle of nowhere?"

"He's the one that owns all that nowhere," Virginia chimed in. "That land's been in his family for years."

"It's not worth what waterfront lots are worth here," Phoebe explained. "Not yet anyway, but you just have to look at what's been happening down on Fort Morgan Road to know how that land's going to skyrocket. If he wanted to, Ben could sell off some of it now and never have to work another day in his life. 'Course, the Stantons were never much for selling their land. That's why that tract is all in one piece."

"So...he didn't need the chief's job?"

"Didn't need it and didn't want it. Ben came home from the army, and we drafted him all over again," Phoebe said.

She sounded pleased with the analogy. It was obviously something she had said before. Maybe the whole town had said it when they'd tried to convince Stanton to become their chief law enforcement officer. Given the aging population of this community, they had probably felt they'd pulled off quite a coup when he accepted.

"He was young, and he was smart," Virginia added, verifying that speculation. "Besides, he'd had experience with criminal investigations with the army. Whatever they call that."

"CID," Callie supplied, remembering Buck Dolan's condemnation of that as Stanton's only qualification—and a poor one—for handling a murder case, especially a high-profile one. "So how long did he hold office?"

"Maybe...two years before the murder," Phoebe said.

"Maybe a little bit more than that. Then those couple of years after it, while he was trying to solve the case. Up until Tom died, I guess. Then it was like he just gave up."

"Delacroix died, and Stanton was fired?"

"Resigned. He thought that as long as Tom was alive, he had a chance of getting an indictment."

"Do *you* think he did it?" Callie asked, watching her eyes.

"I *never* did," Virginia said, speaking eagerly into Phoebe's hesitation. "Tom purely doted on that little girl, and that's a fact. He took her everywhere with him. I never did believe he could do...what they said had been done to her," she said, clarifying without becoming explicit.

Callie didn't remind them that fathers and mothers killed their children all the time, often in ways that seem too bizarre and too horrible for normal people to comprehend. These women had known Tom Delacroix, probably for a long time. And she had asked for their opinions, which she understood would be subjective. That's what she had wanted. What they *felt* about Delacroix's guilt or innocence.

"And if not...?"

Callie deliberately let this question trail, still watching Phoebe's face. She had yet to answer the original inquiry. Maybe out of loyalty to Stanton or because she didn't know what she believed.

It seemed there was something she wanted to say, but for some reason, she was reluctant. Because Virginia was here? Or because she wasn't sure that her opinion wouldn't be repeated? Perhaps in Callie's book.

"If not Tom, you mean?" Virginia asked.

Callie nodded, glancing back at her. "There was another child murder twenty-six years ago in North Carolina. There were several unusual elements about it that were...very much like Kay-Kay's. Tom Delacroix was in rehab at the time, which means that he couldn't have killed that other little girl."

"My stars," Virginia said softly. "Ben know about that?"

"I've told him, but...he doesn't believe they're connected. Maybe because he doesn't want to believe it."

"So whoever killed Kay-Kay was like a serial killer? Is that what you're saying?"

"I'm saying it was someone who had killed before, at least once. And because of the timing of that previous murder, Tom Delacroix has to be excluded as a suspect. So, if it wasn't Delacroix...?" she asked again.

"An intruder," Virginia said, as excited as if she were answering a question in a quiz. "Just like they always said."

That had been the family's explanation. The only one they could make, given the situation.

"Do you believe a stranger would be able to walk into that house," Callie asked, "find the child, and get her out without her father hearing anything?"

"No," Phoebe said.

Callie turned back to her. Phoebe's face had changed, the lines that bracketed her mouth seeming to deepen.

"Whoever killed Kay-Kay had to know the house," she said, conviction strong in her voice. "To know Lorena was gone. And to know that Tom would be dead drunk that time of the night."

"A stranger couldn't have known," Callie reiterated.

Phoebe shook her head. "If it wasn't Tom, it had to be one of us. As much as nobody wanted to admit that, I think we've always known it was true. If you didn't believe Tom had anything to do with Kay-Kay's death, then you had to look at everybody in Point Hope differently after that murder."

"Stanton wasn't willing to do that?"

"I expect because Ben had more reason than just the evidence to want to blame Tom Delacroix," Virginia said.

"You hush," Phoebe hissed, turning angrily on her friend. "That's nothing but gossip, and you know it."

"What is?" Callie asked, feeling a surge of excitement, despite the pall last night's terror had temporarily cast over her enthusiasm for uncovering the secrets this town hid.

Virginia glared back at Phoebe, but she didn't answer.

"What kind of reason?" Callie prodded.

Virginia shook her head, her mouth pursed as if she were physically preventing what she'd hinted at from leaking out.

"Nothing," Phoebe said firmly. "Nothing that's going to be repeated in my house."

"Phoebe, a child was murdered," Callie reasoned. "A little girl you knew and loved. Surely, you want—"

"That's not got a thing to do with what she's talking about. Not one single, solitary thing."

Callie opened her mouth, prepared to argue that anything concerning Stanton and Delacroix probably had had a bearing on the crime. At least on the police chief's investigation of it.

"You see what you started?" Phoebe scolded her friend. "And it's got nothing to do with Kay-Kay's death. You tell her that."

"Ben thought it did, so who are you to say it didn't? You think you're smarter than the chief of police?"

"Ben thought *what* did?" Callie asked again.

Neither of them looked at her, ignoring the question as, eyes locked, they continued what was obviously a battle of wills. A battle in which the two opponents knew one another very well.

"Never you mind," Phoebe said. "That's water over the dam. And it's got no connection to that murder."

The noise Virginia made was both expressive and crude.

"If you're going to act that way, you just go on home," Phoebe told her. "We don't need that kind of commonness here."

Oh, yes we do, Callie thought. *We need whatever commonness will let Virginia spill her guts.*

"What the two of you are talking about is obviously old news," she argued. "Delacroix's dead, so what can it possibly hurt to repeat it? Since last night, I'm not sure we can afford to be particular about any aspect of this," she reminded Phoebe.

Not a very subtle plea for sympathy, but maybe a necessary one. *If* she were going to find out what they were talking about.

"They were just trying to scare you," Virginia said.

"He," Phoebe corrected. "There wasn't any *they*."

With Virginia's about-face, Callie felt as if she had lost an ally. It made her defensive enough to hint at what she had suggested more openly to Stanton last night.

"You think someone held my head under water long enough to make me pass out just to *scare* me? Who in this town could possibly be bothered enough by what I'm doing to do that?"

"There was nothing enjoyable about what we went through at the time of that murder. Nobody who was here then is eager to have that mess stirred up again." Phoebe's eyes released her friend's to focus on Callie. "Nobody."

"Any idea who might be so determined *not* to have it stirred up that they would do that last night?" Callie asked. "And more importantly, *why* they would be that determined?"

She tamped down her disappointment that Phoebe's championing, which had been so welcome last night, had turned into the same resentment she claimed the other townspeople felt.

"I don't know," Phoebe said. "It's not my job to find that out. Doak will talk to the people who were on the beach. Somebody may have seen something. You can't tell until you ask."

Unlikely, Callie thought, since neither Stanton nor Charlie had seen anything. And they'd been *much* closer than anyone else.

"Phoebe—"

"Going on with all this questioning and investigating is just not smart," Phoebe interrupted, her voice almost pleading. "*Or* safe. Surely you can see that. Folks around here aren't happy about what you're doing. Stirring that up again.

You need to examine your heart and see if this is really worth it to you.''

Folks around here aren't happy about what you're doing. Maybe that was true, but it seemed to her that there was only one person in this town who couldn't afford to risk that she might produce some new evidence about Kay-Kay Delacroix's murder.

"Now Virginia's going on over to her house," Phoebe announced, "and I'm going upstairs to take a nap. And if I were you, Callie, I'd think seriously about packing my bags and heading on back home."

"Do you hear what you're saying?" Callie asked softly.

The fact that Phoebe seemed to be turning against her, even though she was couching her objection in the form of "for your own good," was very disappointing. And disturbing.

"You're the one claiming somebody's trying to hurt you," Phoebe said. "Whether that's true or not—even if they were just trying to scare you—I think if I was you, *I'd* stop doing whatever it is that got somebody angry enough to hold my head under the water. *If* I was you," she repeated, standing up. "You go on home now, Virginia. And try not to say something that'll get somebody mad at *you*."

"Don't you be telling me what to do, Phoebe Mae Robinson," Virginia retorted. "You aren't my boss."

"Well, I *am* your hostess. And *I'm* going upstairs for a lie down. You go on home. Callie needs to take a rest, too. And she needs to do some thinking."

It was obvious, as it had been before, who had the stronger will. Virginia sat stubbornly in her chair for another second or two, but eventually, draining the rest of her coffee in one long swallow, she banged the cup down noisily on the saucer and stood.

"Well, I guess I know when I've worn out my welcome."

"Good," Phoebe said.

She turned back toward the door that led into the house as her guest stalked toward the one that led outside. Just before

Virginia reached it, she turned and said in a whisper, "Come on over to my house later. I'll tell you."

A little shocked by that flagrant breech of a long-standing friendship, Callie glanced toward Phoebe's retreating figure. Despite Virginia's whisper, her pace hadn't slowed. Apparently she hadn't heard the offer or had chosen to ignore it.

Callie turned back to find Virginia, her finger across her lips, nodding encouragement and winking at her. Then the old woman opened the creaking screen door and stepped out into the sunlight, leaving Callie alone on the porch.

Her mind on the recent conversation, her eyes again considered the water before her. Glinting in the morning sun, the bay looked serene. Incredibly peaceful. Just as Point Hope itself had when she'd first arrived. Now she knew that for both of them, that tranquillity was deceiving.

"VIRGINIA?" Callie called, tapping on the wooden frame of the screen door.

When she'd gotten no answer at the front, Callie had gone around to the back of the Wilton house, which, like Phoebe's, had a screened-in porch overlooking the water. Although it was early afternoon, too hot to be outside and hours before another of the spectacular eastern shore sunsets, she thought she should at least check to see if Virginia was out here before she gave up.

She had decided to drive out to Stanton's place again. The fact that he'd let Doak do all the talking last night might mean he agreed with everything the chief of police had suggested. Or it might mean that he had been thinking about what she had blurted out on the boat.

If nothing else, she needed to thank him. He had come into the water after her, which she knew he probably would have done for anyone else in that situation. She certainly wasn't attributing Stanton's rescue to any kind of personal concern.

To give him credit, however, he had persisted in his rescue, even after she'd attacked him, believing him to be her assailant. And when he'd realized how truly terrorized she was, he had treated her with a compassion that seemed genuine. All of which deserved some expression of gratitude, which she couldn't remember making last night.

And since Virginia's house was on her way, she had decided to accept the old woman's invitation to come over and hear the gossip Phoebe wouldn't let her repeat this morning.

"Virginia? Are you in there?"

She knocked again, and then tried the screen door. It wouldn't open. She put her hand along her forehead, as Virginia had done this morning, to examine the inside frame. There was an old-fashioned hook-and-eye latch, which had been secured.

So much for going out to Stanton's armed with Virginia's information. Disappointed, she stepped back far enough that she could look up at the second-story windows. There was an air-conditioning unit chugging away in one of the front rooms.

Phoebe usually lay down in her bedroom for an hour or so in the heat of the day. Callie would be willing to bet her neighbor did, too. Given the climate and their age, an afternoon nap was probably a smart move. With the noise the AC-unit was making, Virginia wouldn't be able to hear Callie calling.

Resigned to failure, she turned and began to retrace her steps to the street where she had parked her car. After Phoebe's warning, she hadn't informed her hostess about where she was going. And she certainly hadn't mentioned her intention to stop by the Wilton place on her way.

While they had eaten lunch, that same hint of reproach had been in Phoebe's manner. Maybe she was genuinely concerned for Callie's safety. Or maybe, since Callie was living in her house, she was worried about her own. And if someone *had* tried to kill Callie last night, perhaps she *was* putting Phoebe at risk.

They were just trying to scare you. That seemed to be the consensus. And after all, her attacker *had* let her go. She had attributed that to the arrival of Stanton's boat, but it *was* possible the two actions had had nothing to do with one another.

She had no idea how much time had elapsed between the moment her attacker had pushed her upright, inadvertently restarting the process of breathing, and the moment Stanton's hands had fastened around her upper arms.

Or *had* that hard shove in the center of her back been inadvertent? Had her assailant intended all along to bring her to the brink of unconsciousness and then to let her go? Had he intentionally pushed her upward with such force that it would bring her out of that oxygen-deprived stupor?

She reached her car, parked under one of the massive trees that shaded Virginia's front lawn. As she inserted the key in the door, she glanced down the row of houses. Heat rose off the pavement in waves, distorting the air. There was no one outside on either side of the street. No one sitting on the shaded front porches. No traffic to disturb the stillness.

She climbed into her car, hurriedly slipping the key into the ignition and starting the engine. As cool air began to pour from the vents, she adjusted the one to the left of the steering column so that it was blowing directly on her face.

She tilted her head, letting the cold stream touch the moisture on her neck. Then she turned her face to the right, allowing the vent to blow over her jawline and the dampness that had gathered around her temple. Finally she turned her head the other way, rolling her neck, which was stiff from a combination of tension and too little sleep.

As she did, something drew her eye to one of the windows on the second floor of the Wilton house. The twitching aside of a curtain, perhaps? To allow someone to see out?

There was nothing there now. The white sheers hung limp and still, presenting a blank, unrevealing face to the outside world.

She wondered if Virginia had changed her mind about sharing her gossip. Maybe having had time to consider Phoebe's objection, she had thought better of her invitation.

Maybe she had realized that if she told Callie what she knew, and it ended up in a book, she might very well alienate an old friend for life. Instead of telling Callie directly that she'd changed her mind, had she chosen this way to avoid the temptation to talk?

"You can run, Virginia, but you can't hide," Callie said, the words very soft.

She had a feeling she could talk Virginia into telling her that gossip, which she had obviously considered to be of the "too good to keep" variety. And that would definitely be to Callie's advantage. She'd come by again on the way back into town, she decided, taking one last look at the window where she had seen movement before she pulled her car away from the curb.

CHAPTER SEVEN

THE SOUND of the car broke Ben's concentration on the vibration he was adjusting in the cruiser's engine. He shut it down and straightened, standing upright inside the engine well. His eyes were only slightly above the level of the housing, but he could see enough to make an identification of the vehicle he'd heard. It wasn't the one he'd been expecting.

He'd spent the morning getting ready for tomorrow's charter, so he hadn't been inside to answer his phone. And he had known Doak would want to discuss what had happened last night.

Thinking out loud, his former deputy called it. In reality, Doak's visits were a tacit request for Ben's input on some problem. Apparently Withers wasn't the only one who wanted to talk about what had happened last night, however, because Callie Evers had just parked her car in his yard.

He had left the house open, so it was going to become obvious pretty quickly he wasn't there. When it did, based on what he had learned from their previous encounters, she would come looking for him. The logical place to start would be out here, and he didn't want it to appear as if he were hiding. Not from her. Not from what she had said last night.

Mouthing a profanity, he reached down and retrieved the rag he'd laid on the casing. He used it to wipe grease off his fingers, not hurrying because he needed time to think. A few minutes to get prepared for what he expected her to say.

When he finally started up the steps, he realized she hadn't gotten out of her car. She was still sitting inside, the driver's-side window rolled down as a concession to the heat.

She's no more eager for this than I am, he thought, surprised by that intuition.

It didn't make a lot of sense. After all, she had driven all the way out here again. And there were only a couple of reasons for why she would. Either she wanted to talk about what she'd suggested in the boat last night or she wanted to thank him for getting her out of the water. He wasn't looking forward to either discussion.

He jumped onto the pier as she opened the car door. Eyes shaded with her hand, she seemed to be looking right at him, but she didn't start walking toward the water. Some kind of power play? To make him come to her? he wondered. Of course, since this was his home turf, he had all the advantages.

Still thinking like a cop, he admitted with a trace of bitterness. And he wasn't one. Not any longer.

Whatever had happened to Callie Evers last night wasn't his responsibility. If that's what she had come out here to talk about, he'd refer her to Doak. Not that she'd get anywhere.

Ben had realized that much as he'd listened to his former deputy's interrogation last night. He hadn't interfered, telling himself just what he was telling himself now. Not his responsibility. Not anymore, thank God.

He discovered he still had the grease rag in his hand. As he stood here, dreading another meeting with Callie Evers, his fingers tightened over the fabric, gripping strongly enough to be painful. Annoyed, he jammed the cloth into the back pocket of his jeans.

The same ones he'd been wearing last night, he realized. He hadn't seen any point in changing clothes to run his catch in. And then, knowing he had a full day's work ahead of him to get ready for tomorrow's charter, he had decided to delay showering until after he finished.

He probably reeked of fish and engine oil. He was so accustomed to those smells he was no longer aware of them, but he'd be willing to bet that Ms. Callie Evers would be. *And I really don't give a damn.*

As he stood watching from the far end of the pier, she turned and ducked back inside the car. She put her knee on the driver's seat and stretched across it, reaching for something.

When she stood up again, she settled a pair of sunglasses on her nose. She closed the car door, the sound echoing across the water as it always did. That's how he had found her last night. He had heard her wheezing, trying to get some air into her lungs, long before Charlie's flashlight had picked her up.

"Mr. Stanton?" she called, pitching her voice to carry across the distance between them, although she had already started to close it. "Do you think we could talk? If you have time. I promise it won't take long."

She had just offered him the perfect out. And he wouldn't even have to lie. He really did have a lot more to do before he'd be ready to take the cruiser out at dawn. The problem was, and it surprised him to admit it, there was some part of him that wanted to hear what she had to say. Maybe a natural curiosity about what had really happened out in the bay last night. Maybe even about the other murder she'd told him about.

Or maybe, Ben acknowledged, feeling a tightening in his groin as he watched her approach, his desire to talk to Callie Evers was based on something else entirely. On another, very different kind of desire. Because she looked a hell of a lot better than she had last night. A whole *hell* of a lot better.

She was wearing narrow white trousers, topped by a dark red shirt. The afternoon sun emphasized the blond streaks in her shoulder-length brown hair. He wasn't expert enough to say whether those were natural, but they looked as if they could be. Especially considering that nearly porcelain skin.

She seemed to have gotten some sun since she'd been down here. There was a sweep of color across the bridge of her nose and along the high cheekbones. The beginnings of a tan? With her complexion, that would be a real shame.

"What about?" he asked, raising his own voice.

"About last night," she said.

Her steps slowed the closer she came. As if, just as he'd thought before, she, too, was reluctant to have this conversation. Only, he couldn't figure out why she would be. Anymore than he had been able to figure out what she was after the first time she'd come out here.

Doak said she was writing some kind of true crime book about the murder. He hadn't been around many writers, but her interest in Kay-Kay's death had felt personal rather than professional. And more passionate than a ten-year-old murder should warrant. Even if she expected to turn this tragedy into a bestseller.

Personal, he thought again, jolted by the characterization. Maybe that was just wishful thinking on his part. The idea Callie Evers might be motivated by something other than money.

She came to a halt with less than ten feet of pier between them. He couldn't see her eyes, hidden behind those dark glasses. He had never liked being at that disadvantage. At one time he had considered himself skilled at reading people—especially their eyes. He liked to track the thoughts moving within them as they talked, using those to judge their veracity.

"I wanted to thank you for what you did last night," she said. "I couldn't remember whether I had or not. I guess I was a little...distraught at the time. I truly am very grateful."

There were a dozen responses he could make, some of them ungracious, even if they might also be true. Anybody in this town would have gone into the water last night. He would have done the same thing no matter who had been struggling out there. *With,* he admitted, *a couple of fairly obvious exceptions.*

He nodded without making any verbal response. The first time she'd come here, his reactions had given away more than he wanted them to. It was a mistake he didn't intend to repeat.

"And despite what Chief Withers suggested," she added, "I wanted you to know that I wasn't mistaken about what happened."

"Somebody got carried away," he said, echoing Doak's theory. "They were trying to scare you, and it got out of hand."

"Is that really what you believe?" she asked. "Even after what I told you? Even knowing Tom Delacroix couldn't have been responsible for his daughter's death?"

"I don't know anything of the kind. I've seen no proof of what you said about that other murder. *If* there was one."

"I have the affidavits I told you about in my car. If you'd only look at them—"

"Even if there *was* another murder with similarities to Kay-Kay's, it doesn't prove the same person committed both. Maybe Delacroix read about the other case. Maybe what he did was an attempt to make people believe just what you believe."

He was pleased that the old skills seemed to be coming back. Of course, he was more prepared this time. At his denial, her mouth flattened. After a few seconds, she shook her head.

"I don't understand why you aren't willing to at least consider the possibility. Supposedly, you were a good cop. Whatever you believed, you at least went through the motions. All I'm asking is that you do that again. Just go through the motions on the off chance that I might be right."

He was tempted, but he knew that had more to do with her than with her arguments. With the way she looked. Maybe even with the way she smelled, a subtle fragrance of flowers, which was probably her shampoo. The wind was whipping strands of sun-touched hair across her face, which she caught with her fingers, holding them away from her eyes.

His growing sexual attraction, and the resulting urge to

please her, would be the only reasons to look at the material she wanted to show him. He had known from the beginning who had killed Kay-Kay. He had even known why. And nothing Callie Evers could ever show him would make him forget that.

"Sorry," he said, and on some level, maybe only hormonal, he really was. "It's not my job." He had already started back to the ladder when her voice stopped him.

"Someone tried to kill me last night. If you hadn't been there, they would have succeeded. It seems to me the only person who has that kind of stake in making sure I don't write about Katherine Delacroix's murder is the person who killed her."

He turned to face her. "That person's dead, Ms. Evers. You're eight years too late to make that accusation stick."

"But if I weren't too late, you'd buy into that idea, wouldn't you? Virginia Wilton hinted there had been bad blood between the two of you, long before Katherine's murder."

The question threw him. He wasn't sure what she was trying to get him to say. Or what she'd been told.

"Are you asking me if I believe Delacroix was capable of killing someone else? If, just for the sake of argument, we pretend he isn't dead?" He had intended the sharp sarcasm. If he had expected any reaction to it, he was disappointed.

"Just for the sake of argument," she agreed, her voice calm.

"I think Tom Delacroix was capable of almost anything."

"Even of what was done to his own daughter?"

Ben didn't understand why he hesitated before he could answer that. Maybe because of the way the question had been phrased. Even of what was done to his own daughter.

Kay-Kay's death hadn't been the result of some drunken rage. Nor had it been an accident—a family argument that had gotten out of hand, claiming the life of an innocent victim. That had been the FBI's opinion, but Ben had known the murder hadn't been staged to cover up something like that.

It had been exactly what it had appeared to be. Cold and cruel and deliberate. There had never been any doubt in his mind about that aspect of it. There still wasn't.

"Even that," he said.

"You hated Delacroix," she said softly. "Maybe with good reason. I don't know. But all these years you've been terrified that your hatred made you screw up that investigation. You're afraid you let *it* convince you of his guilt, rather than the evidence, so that you did exactly what they all accused you of doing. You didn't look any place else for the murderer."

"You don't have any idea what I did," he denied, but she was getting to him, just as she had the first day she'd come here.

"Then why are you afraid to listen to me? Or to take a look at the information I've collected?"

"Is that supposed to be some kind of challenge, Ms. Evers? Something my ego just won't be able to resist? I'm supposed to jump into your little literary *investigation* because I can't stand being told I was wrong? Sorry, but I outgrew that kind of knee-jerk reaction a long time ago."

"It was supposed to make you think."

He laughed, the sound short and harsh. "Believe me, Ms. Evers, I think about Katherine Delacroix's murderer every day of my life. I think how sorry I am I didn't strangle that son of a bitch with my bare hands as soon I saw what he'd done."

"But he didn't," she said, her voice intense. "He *didn't* do it. That's what I've been trying to tell you. Tom Delacroix couldn't have killed his daughter."

The passion he had recognized was there again. And the surety. That's what had bothered him the first time. How damn sure she was about what she was saying.

"Because he didn't kill Mary Cameron twenty-six years ago," she went on. "He couldn't have. And if he didn't kill *her,* then he didn't kill Kay-Kay. Which means whoever did is still here.''

''Or maybe he's moved back to North Carolina,'' he said, ridiculing her theory. Ridiculing her. It had no effect. Neither her face nor her voice changed in response to his mockery.

''He's here. I didn't believe that before. I didn't think it fit the pattern. But, after last night…'' She took a breath, deep enough that it lifted her shoulders. ''Whether you help me or not, I'm going to find out who he is, but…I'd really like your help,'' she finished softly.

He was even thinking about it, he realized, caught again in the spell of her conviction. Except his was just as deep.

''If you really believe someone tried to kill you last night, then if I were you, I'd get back in that car, and I wouldn't stop until I was too exhausted to drive. I wouldn't spend another minute in Point Hope. *If* I really believed that,'' he challenged. ''Now if you'll excuse me, I have several hours work left. Good luck, and I hope goodbye. Because if you're smart, Ms. Evers, this will be the last time you and I see one another.''

He turned and walked back to the cruiser. He thought he could feel her eyes following him, but he didn't look back. And a long time after he had the engine running as smooth as silk again, he heard her car start. He straightened, watching, as she drove back down the winding driveway toward the main road.

''MRS. DELACROIX?''

The slender blonde, stopped in the act of closing the door of the silver Mercedes sedan, turned at the sound of her name. The slight smile seemed automatic, probably her normal response to being addressed. As soon as she realized that the person who had called to her was a stranger, delicately shaped brows arched above the frames of the sunglasses she wore, questioning either Callie's right to be on her property or her identity.

Lorena Delacroix was more attractive than her pictures had

suggested. Although her face was soft and pale, in keeping
with the wheat-colored hair, it was not as full as the cameras
had portrayed it. She was also more slender, and more fragile
somehow, than Callie had imagined. Despite the fact that the
woman had yet to open her mouth, Callie's preconceptions
about Katherine Delacroix's mother shifted minutely.

"Yes?" Lorena asked, her tone sharply questioning.

Finally face-to-face with Kay-Kay's mother, Callie was in-
explicably at a loss for words, uncertain how she should begin this crucial interview. And yet the whole time she had
been waiting, standing in the shade of the oaks that lined the
Delacroix's drive, she had been practicing what she would
say.

Only occasionally had she let her eyes consider the second-
story windows, two of which belonged to the room that had
been Kay-Kay's. Whenever she did, "ghoul" had echoed
unpleasantly.

"Who the hell are you?" Lorena demanded.

She took a step away from the car, putting her hand above
her eyes to shade them from the sun. Even from this distance
Callie could hear the soft jingle of the bracelets she wore.
The sound seemed to break the spell that had held her.

"My name is Callie Evers, Mrs. Delacroix," she said, trying to find words that wouldn't get her thrown off the property. "I wonder if I could talk to you. It won't take long, I
promise."

Almost the exact thing she had said to Ben Stanton. And
if this interview had the same outcome as that...

"Talk about what?" Lorena's voice had lost all pretense
to pleasantness. "You *do* know you're trespassing, don't
you?"

"I know your husband wasn't responsible for your daughter's death. I know that he couldn't have been."

The hand that had been raised to shade Lorena Delacroix's
eyes whipped the sunglasses off them instead. Although they
narrowed reflexively against the sudden glare, they didn't wa-

ver from Callie's face. And they were not nearly as hard as they had appeared in those long-ago photographs.

"May I come inside and show you *how* I know?" Callie asked.

The silence lasted so long that she began to be afraid that using this approach had been another mistake. The cupid's bow mouth, carefully outlined in carmine, had a pinched look. Finally, it opened, revealing very even and very white teeth.

"If this is some kind of trick—"

"No trick, Mrs. Delacroix."

"If you're a reporter, I'm not telling you *anything.*"

"I'm not asking you to. But…there are things I think *you* should know. Some things *I'd* like to tell you."

"Like what?"

"Could we go inside? I'm not used to this heat," Callie said, softening the blatant request with a smile. *And if you tell me it's not the heat, but the humidity…*

Another few beats of silence. Then Lorena set her sunglasses back on her nose, its perfection a dead giveaway that some skilled plastic surgeon had created it. The movement of the bracelets this time caught the sun, sending droplets of light glittering between them.

"You alone?" she asked.

"Of course," Callie said, feeling the same anticipation as when she had heard Stanton's voice in the darkness last night.

He was the ally she had wanted, but the barriers he had erected against any suggestion that Tom Delacroix might not be guilty were too firmly in place, and that had left her with only one other option.

"Come on in," Lorena Delacroix ordered.

Without waiting to see if Callie followed, she walked around the front of the car and headed toward the dozen or so steps that led up to the wide front door of her home.

"I CAN'T BELIEVE THIS," Lorena said. "How come nobody ever told me about this drawing?"

"The police usually keep some piece of evidence from the public so they can distinguish between the real murderer and people who confess to crimes they had nothing to do with."

"Wait a minute. Are you saying they thought somebody who *didn't* have anything to do with the murder might confess?"

There had been no hesitation before the words "the murder." They had come out of Lorena Delacroix's mouth as if they had no connection to her own flesh and blood.

"That happens all the time," Callie said. "If the police hold something back, something only the real murderer could know, it makes it easier to disprove those false confessions."

The blue eyes had held intently on Callie's face as she talked. "I'll be damned," Lorena said. "That's...crazy. Somebody confessing, I mean."

"There are a lot of crazy people out there, Mrs. Delacroix. People who would do anything for the attention that being a suspect in a high profile crime like this would give them."

"Then you can bet your ass they've never *been* a suspect."

Callie was beginning to relax. Mrs. Delacroix had never questioned that what she was telling her was the truth. Admittedly, it was very much to her advantage if it were.

"That son of a bitch," Lorena said, her eyes dropping to the photograph on the coffee table.

Although it was only a shot of the back of a small blond head, Callie had been reluctant to bring it out of her leather portfolio. She had finally decided there was no way to discuss the drawing without providing some evidence of its existence. And this photograph was all she had to offer.

That and the two affidavits she had collected in North Carolina were the only proof of her absolute conviction that the same person had committed both these murders. And unlike Ben Stanton, Lorena had been very willing to look at them.

"Stanton?" Callie asked, having little trouble figuring out who Kay-Kay's mother would consider a son of a bitch.

"This proves what a lying jackass he is."

"It's pretty standard police procedure."

Callie was trying to walk the fine line between being truthful and forming this necessary alliance. She had hoped to convince Stanton to work with her, but after this morning—

"You're telling me it's standard procedure to keep information like this from the parents of a murdered child?"

If those parents are suspects. "I'm afraid so."

"Let me make sure I understand what you're saying. The police have known about this...flower thing all along, but they never told anybody, because if they had, somebody might have discovered another child had been killed just like Kay-Kay."

"I wouldn't assign that motivation to—"

"I would." Lorena's words cut her sharply off in midsentence. "That lying son of a bitch."

Although Callie knew Stanton could care less if she defended him, withholding this kind of information *was* standard. It certainly didn't mean he hadn't investigated the drawing of the rose himself. She had never intended to imply that.

"I'm sure Chief Stanton ran the drawing through the national crime databases. When nothing turned up—"

"Why wouldn't it?" Lorena interrupted again.

"Police departments haven't always been good about sharing information," Callie said. "And when the national databases were established, no one could guarantee that all the cold cases were included. That was the intent, of course, but just the physical task of tracking down the information and submitting it would mean hundreds of hours taken away from their regular duties. Small police departments would have been hard-pressed—"

"So you're saying this other rose wouldn't have been in the database?" Lorena demanded, again cutting off her explanation.

"Probably not. Especially since all the original records on that case burned in a courthouse fire. That, itself, was almost twenty years ago. I don't know that anyone has even looked at that particular murder since.''

The blue eyes seemed almost as hard now as they had in the television footage. ''So how come *you* did?''

It was the question Callie had waited for Stanton to pose. And he hadn't. For some reason she hadn't expected it from Mrs. Delacroix. Again, her opinion of Kay-Kay's mother altered.

''I'm a reporter, Mrs. Delacroix,'' she said. ''It's my job to dig up facts.''

The skepticism in that steady blue regard didn't change, despite the smile that moved the too-small mouth. ''I wasn't born yesterday, Ms. Evers,'' Lorena said. ''And I'm not a fool. You better start telling me the truth before I call Doak Withers and tell him I've got another trespasser for him to pick up.''

I'm not a fool. It was the third time in the past few days someone had made that claim. And, Callie acknowledged, they'd all been right. These people had been tempered by the fire of the media scrutiny they had passed through. There was nothing left in them that was naive or trusting.

''I knew the family involved,'' she said.

''In that other murder?''

Callie nodded, her throat tight.

''Twenty-six years ago,'' Lorena said, speculatively. ''You must have been just a kid.''

With the speed and approximate duration of a flashbulb's explosion, the image of that basement was in Callie's head. She could smell the mold and feel the dampness.

''I'm surprised you remember it after all that time.''

Callie heard and even understood the words Lorena had just said. She just couldn't concentrate on them. Not even when the memory faded. For a few seconds the after-image of that swinging lightbulb burned in her consciousness, as the retina will retain the glare of a flash after it's gone. It had been a very long time since that had happened. Long enough that she had almost forgotten how intense it was. And how devastating.

She allowed her lips to part slightly, trying unobtrusively to breathe through her mouth. Trying to pull in the oxygen she needed to defeat her lightheadedness. And the whole time she was doing that, she was also aware that she was expected to make some answer. Aware of the slow seconds ticking by as Lorena waited. Suspicion had begun to seep into the blue eyes before Callie could manage to align words into a coherent sentence.

"It's hard to forget something like that. Especially hard when you're a child," she added, wondering as she said it whether her answer made sense. And if it were too revealing.

Lorena nodded as if what she said had been perfectly rational. Then her eyes fell back to the photograph of the back of her daughter's head.

"The fact that there was this other case *proves* Tom didn't have anything to do with Kay-Kay's death."

For some reason, the triumph, the sense of vindication Callie would have expected, was missing from Lorena Delacroix's declaration. Her voice was flat instead, almost without emotion.

"It should. But I'm afraid there are…some problems."

"Problems?" The blue eyes lifted.

"The fire I told you about destroyed the official documentation. All we have is some secondary corroboration of the existence of that first drawing."

"What does that mean? Secondary corroboration?"

"Statements from people who talked to those who actually saw the drawing of the rose. People who, for one reason or another, were told it was an integral part of the investigation."

"Like that guy's wife? The sheriff's wife, whose statement you showed me?"

"That's right."

"So?"

"So…they probably won't be enough to convince the police to reopen the case. Especially since Stanton never acknowledged there was a similar drawing on...your daughter's body.''

''Damn straight they aren't going to reopen the investigation,'' Lorena said, her voice bitter. ''Not as long as Ben Stanton is alive. They wouldn't if you brought them the real murderer, begging to confess.''

''If we can convince Withers—''

''Doak don't take a piss unless Ben tells him he needs to.''

The crudity didn't fit with the persona Lorena had tried to convey, again shifting Callie's perceptions of the woman seated across from her.

''And you aren't ever going to convince Stanton,'' Lorena went on, seeming oblivious to the effect of her vulgarity. ''This is personal with him. So...we go over his head.''

''I'm not sure—''

''We don't mess around with the law,'' Lorena said, seeming to relish the words. ''We go straight to the media instead.''

''Without more concrete proof, they aren't going to be any more inclined to believe this than Stanton is.''

''He hasn't got any authority to stop us.''

''Maybe not,'' Callie admitted, ''but the real question is whether or not the media would be convinced by what we say. Especially since no one involved in *this* investigation is going to admit that rose was there.''

''They won't have to be convinced. Those people don't care about proof. The only thing they care about is whether or not this'll sell papers. You just give me those affidavits—''

''Mrs. Delacroix, I really believe—''

''Look,'' Lorena interrupted again, her voice harsh, ''I've lived with this hanging over my head for ten years. It killed my husband. Drove him to an early grave, God rest his soul. And all along there was proof that somebody outside this family killed Kay-Kay. And that son of a bitch Ben Stanton made sure we didn't know about it.''

"*He* didn't know," Callie said, again wondering why she was defending Ben. "That's what I'm telling you. And even if he now admits it was there, the rose on your daughter's body can't exonerate your husband. Not alone. It can only do that in conjunction with proof of the existence of the other one."

"So that's what we show them," Lorena said, sliding the papers around until the two affidavits covered the photograph of the back of her daughter's head.

"If we release this information prematurely, and then they find out how flimsy our evidence is, we destroy our credibility. I think we have to wait until we find some solid link between the person who committed that first murder and this."

"What kind of link?"

"Something that ties him to the other family. Or at least to the area. I think that's the safest way. *And* the most likely to get the results we want."

The blue eyes considered her face a long time. "I've never much believed in playing it safe," Lorena Delacroix said finally.

"But surely if there's anyone who can understand the kind of harm that can be inflicted by having people speculate on someone's guilt or innocence..." Callie said, letting the suggestion speak for itself.

"You think I give a damn about somebody else being a suspect for a change? Hell, I wasn't even here that night, and they *all* think I had something to do with it."

Callie couldn't deny the truth of that. There were plenty of people who believed Lorena Delacroix knew more than she had told the authorities about her daughter's death.

"I think our best chance of putting this to rest, once and for all," Callie reiterated, "lies in working together to make that connection and waiting to go public until we have enough to convince any reasonable person."

Lorena laughed again. "Honey, if there is one thing I've

learned, it's that reasonable people don't exist. Not when it comes to something like this.''

''I know it must feel like that—''

''You don't know anything,'' Lorena broke in. ''*Nobody* knows unless they've been there. Unless it's your picture on the covers of those sleazy little magazines stacked along every check-out counter in this country. You don't have any idea what we went through.''

''Mrs. Delacroix—''

''I'll wait,'' Lorena said, holding up her hand, its palm toward Callie. Jangling, the bracelets slid off her wrist and lodged on the fleshy part of her forearm. ''Hell, I've waited this long. A little longer isn't gonna kill me. But I'll tell you this, Ms. Evers. When it's time…''

''Yes?'' Callie asked, obeying the unspoken prompt as Lorena let the pause lengthen dramatically.

''I want to be the one who blows the whistle on that bastard. You understand me? I want to be the one who tells the press that for ten years Ben Stanton sat on evidence that could have cleared my husband of any suspicion in my daughter's murder. And I want to see the look on that bastard's face when I do.''

CHAPTER EIGHT

SHE SHOULD HAVE enough time for one more stop before Phoebe expected her for dinner, Callie decided, stealing a glance at her watch. She double-checked the numbers on the mailbox she was approaching, verifying the neatly lettered address.

The box itself was huge, carved and painted like a mallard decoy, with the opening for mail cut into the duck's broad breast. As she pulled her car into the gravel drive beside it, the wings attached to the wooden body spun madly in the hot wind.

Unlike most of the houses in the area, the cottage wasn't shaded by the ubiquitous live oaks. Instead, fruit trees stood like sentinels, guarding one side of the lot. On the other, neat wooden stakes defined the rows of a garden, green and flourishing despite the heat. Someone had devoted a lot of time and effort to seeing it stayed that way.

She turned off the engine and sat in the car a moment, studying the house. It was late Victorian, or at least it was garnished with the trappings of the period, including intricately cut gingerbread trim. Everything appeared to have been freshly painted; the shrubs and the lawn recently trimmed.

Glancing again at her watch, Callie gathered up her purse and the portfolio containing the photograph and affidavits. Then she stepped outside the car to be assaulted again by the heat, which had grown more oppressive as the long afternoon wore on.

"I got lemonade, but no air-conditioning."

The voice drew her eyes to the right-hand side of the porch where an old-fashioned swing hung from the ceiling on chains. Seated in it was the man she had come to see.

"But air or not," he went on, "it's bound to be cooler up here than it is out in that sun."

"Dr. Cooley?"

"Now I know you're from out of town. Nobody's called me *Doctor* Cooley in forty years."

"What do they call you?" Callie asked with a smile, responding to the vein of humorous self-deprecation.

"To my face, you mean?"

She laughed, and after a second or two, the sound of his laughter, as deep and rich as his accent, joined hers.

"Come on up here where I can see you," he urged. "I don't get many good-looking women paying me afternoon calls anymore. They all act like I got old or something."

Relaxing at the warmth of his welcome, after the strain of the taut-string hour she had just spent with Lorena Delacroix, Callie climbed the low front steps. It took a moment for her eyes to adjust to the relative dimness of the porch.

The figure that materialized as they did was stereotypical. White-haired and portly, Dr. Everett Cooley looked exactly like what he was. A retired country doctor.

He wore an open-necked cotton print shirt. Khaki pants, held up by suspenders, stretched over a rounded belly. His feet were encased in beige tennis shoes. As their toes touched against the planks of the porch, propelling the swing gently back and forth, his trousers rode up a little, exposing white athletic socks banded at the top in red.

"Am I supposed to know you?" he asked, the movement of the swing smooth and measured, its chains creaking softly with each rhythmic push. "Neither my eyes nor my mind is as good as they used to be. And don't you be insulted if I delivered you or something. I've seen a heap of baby bottoms in my day. Can't be expected to try to sort all of them out at my age."

Callie laughed again. "You can relax. We've never met."

"You selling something?" he asked.

A different version of an old story, she thought. A story Everett Cooley was very familiar with.

"Makes me no never mind if you are, you understand," the old man hurried to assure her. "I like visitors, even salesmen. And I might just buy whatever it is you got for sale. Except magazines. I already take more of those than I can get read."

"Not a salesman, but a writer," Callie said.

The white head tilted slightly, as the shrewd brown eyes examined her face. "What you write?"

"A column for a weekly up in Charlotte. And a lot of freelance articles. Maybe even for some of those magazines you subscribe to."

"Well, why don't you sit down and talk to me about what you're writing," Cooley said.

Callie chose the rocker aligned at an angle from the swing. She set her purse and the portfolio on the floor beside it, and then leaned back, setting her own chair into motion. Neither of them said anything, listening to the creak of the chains and the low thump of the rocker against the wooden planks.

"You famous?" the old man asked after a moment or two.

"I'm terribly afraid I'm not, Dr. Cooley," Callie said.

"But you're hoping to be. Every writer's hoping to be or you wouldn't stick with it. Too damn hard, otherwise."

She laughed. "Then maybe I am hoping, at that."

"So what do you write?"

"Articles about dogwood festivals and art shows. Nature things. Caves, forests, rivers. Articles telling people where to go for their next vacation. You name it, I've done it."

"I probably read something of yours. What's your name?"

"Callie Evers."

"Evers. Don't ring a bell. You making any money?"

"Not as much as I'd like to," Callie said, laughing again in response to the overt teasing. His good humor was infectious.

"And I expect that just might be why you're here," Doc

Cooley said, the amusement suddenly stripped from his voice.

At the abrupt change in tone, there was an increase in Callie's heart rate and the beginnings of a blush spread upward into her throat. She had been lulled into relaxation by the old man's friendliness—just as he'd intended.

Obviously, Cooley was as shrewd as the stereotype suggested. She wished she'd remembered that part. Her smile had become strained, but somehow she managed to hold onto it.

"You came here looking for fame *and* fortune, I'd imagine," the old man said softly. "Or would I be wrong about that?"

"I came here to write a book."

"About Kay-Kay Delacroix. Well, you ain't the first. Unfortunately, I doubt you'll be the last. 'Course, it's been a while, 'cause there's nothing new to write. But then I forgot we got the tenth anniversary coming up. Guess folks'll be wanting to speculate some more about what *really* happened."

"And you believe you already know," Callie suggested.

"Me? Hell, no. I never claimed to know any more than *how* that baby died. Medically, I mean. That was my job, and I did it, sick as it made me. You want theories about anything else, you go see Ben Stanton."

"Do you think his is the *right* theory?"

"Ben shore believes it is."

"You didn't answer my question, Dr. Cooley. Do *you* think Tom Delacroix killed his daughter?"

"Tom was a friend of mine. We grew up together. Hunted and fished together a thousand weekends. Slept in the same tent. Ate the same food out of the same pan. So I'm not exactly what you'd call an impartial observer." His mouth moved, lips pursing, and then he leaned back in the swing, looking up at the ceiling above their heads. "You want the God's truth about what I think?" he asked, his eyes still raised.

"Yes."

"I've seen a lot of purely awful things in my time. Some I don't like to think about. But what they did to that baby—"

"They?" Callie broke in, her voice sharpened with surprise.

His chin came down at the tone, eyes meeting hers. "Him. Her. Whoever did it."

"Are you saying…it could have been a *woman?*"

Despite the speculation about Lorena's complicity in her daughter's death, Callie had never seen any suggestion in print that Kay-Kay Delacroix's murderer might have been female.

"Why not. It might have been easier for a woman to lure her out of the house. And the rest wouldn't have taken any more strength than a normal-sized woman would have. 'Course it never was the strength that was the sticking point for me. It was the other."

There were so many possible "others" that Callie was afraid to guess which he might mean, so she didn't interrupt again.

"Tom Delacroix doted on that little girl. Never seen anything like it. She went everywhere with him, almost from the day she was born. And despite all I know about the sorriness of the human condition, I can't believe a man who loved a child like Tom did Kay-Kay could do that and *then* have the presence of mind to take the precautions he took afterward."

"You mean the water," Callie said softly.

"Washed her as clean as she was when I handed her to her mama to take home from the hospital. Cleaner maybe."

The killer had lured or carried Kay-Kay Delacroix from that pink-and-white bedroom on the second floor of the house Callie had just left. The site where the murder had taken place had never been determined, not to anyone's satisfaction. It was another of the anomalies that had made the case so fascinating to the media.

But after the murderer had finished, he had taken the little girl's body down to the dark waters of the bay and washed it. He had wrapped her in a sheet, one that had been taken from the Delacroix linen closet. Then he'd hidden the body in the marshy grasses near the edge of the water behind the Delacroix house. Where Ben Stanton had found it the next morning.

"Whoever killed her even scrubbed under her nails," the old man said. "Scrubbed 'em clean, too. There wasn't nothing on that little girl's body that gave us one single clue we could use to find her killer. Not a hair or a thread or a scraping of skin. And in my opinion, professional *and* personal, it would take somebody a lot colder and a lot less drunk than Tom Delacroix would have been by that time of the night to do that."

The silence after Cooley finished lasted so long that the low buzz from the yard seemed to fill Callie's head.

"He left *something*," she said, her voice no louder than the creak of the chains. "Something I think you found when you examined the body."

Cooley had to know about the rose Stanton wouldn't admit existed. He *had* to. And that was why she was here, of course. If she could get an affidavit from him—

"Something *I* found? You tell me what you think I found. I'd be real interested in hearing that."

"He cleaned the body, to remove any evidence that might link the murder to him, but then he marked it."

"What kind of a mark?" he asked, sounding genuinely curious.

Obviously he was testing her. Trying to find out how much she knew. He had been fairly forthcoming so far. Maybe when he realized that she really did know what she was talking about, he would be even more so.

"Whoever killed Kay-Kay drew a small red rose on the back of her neck, hidden under her hairline."

The doctor's eyes widened, but not in the same way Ben Stanton's had. Not at all in the same way, Callie acknowledged. Cooley looked bemused rather than shocked. And he shook his head, smiling a little.

"I don't know who you been talking to, young lady—"

"The end of the stem is visible in one of the autopsy photographs."

"And I'll bet you got that photograph real handy in that satchel there."

"Would you like to see it? To refresh your memory."

"My memory's fine," the old man said. "I don't need it refreshed. Not about what was done to that little girl."

As the silence stretched, it became obvious he wasn't going to respond to what she had told him about the rose. There were other questions that only Cooley could answer, however.

"She was your patient, wasn't she?" Callie asked. "Before the murder."

Even after all these months, Katherine Delacroix was only a series of photographs to her. Everett Cooley had known her. And as he had talked about the murder, the sense of Kay-Kay as a real child, a person, an individual, came through more clearly from the old man than it had from Lorena Delacroix herself.

"I brought her into this world, and I saw her laid out for the next. And there weren't nearly enough years between."

At the sudden quaver in his voice, it seemed a sacrilege to continue. Except two little girls were dead. And there was no one to speak for them. No one was looking for their murderer. No one but her. So Callie steeled herself against Cooley's emotion.

"About the rose, Dr. Cooley…"

"I didn't find any roses on that baby's body, Ms. Evers. I took those pictures myself, and I expect whatever you think you see in that photograph was just that—something you *think* you see. Now I'm telling you flat out it's time to let this thing go. Let it rest. Let *us* rest. Whatever you write ain't gonna bring Kay-Kay back. It's just gonna stir up a lot of pain and unhappiness. And you sure ain't gonna solve that crime, if that's what you're thinking. Not after all this time.

Ben Stanton couldn't, not as bad as he wanted to. And he *did* want to. Believe me.''

"But he was wrong," Callie argued. "His premise was wrong from the beginning, and it tainted everything he did."

"I know there's folks who'll tell you that—that the police didn't look at anybody but Tom—but I know for a fact that ain't so. Ben's a good cop, and he conducted a good, thorough investigation. Once he knew what he had, he went at it from every angle you could imagine. There wasn't nothing there. Nothing that could *prove* who did it.

"Ben thought he'd figured it out, all right. He'll probably think that until the day he dies, but I can tell you for a fact that he didn't leave any other possibility unexamined. If that baby's murder *could* have been solved, Ben would have done it.''

The brown eyes were earnest. And she found that she believed what Cooley was telling her. There had been no shock in his eyes when she revealed that she knew about the drawing. Not as there had been in Stanton's. And there hadn't been any pictures of it included with those that had been stolen and released to the media, which must mean...

What? she wondered. That Stanton had never told *anyone* about that mark? Had that been for the very legitimate reason she had just suggested to Lorena Delacroix? Or because it didn't fit with his theory about the identity of the murderer?

"Now you pick up your purse and your picture with whatever you thought you saw in it, and you carry them on back home with you," Dr. Cooley said. "Let these good folks here alone. And let Ben Stanton alone, too. He did all a man *could* do. He don't need you and everybody else second-guessing him. Stirring everything up again. Don't you think he feels bad enough?''

"Does he?" Callie asked. "You know him. I don't. I don't have any way of judging how he feels."

"Ben would have given his life to protect that little girl. He wouldn't have thought twice about it. He couldn't do that, so he did the only thing he could do for her. He devoted two years of it trying to catch her murderer. And when he couldn't do that either, I thought it would break him, strong as he is. I'll tell you the truth, Ms. Evers. I prayed God it wouldn't. And my prayers were answered. That baby's murder changed Ben Stanton, but thank God, it didn't destroy him. Now you get on home. Take your roses and your photographs and your book writing with you. And you leave that man *and* this town alone.''

IF IT HAD BEEN Doc Cooley's intention to change her opinion of Ben Stanton, it had worked, Callie admitted, as she drove the now familiar route back to the bed-and-breakfast.

Ben Stanton would have given his life to protect that little girl. He wouldn't have thought twice about it...

Just as he had come into the water last night to rescue her. Without any hesitation. Without any idea of what he might find out there. Without any consideration of his own safety.

He devoted two years of it to trying to catch her murderer. And when he couldn't do that either, I thought it would break him, strong as he is.

The phrases ran through her head like a litany, more powerful because she knew they were true. Instinctively, from the beginning, she had known this was the kind of man Ben Stanton was, despite his refusal to help her.

And why should he? To him, she was exactly what he had called her. A ghoul. And that's all she was.

What she had never realized was the depth of his emotional involvement in this case. She had believed Stanton was belligerent to her because he couldn't stand to give up his cherished theory about the identity of the murderer.

But maybe his reluctance to consider her evidence had more to do with what would be an unbearable sense of failure than with any personal animosity he had felt for Kay-Kay's father. Even as she acknowledged that possibility, she realized she still didn't know the source of that supposed animosity.

She had just turned down the street beside the bay—the

quiet, shaded avenue on which both Phoebe and Virginia lived. She looked at her watch again as she approached the Wilton house.

She was already late for supper because she had spent so long with Cooley. If she didn't take one more shot at getting Virginia to talk to her, she might never understand the relationship between Ben and Delacroix. And on the chance that it had some bearing on the identity of the real murderer...

She pulled the car up to the curb in front of the Wilton house, looking up at the second-story windows as she turned off the ignition. The sheers covering the one where she had seen movement earlier this afternoon were still.

She opened the car door, slipping her keys in the pocket of her slacks and leaving everything else where it was on the passenger seat. She stepped out onto the sidewalk, hit the auto-lock on the handle and closed the door.

When she turned to face the house, she felt a strange reluctance. In the emotional aftermath of Cooley's tribute to Stanton, this felt very much like a betrayal. As if she were going behind Ben's back in an attempt to acquire damaging information about him.

Did it really matter what personal hatreds had once existed between him and Tom Delacroix? Cooley had assured her that Ben had conducted a thorough investigation, no matter what he had felt about Kay-Kay's father.

Her hand dipped back into her pocket, closing around her keys. Then, remembering what was at stake, she forced her fingers to release them and walked up to the door. She pushed the bell, listening to its old-fashioned chimes in the distance.

As she waited, she turned to look along the street. A few of the neighbors on the other side were sitting on their front verandas. With this row of houses between them and the bay, she wondered if they could see from that vantage point the nightly display the setting sun provided.

She turned, pressing the bell again, and waited once more as the long seconds of silence slipped away. Finally she turned, intending to head back to her car.

Out of the corner of her eye, she caught sight of the brick walkway that led to the back of the house. It wouldn't take half a minute, she thought, to see if Virginia were sitting on her screened porch, preparing to watch the nightly spectacle.

It didn't, but because of the rain roof and the approach of dusk, the porch was too dark to see into. As she had this morning, Callie put her hand along her forehead and leaned close to the screen door. The wicker chairs, almost identical to Phoebe's except for the colors of the flowers in their cushions, were all empty.

She noticed the latch that had been hooked earlier this afternoon no longer was. It would take only another half minute to cross the porch and knock on the back door. Virginia was probably in the kitchen fixing supper. It was entirely possible, considering the volume of her whisper this morning, that her hearing, like Phoebe's, wasn't what it used to be.

Callie eased the door open, the movement almost furtive. She walked across the porch, sandals echoing on the planks. The curtains over the glass portion of the back door had been drawn to each side, but there was no light on in the kitchen.

There seemed to be a faint glow from the front of the house. She hadn't noticed it when she'd pulled up to the curb, so obviously it wasn't coming from any of the rooms facing the street. Again she put her hand against her forehead and pressed it against the pane of dark glass, trying to determine where the light was originating.

As she leaned against it, the door opened, swinging inward without a sound. She straightened, startled and slightly off balance. The door continued to move, exposing an expanse of black-and-white floor tile and old-fashioned metal cabinets that had been painted white.

There was a wicker table, with colorful place mats and two settings of china on it. Matching napkins were folded on each plate. There was no smell of food. And no evidence in the sink or on the counters that anyone had cooked tonight.

Maybe Virginia had decided to walk down to the shore

before supper. Callie turned, looking out through the screen of the porch at the colors the sinking sun painted over sky and water. She scanned the area under the trees, starkly silhouetted against that backdrop.

There was no one there. Nothing but the row of long piers, reaching out into the water. And an equally empty darkness inside, she acknowledged, turning to look across the kitchen.

''Virginia?''

She waited, listening to the tree frogs and the low, soft lap of the water. *Close the door,* she told herself, *get back into the car, and drive three houses down the street to Phoebe's.*

Her growing sense of unease prevented her from doing that. For some reason—a reason that had nothing to do with the gossip she had come here to hear—she wanted to see Virginia Wilton. She wanted verification that the old woman was all right. That she was as sharply contentious as she had been this morning.

Without allowing herself time to think about the propriety of what she was doing, Callie stepped over the threshold and walked across the kitchen. The sound of her footsteps seemed magnified by the tile, the metal, the emptiness.

''Virginia?'' she called, when she reached the opposite door.

There was no answer. As she strained to hear one, she became aware of the music, filtering faintly downward from somewhere upstairs. Her lips relaxed into a smile.

She couldn't have named the song if her life depended on it, but she knew the era to which it belonged. The 1940s Big Band sound fit with the peaceful, dusky atmosphere of the house, and it would also explain why Virginia hadn't answered the bell or heard her calling.

Reassured by the simple explanation, Callie stepped into the hallway, walking forward boldly now, guided by the music. From the foot of the stairs, she could see an open door on the second floor. Muted light flooded from it into the dark hallway.

''Virginia?'' she called again, more as a matter of courtesy than because she expected the old woman to be able to hear her over the strains of Glenn Miller or Tommy Dorsey or whatever orchestra was playing.

She was surprised that, if Virginia had retreated upstairs for the night, she'd left the back door unlocked. Of course, in Point Hope that probably wasn't all that unusual.

We haven't had a crime… The remembrance of Phoebe's claim triggered in her consciousness the same response it had then. *Not since someone killed a little girl.*

The sense of apprehension she had felt before she heard the music washed over her in a great, roiling wave of anxiety. She hurriedly climbed the carpeted stairs, her footsteps this time making no noise at all. She intended to call out again, but the volume of the music increased as she neared the open bedroom door and her throat tightened.

She had at last recognized the song. A half-remembered snatch of lyrics echoed through her memory as she climbed. *I'll be seeing you in all the old familiar places…*

She topped the stairs, the thickness in her throat a hard ache now. *Something was wrong. Something…*

She would wonder later if she had smelled the blood before she had seen it. Or if the scent she had unconsciously attributed to an old house occupied by an old woman hadn't also been a memory.

One as elusive as the words of that song, which had played over and over again on Virginia's record player as her blood had inexorably seeped out of the wound in her head, slowly congealing in a glistening, ever-expanding puddle.

There was no need to check for a pulse. No need to call 9-1-1. Callie had never known anything in her life with such absolute certainty as she knew that.

Virginia Wilton was dead. She had been dead for a long time. And the secret she had promised to tell Callie this morning would never be revealed. Not by lips that were so ghastly white.

CHAPTER NINE

CALLIE TURNED, stumbling in her haste to get away. The banister wavered into sight, and her hand reached out for it. She leaned weakly against the balustrade—eyes closed, mouth open, breathing deeply.

After a few seconds, she pushed away from its support and ran down the stairs. She never even considered trying to find the phone and calling the authorities. She wanted out of the house. The smell of it, combined with what she had seen in that upstairs room, was more than she could bear.

She turned at the foot of the stairs, skidding on the hard-wood floor. She hadn't headed toward the front door, which was nearer, but unthinkingly retraced the path she had taken here. Only as she neared the end of the hall into the kitchen did she slow. While she'd been upstairs, the sun had sunk into the bay, leaving the back of the house in total darkness.

She hesitated on the threshold, unable to see anything but the white tiles of the floor, paler than the alternating black ones. That same sense of foreboding she had felt as she approached the house closed over her again.

She did not want to cross that dark expanse. Not even to escape what she had found upstairs. Not even to summon help from the neighbors, sitting tranquilly on their porches across the street. Not even to avoid the stench of blood and mildew.

Trembling, she collapsed against the wall. She put the back of her head against it, listening to the harshness of her own breathing. Her mother's voice, calm and reasoned, echoed in her memory. *You're going to have to go back to your own bed.*

This was the same nameless terror she had fought so long ago. And into it came the shrilling of the phone, the sound so unexpected she jumped. Hanging on the wall beside the doorway where she was standing, it seemed preternaturally loud. Panicked, she ran across the kitchen and slammed into something big and solid, something that grunted with the impact.

"What the hell?"

Her recognition of that voice was instantaneous. And just as she had in the water last night, Callie put her arms around Ben Stanton, clinging to him mindlessly. Exactly as she had once clung to her mother, fighting the formless horror of nightmares she could never articulate.

After a few seconds, as the phone continued to ring, Ben's arms closed around her. She laid her cheek against his chest, listening to his heartbeat. Reassured by its steadiness.

And then she remembered what she had to tell him. She raised her head, looking up at his face. She could barely make out his features in the darkness, and she wondered how she could possibly have known with such certainty whom she had run into. There had been no doubt in her mind. No question. And no fear.

"She's dead," she said. "Virginia's dead."

"Dead?" he repeated, as if the word or the concept it conveyed were unfamiliar.

"Upstairs. In the room with the music." In the silence between the measured ringing of the phone, she could still hear the tinny strains of that old melody drifting down the stairs.

"What happened?" he asked.

She shook her head, the motion so slight it was barely movement.

"Callie?"

"I don't know. She was just…lying there."

"Are you sure…?"

"Oh, yes. Oh, God, yes."

She was. Even now, even at this distance, she was sure.

"Stay here," he ordered, stepping back to break her hold.

It didn't work. She wasn't about to let him leave her here alone. Not in this darkness. "No," she denied.

She clung to him, even when he put his hands on her upper arms, attempting to set her away.

"I have to go see about Virginia. You know that."

"No," she said again. Despite the knowledge that she was acting like a child, she thought she couldn't stand it if he left her alone. Not in this house. Not with that miasma of rot and mold and blood still in her nostrils. In her head.

"Then come with me."

The lesser of the two evils, but she wanted to be out of here. Away from what she had seen upstairs. Out in the fresh, heat-laden night air.

"*Damn* it."

For an instant she thought that had been directed at her, but he stepped to the side, breaking her hold by pushing her arms downward. He succeeded because he finally used his strength against her. He strode across the kitchen and picked up the receiver, mercifully cutting the phone off in midring.

"Hello?" And then he listened.

As he did, Callie crossed the room. She positioned herself behind him, her back to his, facing the blackness where she knew the outside door to be. She stood as near to Ben as she could get without physically touching him. Shoulders hunched, she crossed her arms over her chest as if she were cold. She was. She was shivering, from fear or reaction.

"It's Ben Stanton, Phoebe," he said into the receiver.

Eyes gradually adjusting to the darkness, Callie could make out the shadowed shapes of table and chairs. And then the door to the screen porch, standing open, just as she had left it.

"I'll have to call you back," Stanton said.

His voice reflected a calmness that was as comforting to her as the rhythm of his heart, beating steadily under her cheek, had been. He reached out, wrapping his arm around her shoulders and drawing her against his side.

Tears burned her eyes at the gesture. Gratefully, she pressed her face against the cotton of his shirt, and took a deep breath, seeking control of the terror that had seized her upstairs. The fabric under her cheek smelled of washing powder. Underlying that was the unmistakably masculine scent of his body. A hint of soap. The clean, salt-tinged fragrance of the sea.

"As soon as I can," Ben promised. Then he listened, briefly this time, before he spoke again. "Callie's here. She's fine. Give me a few minutes, and I'll call you back. I promise I will, Phoebe. Don't you come over here until you hear from me."

He put the receiver on the hook, still holding Callie against his side with one arm.

"You sure you want to go back up there?"

If the option is to be left down here in the darkness...

She nodded, her skin brushing against the cloth-covered wall of his chest. His fingers squeezed her shoulder reassuringly, and then he turned, guiding her through the doorway and leading the way toward the stairs. Back toward the light and the faint, hauntingly familiar music.

THE STREET that had been so peaceful when she had parked her car in front of Virginia's house was alive with activity. Emergency vehicles, their light-bars garish in the darkness, were parked along either side, blocking traffic. People stood on the sidewalks, the alternating colors of the strobes reflecting off their shocked faces.

Even though she had gone upstairs with Ben, his arm around her, she hadn't gone into Virginia's bedroom. Not even to the door. She had stood at the top of the stairs, leaning against the banister. Ben had left her there only a matter of seconds.

It had taken him no longer than it had taken her to arrive at the same conclusion. He had reacted to it far more efficiently, however, calling the dispatcher as soon as they got back downstairs. Callie had retreated to the veranda when the first of the emergency units arrived.

That had been maybe thirty minutes ago. Now Ben and Doak Withers were standing out in Virginia's front yard, talking to one of the paramedics who had been upstairs.

They were too far away for her to hear any of the conversation, but the medic kept shaking his head. Once Doak raised both hands, palms up, the gesture questioning.

Remonstrating with the opinion he'd just been given? she wondered. An opinion about the cause of death? Whatever that was, no one had bothered to share the information with her.

Finally, Doak put out his hand, talking the whole time. After the fireman had gripped it and then Ben's, he stepped away, heading toward one of the units parked along the curb. The two men watched his retreat, their backs to Callie.

Withers said something to Ben. Then both of them turned to look up at the porch where she was standing. Ben shook his head, the movement slight. His mouth never moved, although Doak made another comment. Without answering it, Ben started across the yard, his ex-deputy following. They climbed the steps together.

"Ms. Evers?" Withers said. "Like to ask you a few questions, ma'am. If you don't mind."

Despite the way that had been phrased, she knew it wouldn't make any difference if she did.

"What happened to Virginia?" she asked, instead of bothering to agree to something they both knew was a foregone conclusion.

"The paramedics think she must have fallen and hit her head hard enough to knock herself unconscious. Hard enough to open up a gash on her temple. And then…she just never woke up."

Callie allowed the scene she had just spent the last half hour trying to forget to reform in her head. The explanation for what she'd seen upstairs seemed to be that Virginia Wilton had bled to death as a result of a minor accident.

"Fell over what?" she asked disbelievingly. "She was in her own bedroom, for God's sake."

Virginia had lived in this house for years. She would have known the position of every piece of furniture, especially that in her own bedroom.

"I don't guess we'll ever know what happened for sure," Doak said. "Maybe she got up too fast and felt a little faint. Paramedic said that kind of thing happens all the time."

She had heard about cases like that. Usually there was something else involved. Drugs or alcohol. Maybe in this instance the contributing factor had simply been age.

"There was so much blood," she said, her voice low.

"They think with her history she may have been on medication that contributed to that," Ben said.

"What kind of history?"

"A couple of strokes, the last one only a few months ago. They were relatively minor, but still…"

Callie nodded. Apparently there had been nothing sinister about Virginia's death. A simple accident. One of thousands that befall the elderly every year. This one with more tragic results than most.

"We were curious as to why you were here," Doak said.

Their eyes were fastened on her face, the same detached, professional interest in both. Her gaze met Ben's, wondering if he suspected what had brought her here. And then, suddenly, wondering if her careless revelation this afternoon had been what had brought *him* here.

She hadn't thought to question why Stanton was standing in the middle of Virginia's kitchen in the darkness. She had been far too relieved to find that he was.

"Ms. Evers?" Withers prompted.

"I wanted to ask her some questions," she said, pulling her eyes away from the steady regard of Stanton's.

"Questions about…?"

"The Delacroix case. I told you when I came by your

office. I'm writing a book about Katherine Delacroix's murder.''

She didn't look at Ben again, but those unanswered questions still troubled her. Had he come to Virginia's to try to find out what the old woman had told her? Had he been that concerned about whatever Virginia knew?

''You thought *Mrs. Wilton* would have some information about the murder?'' Doak asked skeptically.

''I'm trying to talk to as many people as I can who were residents at the time of the murder. To get a feel for atmosphere. For the town's reactions, if nothing else.''

Withers nodded as if that made sense. What Virginia had intimated she knew was none of his business, Callie decided. Phoebe had been adamant that the old gossip had nothing to with Kay-Kay's death, and Virginia hadn't denied her contention. Although that begged the question of why Callie had been so determined to hear it.

''You come in the back?'' Doak asked.

''The door to the screened porch was unlatched. I thought Virginia might be cooking supper. I came in, intending to knock on the back door, but…'' She hesitated, trying to remember.

''Yes, ma'am?''

''It was unlocked. Actually, it wasn't completely closed. It opened when I tried to look in. I wondered why Virginia would go upstairs at night and leave the door unlocked.''

''Most people around here don't bother to lock their doors,'' Withers said, his tone a little patronizing. ''We aren't like other places where you have to be afraid all the time.''

We haven't had a crime…

''Virginia locked *hers,*'' she said.

There was a small silence.

''How would you know that?'' Ben's tone was more assertive than Doak's. And again professional.

''It was locked when I came by earlier this afternoon.''

''The back door?''

''The door to the screened porch. The hook was latched.''

"Did you knock?"

She nodded. "I rang the bell, and when there was no an-swer, I went around to see if she might be out on the back porch."

"About what time would that have been," Doak asked.

Right before I drove out to his place, Callie thought, her eyes locking with Stanton's. "Maybe...one. One-fifteen," she guessed. "After lunch."

There was a subtle change in the blue eyes, and she knew Stanton had just put those times together, but he didn't men-tion her visit to his place either.

"And that's when you found the screen locked?" Doak asked.

"I called up to her, but the window unit was so loud I knew she wouldn't be able to hear me."

"Maybe she was out shopping or something," Doak sug-gested.

She shook her head. "I saw movement. At the window upstairs. Someone pushed aside the curtain." She turned and looked up, as if she could see through the roof of the veranda. "It was the window right above our heads."

Both men looked up, and then quickly back down, as if embarrassed by that lapse of logic. And neither of them voiced the obvious. The room directly above their heads was the corner bedroom where she had found Virginia's body.

"You're sure of the time?" Ben asked.

She turned, again meeting his eyes, wondering why he had asked. "I stopped by here on the way out to your place."

Withers' brows lifted in surprise, but he didn't question the reason for that visit.

"Is she right?" Doak asked. "Between one and one-fifteen?"

"About then," Ben acknowledged.

There was a prolonged silence. A radio in an emergency vehicle out on the street squawked, its message unintelligible.

"That doesn't make sense," Withers said finally.

"What doesn't?" Callie asked, sensing that the atmosphere had altered somehow, without understanding what she'd said to bring that change about. "Ben?"

This was the first time she had called him by his given name, and despite their physical proximity in the kitchen, saying it felt strange. Out of place. Less comfortable than his arm around her shoulders had felt.

"The paramedics placed the time of death earlier," Stanton said. His features were set, his mouth almost stern.

"Earlier? How much earlier?"

"Around eleven o'clock this morning. That's just an estimate," Doak said. "And very preliminary. Based on their observations of the condition of the body. Amount of rigor. The way the blood had settled. But hell, in *this* heat…"

Withers continued to talk. After the phrase "in this heat," however, Callie heard nothing else, her mind racing along its own track instead. She had just realized that, despite the late afternoon heat, the window unit in the bedroom hadn't been running. As loud as it had been this morning, she would have noticed it. There had been no sound in that room but the record, playing over and over again on the old-fashioned turntable.

She looked up to find Ben watching her again, a question in his eyes. As if he knew she had just thought of something that didn't fit.

"…so don't go feeling this was your fault," Doak was saying. "They're probably right about the time of death. They're usually right on the money."

The statement was just bizarre enough that it broke through her abstraction. "That *what* was my fault?" Surely he couldn't mean Virginia's death.

"I don't want you to worry that she got up too quick when she heard you calling her and fell."

Was that possible? The idea that this might be her fault hadn't crossed Callie's mind until he'd planted it. And now that he had…

"If that were the case, then who unlocked the screen door?" Ben asked.

The possible answers to that were undoubtedly running through their minds just as they were through hers. The simplest was that it had been Virginia at the window this afternoon, just as Callie had thought at the time. And Virginia who had shut off the window unit in the bedroom and then come back downstairs sometime later in the day to unlock the screen door.

If the paramedics were right about the time of her death, however, then it would have had to be someone else at the window. Someone who had entered the house and locked both doors behind him. Someone who had watched through that upstairs window as Callie drove away. Someone who had turned off the air conditioner—to make it more difficult to pinpoint the time of Virginia's death? she wondered—and had then left the house through the kitchen, leaving both doors at the back unlocked.

"Are you saying...?" Doak paused, seeming to want someone else to put it into words.

Callie wasn't sure she was capable of doing that, although she understood what Ben was thinking.

"I'm saying that Virginia might not have been alone when she died. Not if Ms. Evers is certain about the time she was here this afternoon."

"It was after lunch," she said, trying to remember if she'd looked at the clock before she'd left. "Phoebe and I ate late because we'd been up most of the night. She took a morning nap."

She didn't mention Virginia's early morning visit. And she wasn't sure why she didn't. Maybe to avoid questions about why she hadn't conducted the interview she'd mentioned then?

"What you saw could have been the air conditioner blowing on the curtain. Making it flutter or something," Doak suggested.

"Then who shut the air conditioner off?" she asked. "It *was* off, wasn't it?"

The last was addressed to Ben, and he nodded.

"Now let's not go off half-cocked here," Doak protested. "There are probably a dozen explanations. We need to wait until the coroner gives us a definite time of death. Until then—"

"Secure the scene," Ben said.

The chief of police didn't respond immediately. Finally, as he realized the implications of that quiet command, Withers' brows lifted.

"Hell, Ben," he said, his voice subdued, "it's too late for that. There must have been ten paramedics tramping around up there. Volunteer fire department," he explained to Callie. "We get an emergency, and everybody wants in on the action."

"Do it anyway," Ben urged. "At least keep anybody else out of there."

"You were the first one here," Doak said, turning his attention back to his ex-boss. "You see anything strange?"

"I wasn't looking for anything strange."

Just like before, Callie thought, the realization chilling.

The same scenario Stanton had faced with Kay-Kay's death. And it must be a cop's worst nightmare: to believe you are dealing with one situation, which calls for one kind of reaction, and then to find out after it's too late that you were dealing with something very different.

"Secure it now, Doak," Ben said, the note of authority clear. "And tell the coroner we need something definitive on time of death as soon as possible."

"Look," Doak said, "I understand what you're suggesting, but...if Mrs. Wilton died at eleven, why would someone still be up in that room at one?"

"Most of the houses along this stretch are occupied by the elderly. Lying down after lunch is the norm rather than the exception. And those who are awake aren't going to be out in the heat of the day. Waiting a couple of hours to leave would mean less chance that whoever was here would be seen."

Doak nodded. "Anything else?"

"Dust it. And do it yourself. Check for prints on the air conditioner. The arm of the turntable. Both back doors. You didn't touch the knob on the door into the kitchen?"

It took a second for Callie to realize he was talking to her. She shook her head. "It opened when I leaned against the glass. I never touched the knob."

"That door first," Ben ordered, turning back to Withers. "My prints will be on the inside knob of the front door where I let the paramedics in. Both our prints will be on the handle of the screen at the back, but I don't think anyone else came in that way."

I don't think anyone else came in that way. She wanted to ask why he had come in through the back, walking into Virginia's kitchen in the dark. She didn't, though. Not in front of Doak. And she couldn't explain why she was so reluctant to do that.

Of course, she herself had been less than forthcoming about several things. Like why she had come here twice today to talk to an old woman who had nothing relevant to tell her about Kay-Kay Delacroix's death. And why she hadn't mentioned Virginia's visit and the argument she'd had with Phoebe this morning.

"Is that it?" Withers asked.

"It'll do for a start," Ben said. "Just keep everybody else out. That's the most important thing we can do now."

Doak nodded, and then he hurried down the steps toward the patrol car he'd parked on the street. Behind him there was a small, strained silence. Both she and Ben had left things unsaid. Things Withers might need to know if this turned out to be what Ben was suggesting it was.

"Did you call Phoebe back?" Callie asked.

She didn't want her to come over here and discover what had happened without some prior preparation.

"I phoned Doc Cooley and asked him to go over there. I asked him to tell her what had happened to Virginia and, whatever he had to do, to keep her from coming over here."

"I'd like to go see her. If I'm free to leave."

The inflection of the last was questioning. Not that she expected him to tell her she couldn't. Even after the possibility had been raised that there might have been someone in Virginia Wilton's house this afternoon, no one seemed to be questioning any of Callie's actions.

"I'll go with you," Ben said.

"Don't worry. I'm not planning to leave town," she said, stung by his mistrust.

"I'd feel better if you were."

"If I were leaving?"

That hurt, too, and she couldn't imagine why it should. Just because he had put his arm around her when she'd been terrified didn't mean he owed her any special consideration.

"It might be safer," he said.

She shook her head, holding his eyes as the implication washed over her. "You think…" She didn't finish, because she didn't want to articulate what she believed he was thinking.

"I don't like what's going on. I didn't like what happened last night. I don't like the idea that someone else might have been inside Virginia's bedroom this afternoon. I don't like the way any of this looks."

A good cop looks at a scene like that and smells the wrongness of it. From everything she'd been told since she'd been in Point Hope, Ben Stanton had been a good cop.

"You think someone murdered her," she said flatly, finally putting into words what they all had been avoiding.

"I never said that."

He didn't have to. His instructions to Doak had implied the possibility. The unavoidable conclusion to be drawn from those precautions was that this was now a crime scene.

"Whoever it was…whoever was at that window," she amended, "saw me. And he had to have known I was here to talk to Virginia. I haven't made any secret of what I'm doing."

"If they're right about the time, Virginia was dead long before you arrived."

"That's what bothers me," Callie said softly. "The possibility that Virginia really did know something about Kay-Kay's murder. And the possibility that someone killed her to keep her from telling me what it was."

CHAPTER TEN

PHOEBE'S KITCHEN was crowded with neighbors and friends when they arrived. Some, like Doc Cooley and Tommy Burge, Callie knew. A couple of women she didn't recognize were attempting to make coffee, searching through the cabinets and setting mugs and spoons and neatly folded linen napkins out on the counter.

She was surprised Buck Dolan wasn't here. She thought she'd seen him while she'd been standing out on the veranda at Virginia's. As the neighbors gathered in quiet groups along the sidewalks, a man leaned against one of the oaks across the street. She had followed the glowing tip of his cigarette in the darkness as he periodically brought it to his lips.

Maybe Buck was still out there, watching as Doak and his deputy carried out Ben's suggestions. More concerned about observing the investigation of one friend's death rather than seeing to the welfare of another.

"Phoebe," Callie said gently.

The old woman was sitting at the kitchen table, forehead in her hands. At the sound of Callie's voice, she straightened, turning toward her almost eagerly. Her eyes rimmed with red, nose and cheeks blotchy, it was obvious she'd been crying.

"I didn't mean it. You know I didn't mean it," Phoebe said, reaching out to take her hand.

Callie nodded, as she knelt beside Phoebe's chair. Freeing her hand, she put her arms around the thin shoulders and hugged her close. The old woman sobbed audibly, melting into her embrace. After a few seconds, she pushed away, wiping her eyes with the paper towel she held crushed in her hand. She sniffed, and then took a deep, ratcheting breath before she spoke.

"Everett says she must have fallen."

It was almost a question. As if she expected Callie to tell her the details of Virginia's death. Resisting the urge to look at Ben or Cooley for guidance, Callie nodded again. With that encouragement, words spilled from Phoebe's lips in a torrent.

"The paramedics told him it looked like she hit her head on something. I think it was that bedside table. I *told* Virginia it wasn't a real bedside table, but she said it held a lot of things. That table was way too tall to use for a bedside table. If I told her once, I must have told her a dozen times."

Callie nodded again, as if that could make a difference now. Her eyes held on Phoebe's face, trying to evaluate her emotional stability.

"She knew I didn't mean it, didn't she?" Phoebe asked, her voice lowered to a whisper so that the question was only between the two of them. "I was upset about... You know." Her eyes lifted, quickly touching on either Ben's face or Dr. Cooley's before they came back to Callie. "Virginia never did know when to keep her mouth shut, but...I loved her. She was my best friend for more than fifty years. Ever since she married Beau Wilton and moved into that house."

"She knew you loved her, Phoebe. Don't worry about what happened this morning. Virginia knew how much you loved her."

With the questions that had been raised about Virginia's death, Callie had almost forgotten the spat. Now she felt guilty that her curiosity caused the breech in the two women's long-standing friendship.

"Everett says it was her medicine that killed her," Phoebe continued, pushing the crumpled paper towel against her nose and sniffing again. "It was supposed to thin her blood." She shook her head, eyes focused on a spot beyond Callie's shoulder. "If I'd just gotten my nose back in joint and gone on over there to make up with her, maybe..." She shook her head again, her shoulders trembling with the force of her breathing.

"There's nothing you could have done."

"Now what'd you get your nose out of joint about in the first place?" Doc Cooley asked.

Callie turned, realizing that he was standing right beside her. His tone seemed a little condescending, almost as one might talk to a child. Or, Callie acknowledged, as a long-time friend and physician might talk to his elderly, hard-of-hearing patient.

"Me and Virginia had words this morning," Phoebe admitted.

"So what else is new?" Doc asked, smiling down at her. "Virginia would *really* have thought you didn't love her if the two of you didn't go at it now and again. What was this one about? Whether the Winn Dixie or the Piggly Wiggly has the best price on broilers?"

Despite her true and heartfelt grief, Phoebe's lips moved into a reluctant smile at his teasing. "That was last week."

Doc laughed, reaching down to pat her hand. "Now I ain't seen Virginia, so what I'm telling you isn't a medical opinion, you understand. But if the drug she was taking is what I'm thinking it was, there wasn't anything you could have done to save her, even if you'd been over there with her. So I want you to quit worrying about that. Virginia would want you to. You know that, Phoebe. You just buck up, now, you hear me. And put that kind of foolishness out of your head."

"You really think that's true, Everett? That I couldn't have done anything even if I'd been there."

"I doubt you could. I doubt *I* could. So don't you go worrying anymore about that fuss y'all had."

Phoebe nodded, obviously comforted. Callie didn't see how Cooley could make that assessment without knowing Virginia's prescription. Of course, maybe what he'd said had simply been a kindness. And if it was a white lie, Callie couldn't blame him for having told it. She put her hand on the back of Phoebe's chair and got to her feet.

"Callie was gone most of the afternoon," Phoebe said. 'Working on her book. The whole time, I kept thinking I ought to go over to Virginia's, but I just kept putting it off. My daddy used to say not to let the sun set on your anger, so the later it got, the more I knew I needed to put things right. To tell you the truth, I was halfway expecting her to come over here."

Having watched that battle of wills this morning, Callie imagined that would have been the usual sequence. Virginia would be the one who would give in. She would have been the one to make the first move to set things right between them.

"Then, as the day wore on, and she didn't come, I got real uneasy. I just had this feeling that something wasn't right. I called her a couple a times, but she didn't answer. Then the last time I called... That's when you picked up," Phoebe said, looking up at Stanton as she wiped her nose again. "And she'd been lying there dead all that time I'd been thinking about her."

"Doc's right, Phoebe," Ben said. "There was nothing you could have done."

"Did she go peaceful, you think?"

That was addressed to Ben, although it might have made more sense to ask that question of Cooley. It seemed especially ironic that Phoebe would ask Ben. After all, he was the one who had suggested there might have been foul play involved in Virginia Wilton's death. And if he were right, then her last few minutes wouldn't have been peaceful. Not if she had realized what was about to happen.

Callie shivered, just as she had in Virginia's dark kitchen. Again, she crossed her arms over her chest, unconsciously rubbing her hands up and down them. The silence between Phoebe's question and Stanton's answer seemed revealing, but his tone was completely normal when he gave it.

"If the paramedics are right, she just bumped her head and never woke up. There's lots worse ways to go, Phoebe."

For a second the scent of blood and mildew was strong in

the room. Or maybe that was only in her head. She had never before noticed the musty, old-age smell that had seemed to permeate Virginia's house this afternoon in this one.

"Come on, Phoebe. Why don't you let me take you upstairs," Callie said, closing her mind to that. She had noticed that the old woman's hands were trembling more then they usually did. If they weren't careful, Phoebe would have a stroke. "Maybe Doc can give you something to help you sleep," she added.

She glanced at the doctor and found his eyes on her face. She tilted her head, questioning.

Cooley looked down at Phoebe, reaching out to take her hand. He lifted her arm and placed his fingers around her wrist, obviously checking her pulse. No one said anything, waiting until he released the bony forearm. Finally he took Phoebe's hand between both of his and smiled at her again.

"Steady as a rock. You're gonna outlive all of us, Phoebe Mae," he pronounced before he turned to look at Ben. He continued to hold Phoebe's hand in his left palm, his right hand stroking the top of it. "I asked Tommy to call Phoebe's son. Going to stay with him for a couple of days will be better for her than staying here alone and working herself into a state."

"Sam said he'd be here in about an hour," Burge said.

"I told Everett I don't *need* to go to Sam's," Phoebe said, looking up at Callie. "That's my son that lives in Mobile. As soon as he heard, though, he told Tommy he was coming over to get me. Promised to bring me back as soon as we know about the arrangements. You called Peggy Ann, didn't you, Tommy?"

"I called her," Doc said. "That's not the kind of call anybody wants to make, I can tell you. She's gonna come up as soon as she can get a flight out of Tampa."

"That's Virginia's daughter," Phoebe explained for Callie's benefit, since everyone else seemed to be aware of these relationships. "I don't know if they'll want to bury her here.

Surely they will, though. Beau's buried here. All her friends.''

"That's not anything for you to fret about, Phoebe," Cooley said. "Her family'll handle that. You just let it be."

An echo of what he'd told Callie this afternoon, she realized. And in the same tone. *Let it be. Let that man and this town be.* She hadn't, and now...

"Land sakes, Callie, I didn't even *think* about you," Phoebe said, shocked at her lack of consideration for a guest, even a paying one. "You're welcome to stay here. You'll have to do your own cooking, but I can give you back part of the rent—"

"Phoebe," Callie protested, stopping the spate of words. "It doesn't matter. I'll be fine, I promise."

"Well, I don't feel right leaving you, but once Sam and Debbie have made that trip... It'll just be for a couple of days. Just until Peggy Ann gets here and makes the arrangements," Phoebe promised.

Callie nodded. She knew, however, that no matter how long it was, she wouldn't stay in this house alone. She raised her eyes, looking directly into Ben's. He'd been watching her, just as Doc had. And she wasn't sure what her face revealed.

She had come to Point Hope assuming that Katherine Delacroix's murderer had killed and then moved on, as he had so long ago. She had been a fool not to consider the possibility that he might still be here. And that what she was trying to do might put her—or others—in danger.

That she should be afraid of Kay-Kay's murderer, however, had never crossed her mind. Not until last night. And even then, everyone else's explanation had been more palatable.

Someone was trying to frighten her, they had suggested. If they were, she acknowledged bitterly, they had succeeded. It seemed that every ounce of courage she possessed was gone. In the course of the last two days she had been reduced again to that frightened little girl, crying in the darkness.

Holding her eyes, Ben moved his head from side to side. Obviously a negation. Of Phoebe's suggestion? If so, she was in complete agreement. She would get a motel room. Or she would pack her bags and get out of Point Hope.

This was a case that had been unsolved for ten years. The other murder for more than a quarter of a century. What idiocy had made her believe she could figure out what had happened to those two little girls?

"I'll help you pack," she said again, the offer out before she had time to acknowledge her reason for making it. One last chance. *One last chance to learn the truth.*

PHOEBE FINISHED folding the worn nightgowns and cotton underwear she had laid out in a stack on the bed. Callie watched her, trying to think of some way to ask her questions without revealing that there had been something suspicious about Virginia's death.

As Phoebe started to fold the first of the three pairs of slacks and the matching knit tops she had taken out of the closet, Callie admitted there might not be a way. And since she had been thinking only five minutes ago that it was time to leave Point Hope, she wasn't sure why it seemed so important she learn the secret Virginia had hinted at.

She didn't suspect Ben of any wrongdoing, despite the fact that he'd been in Virginia's kitchen tonight. She couldn't explain her surety that he had had nothing to do with either Virginia's death or what had happened during the jubilee.

Not logically, anyway. And in a situation as fraught with danger as this, logic, not emotion, should be the guiding force in everything she did. Instead, she was basing her judgment of Ben Stanton on factors which involved nothing *but* emotion.

The feel of his arm around her shoulders, comforting, drawing her close. The way he had looked at her as he'd knelt beside her in the boat, his eyes concerned and compassionate.

Only last night, she thought, watching Phoebe's palsied

hands move over the garments, smoothing them one by one as she laid them in her suitcase. Last night. Time had telescoped since her arrival here.

Everything was moving too quickly. A new and far more terrible event had occurred before she had had time to understand the significance of the threat against her that had preceded it. There were too many things she was missing. And if she didn't figure some of them out before Phoebe left—

"I need to know what Virginia meant," she said aloud.

Phoebe's eyes, looking old and tired, lifted. "Meant about what, dear?"

"About why Ben Stanton hated Tom Delacroix. About the bad blood that had nothing to do with the evidence. Why Ben was so sure Delacroix killed his daughter."

"That's nothing but gossip. Virginia should never have brought it up."

But she did. And now she's dead. And I have to know if that gossip had anything to do with her death.

She couldn't say any of that to Phoebe. Or to anyone else. Officially, Virginia's death was an accident. Right now at least. And it might very well *have* been. Just as what had happened to her last night *might* have been someone trying to scare her. She doubted both those suppositions.

"Virginia thought it was important," she said.

"Well, it wasn't. Virginia was wrong. Kay-Kay's dead, and so is Tom. Digging up that old dirt isn't going to bring either of them back to life. I'm not about to let you or anybody else speak ill of the dead."

Something that reflected badly on Delacroix then, and not on Stanton. With that realization there was an easing of the unacknowledged dread she hadn't realized she harbored.

"Was it true?" she asked.

A crease formed between Phoebe's eyes. "True?"

"The gossip Virginia was talking about? Just tell me if it was true, Phoebe."

"I told you it isn't important—"

"But it *is*. I promise you that. I won't put it in any book, if that's what you're worried about. It'll stay between you and me, I swear. Just tell me that much. Was it true?"

The old lady's eyes held on her face, and Callie waited, unconsciously holding her breath.

"Only three people know the answer to that," Phoebe said finally. "And one of them's dead. If you want the truth…"

She hesitated, looking down on her trembling hands. Suddenly, she pressed them together so tightly the swollen knuckles whitened. She brought them to the center of her chest, holding them against her breastbone.

"I hate being old," she said, tears welling. "I hate never knowing anymore what's right and what's wrong. You'd think I would by now. You'd think I'd always be sure what was the right thing to do." She shook her head, the palsy making the gesture infinitely sad. "I don't gossip," she said softly. "I don't hold with those who do. You can ask Ben if it's really all that important."

"Phoebe—"

"That's all I'm saying, so don't you ask me anymore. I don't think I can bear it tonight," she said, with a break in her voice. "You ask Ben. And whatever he tells you—if he tells you—then you'll know it's the truth."

"SHE'LL BE ALL RIGHT," Cooley said, as the four of them stood in Phoebe's front yard, watching the taillights of her son's van disappear down the again-peaceful street. "Phoebe's a tough old bird. All that generation is."

Callie realized that she had mentally assigned Cooley and Phoebe to the same generation. Forced to think about it, she acknowledged that there could indeed be a generation's span between their ages. Phoebe was in her eighties, while Doc, only semiretired, might very well be in his early sixties.

"They survived a depression and a world war," Burge said.

"And lost their sons in Korea and Vietnam," Cooley added.

Phoebe had, Callie remembered. And then she had lost her beloved Hobart, too. Facing the deaths of those she loved was not unfamiliar to someone who had lived as long as Phoebe.

"I'm heading home," Tommy said. "Let me know if there's anything else I can do, Ben." Again, there was that unconscious assigning of authority to Ben Stanton.

"Guess I'll get on back, too." Doc said. "Give you a lift, Tommy? You're on my way. Unless you need me for something else." The last was addressed to Stanton.

"Thanks," Ben said, shaking hands with Burge. Then he turned to the doctor, enclosing Cooley's hand in both of his. "You always get stuck with the dirty work, Doc. Thanks."

"Goes with the territory. I knew that going in."

"Does it get any easier?" Callie asked, thinking about having to tell someone a friend was dead. Or having to tell a daughter that her mother was gone. Cooley had done both tonight.

"At least I know what to expect. That's the main difference between now and when I started practicing."

"I appreciate you coming over to check on Phoebe," Ben said. "I was afraid she was going to show up at Virginia's."

"Phoebe's not only my patient, she and Hobart were friends."

Tommy had started off across the lawn, heading toward Cooley's car. The doctor, however, didn't seem in a hurry to put his decision into action.

"How about you, Ms. Evers? You gonna stay here like Phoebe suggested?" he asked.

"Long enough to straighten up in the kitchen at least," she said. Her eyes touched on Ben's face before they moved back to Cooley's. "I'll decide what I'm going to do after that."

"You need a little something to help you sleep?"

The offer was tempting. Wherever she ended up for the night, she suspected the events from this day would play over and over in her head.

''I don't think so,'' she said. She had never used drugs as an escape, not even a temporary one. She was too old to start now. ''Thanks for the offer, though.''

''Suit yourself,'' Doc said.

He turned, following Burge across the lawn. His back to them, he lifted one hand, waving goodbye with a single, side-to-side motion of his wrist.

''How about it, Tommy? You game for a nightcap?'' he called.

Burge's reply was unintelligible, but whatever it was, it made Cooley laugh. She and Ben listened as their voices faded away under the shadows of the oaks. After a few seconds, car doors slammed, followed by the sound of an engine starting. Then, just as they had with Sam Robinson's car, she and Ben watched the taillights disappear down the street.

''You aren't staying here,'' he said.

''I know.''

''Were you serious about straightening up?''

''I can do it in the morning,'' she said. ''I need to make sure everything's turned off. Check the coffeemaker. And then I guess I should find a motel. Any suggestions?''

She looked up, but his eyes were still directed toward the end of the street where Doc's car had disappeared. Toward Virginia's house, she realized.

''Come home with me,'' Ben said.

She examined the words, unsure that he'd said what she thought she'd heard. They had been straightforward enough, however, not to lend themselves to any other interpretation.

''Why?''

''Because I think you'll be safer. Safer than being by yourself in a motel.''

She let the silence build as she thought about the offer. *Come home with me.* Protection wasn't usually the motive for a man to issue that kind of invitation. And in this case...

Logic versus emotion. Despite her instincts, it certainly wasn't logical for her to trust Ben Stanton. Not in this situation. Not enough to be alone with him. Especially since no one would know where she was or who she was with.

No one would know where she was...

"Callie?"

"I need a few things from inside," she said.

"I'll go with you."

Protection, she thought again. Maybe Stanton didn't have any motive other than that for his invitation. But, of course, she did in accepting it.

Ask Ben, Phoebe had suggested. *And if he tells you anything, you'll know it's the truth.*

There were a lot of truths that had not been revealed about what happened the night Kay-Kay Delacroix died. Just as there were other truths about what had happened today. *Ask Ben.*

She turned, walking up the sidewalk to climb the front steps of Phoebe Robinson's old house. Very much aware of the man who followed her.

CHAPTER ELEVEN

"You hungry?"

She was, Callie realized with a sense of shock. It didn't seem as if she should be, not after what had happened today. But it had been a very long time since she and Phoebe had shared lunch and some very strained silences during the conversation that had accompanied it.

It was too dark to see her watch. The last time she remembered noticing the time was when she had been helping Phoebe pack. It had been after eight then, and that had been at least a couple of hours ago.

"Actually...I am."

She was aware that Ben turned toward her, pulling his eyes from the road for a few seconds. "What sounds good?"

The exchange was surreal, given their previous relationship and the events of the past few hours. It reminded her a little of those two women, laying out linen napkins and Phoebe's silver spoons alongside the too-weak coffee they'd made, as if those acts might in some way ease the pain of Virginia's death. There was something very human about going on with the ordinary things of life, no matter the chaos that surrounded you.

"Nothing really," she said. "I just know I need to eat."

She was both nauseated and lightheaded. Almost disoriented. Maybe part of that was because she was riding in a truck with Ben Stanton *and* planning to spend the night with him.

Despite however practical her reasons for that might be, the situation was decidedly unreal. It was suddenly made more so by the abrupt turn Ben made, heading the pickup down an unpaved road, without any lessening of its speed. And it was not the drive that led to his house.

Through the open driver's-side window, she heard the music before they topped the rise, revealing the restaurant below. The ramshackle structure seemed to totter on top of its stilts, hanging haphazardly over the edge of the water.

Someone had wrapped strands of miniature Christmas tree bulbs along the top railing of its attached pier. Their lights were reflected in the bay like stars. That touch of elegance warred with the reverberating bass from the country ballad that was blaring through an outside speaker.

"I know it doesn't look like much," Ben said, guiding the pickup over a series of bone-jarring potholes in the dirt parking lot. "But the food's good."

It would have to be, she thought, as he pulled in between a mud-splattered SUV and another truck, bass boat attached. He shut off the engine and rolled up his window, mercifully lowering the volume of the music.

"We have to eat somewhere," he said in explanation, maybe even in apology. "We'll have to go inside," he added, when she made no move to get out of the truck. "They don't do takeout."

Meaning they would have to sit at a table like an ordinary couple out for the evening. *And if there had ever been a less ordinary evening... Or two people who were less likely to be a couple.*

"Unless you'd rather not be seen with me."

Surprised, she looked up to find he was watching her again. The flickering red neon sign atop the restaurant gave a ruddy glow to his sun-darkened skin.

"What does that mean?"

"I tend to forget what the world out there thinks of me."

Son of a bitch. Botched investigation. It was all right for him to play cop when all he had to do was write the occasional speeding ticket...

All the derogatory remarks that had been made about Ben

Stanton since she'd been in Point Hope echoed in her mind.
And considering them in light of what he'd just said, she
laughed.

His head tilted, questioning her reaction.

"I should probably tell you that there are a few people
here who aren't exactly admirers of yours."

His lips flattened, and then, as she watched, the corners
lifted. Almost a smile.

"I ignore them, too. I'd forgotten how many people
you've talked to."

"Not nearly as many as I'd intended to. Things..." She
shook her head, thinking about the past couple of days.
"Things keep happening."

He turned, staring out at the bay through the windshield.
He laid his forearms on top of the steering wheel, crossing
them at the wrists. She was relieved to escape, even briefly,
the intensity of those eyes.

"I think you may be right," he said. He hadn't turned his
head, his gaze still focused on the water.

She almost asked, "Right about what?" Then, as the possible connotations of that statement filtered through her exhaustion, she found she was incapable of saying anything for
a long time.

"Right about Delacroix?" she asked finally, her voice
husky from the constriction of her throat.

"I don't think this is about scaring you away."

"Then you think... You think whoever is doing this might
really *be* the same person who killed Kay-Kay?"

His head moved slowly from side to side, the motion not
strong enough to indicate denial.

"I would have staked my life," he said softly.

On Tom Delacroix's guilt. In a way, he had. Ben Stanton
had spent two long, frustrating years trying to indict Kay-
Kay's father for her murder. And he had just confessed he
was no longer certain Delacroix had committed the crime.

"Why did you go to Virginia's?" she asked.

He turned to face her. A crease had formed between the

dark brows, and she supposed her question did seem a non sequitur.

"Tonight?"

She nodded.

"You said Virginia told you there was bad blood between me and Delacroix. I wanted to know what she meant."

"Was there? Bad blood, I mean? Before the murder?"

"Lorena didn't tell you?"

She wasn't sure if that was another accusation that she was aligned with Mrs. Delacroix, or if, given the efficiency of small-town gossip, he was aware she had met with Kay-Kay's mother this afternoon. She decided to give him the benefit of the doubt and go with the latter interpretation.

"She told me you were a son of a bitch," Callie said. "I don't know if that's got anything to do with her husband, but I took it to mean there was bad blood between you and her."

He laughed, the sound unexpected, and without amusement. "You could say that."

"Because you accused Delacroix of murder?"

The tempo of the music changed, becoming more upbeat. The bass wasn't strong enough anymore to rattle the windows, but it filled the silence, which lasted long enough to become edgy.

"Virginia didn't tell you anything, did she?" Ben asked. "I couldn't figure out why you'd go back to see her, when I knew damn well she didn't have any information about Kay-Kay's murder. But that wasn't why you wanted to talk to her. She hinted there was animosity between me and Tom. *That's* what you wanted to ask her about."

Cooley had told her Stanton was a good cop. A good investigator. From their previous encounters, she had known he was bright, so she supposed she shouldn't be surprised that he'd arrived at that conclusion.

"Her exact words were that you had more reasons than just the evidence to think Delacroix had killed his daughter. Phoebe wouldn't let her say anymore, but when her back was turned, Virginia promised she'd tell me what she meant. *If* I'd come to her house later on.''

"When did she tell you to do that?"

"She came over to Phoebe's this morning to make sure I was all right. That's what she said, anyway. I think she was just curious.''

"Did you tell her you thought somebody tried to kill you?"

She hadn't. Not in so many words. Certainly not words as blunt as those she had used to Ben.

"I suggested someone had a reason to try to keep me from asking questions. Something more than just to prevent interest in Kay-Kay's death from being stirred up again.''

"Make any suggestion as to who you thought that might be?''

"I don't *know* who that might be," Callie said truthfully, bewildered by the question.

"Obviously someone who had a connection to that other murder in North Carolina.''

She had said that to Lorena Delacroix, and for a moment, she wondered if Lorena had relayed that information to Ben. But the necessity of such a link would be obvious. It was what had brought her to Point Hope.

She nodded. "To the location. Or the family.''

"But you haven't found that connection?"

"Not yet.''

"And Virginia didn't offer any possibilities?''

No one had. She hadn't really told all that many people about the other murder, she realized. Ben. Lorena Delacroix. The two old women this morning. She wasn't sure she had mentioned it in her conversation to Cooley, but she knew she hadn't said anything about it to Withers or Dolan or Tommy Burge.

"She... Actually, I'm not sure how much of what I said made an impression on her. That there had been another murder did, but... She asked me if you knew about it. I told her that you did now. That I'd told you.''

Again the music from the speaker was the only sound in the cab of the truck. The nasal twang of the vocals, something about lost love, seemed out of place with what they were discussing. She had time to listen to a couple of verses of the lament before Ben spoke again.

"Did you tell Virginia and Phoebe about the flower?"

She had told Lorena. And Cooley. She knew she should confess those disclosures, and she would at some point. But that wasn't what Ben had asked. And after all, neither of those people had turned up dead.

"I told them the murders shared some unusual aspects."

"But you didn't mention the drawing specifically?"

She shook her head, again feeling a trace of guilt that she had mentioned the information to the others. Ben had kept that secret for ten years, and it now felt like a betrayal that she had revealed it.

"We need the phone records," he said.

"*Phone* records?"

"Virginia wouldn't have been able to keep that kind of information to herself. She would have wanted to tell somebody about the other murder. About the similarities to Kay-Kay's. Since Phoebe was there when you mentioned it, that wouldn't have been who she called. Not after their argument about gossiping."

"You think she *called* someone to tell them what I'd said."

"Knowing Virginia, I'd be willing to bet on it. At least we have to hope she did."

Because if they could find out the name of the person she'd called, then...they'd know who had killed her? And who had killed Kay-Kay? It seemed too easy. Too simple a solution for this convoluted, decade-old mystery.

"Unless she called everybody in town," Ben added, putting that speculation into perspective.

"Or nobody."

"Knowing Virginia, I don't believe she could have managed that."

"I don't know. Phoebe was pretty hard on her. I thought that's why she wouldn't let me in this afternoon."

"Hard on her how?"

"When she mentioned whatever had been between you and Delacroix, Phoebe told her that it was nothing but ugly gossip and then she sent Virginia home. She told her…" As she remembered them, Phoebe's words seemed eerily prophetic, but she made herself repeat them. "Phoebe told her not to say something that would get somebody mad at *her*. When I went to see Virginia and the door was locked, I thought she'd had second thoughts about sharing her gossip, since Phoebe felt so strongly about it.

"But…even if she did call someone, we can't know what she talked to them about. Maybe she talked about the old gossip or her fuss with Phoebe and *not* about the other murder." She hadn't asked him directly, but it must be obvious that she wanted to know about the bad blood Virginia had mentioned. After all, she had gone to her house twice today to find out. "Unless everyone in town already knew whatever she was alluding to."

Phoebe and Virginia had. Maybe this wasn't nearly the dark secret she had supposed it to be this morning.

"In Point Hope everybody knows everything," he said. "At least they think they do."

"Do they know this?"

"Most of it. Lorena and I have…some history."

The pause had been infinitesimal, but with his linking of their names, Callie had already arrived at that conclusion before he confirmed it. For some reason, the nausea she had been blaming on an empty stomach stirred again.

"A sexual history?" she asked.

And felt like a fool as he let the words lie, unanswered, between them. That pale, round face with its perfect nose and shrewd blue eyes was unforgivably clear in her mind's eye.

She was disappointed, she realized. Disillusioned with the image of Ben Stanton that she had created in her own mind. A creation begun long before she'd arrived in Point Hope.

She couldn't imagine why she was. After all, he was very attractive, obviously virile and an unattached male. He undoubtedly had a long and varied "sexual history," involving a lot of women. She had to have known that, somewhere in the back of her mind. None of it had mattered. Not as long as it *stayed* in the back of her mind.

Hearing him confess to a liaison with Lorena Delacroix, however, created pictures she didn't want in her head. It wasn't as if she herself had made impeccable decisions in her personal relationships. And it was patently ridiculous for her to presume to be disapproving of anything in Ben Stanton's past, even considering her unfavorable impression of the woman involved.

She hadn't liked Lorena Delacroix. Everything about her had rung false. From her pious invocation for God to rest her husband's soul to her lack of emotion over her daughter's death to her blatant hatred of Ben Stanton.

Just as her instinct had been, almost from the beginning, to trust Ben, her emotional responses to Lorena Delacroix had all been unfavorable. She had fought them because she needed the information Kay-Kay's mother could provide, but from the first, she hadn't liked her.

"We come from the same place," Ben said, his voice low. "Share the same background. I've known Lorena all my life. And I understand why she is…what she is."

His gaze was again directed toward the dark water. Hands crossed at the wrist, the long, tanned fingers hung relaxed on the back side of the steering wheel.

"Maybe it's hard for someone who's not from here to know what it's like to grow up on the wrong side of the tracks in a place like Point Hope. You're always on the outside looking in. It's more than money. More than family. Mine and Lorena's have been here as long as anybody else's, but…

"Maybe it's because they made their living from the bay. Suffered through the good times and the bad associated with it. For Lorena's family, those times were mostly bad. Her

daddy was a drunk. A mean drunk. I never thought she'd end
up with another one."

"Tom Delacroix," Callie said.

"Except for his drinking, he represented everything Lorena had ever wanted."

"And that's why she married him?" *Him instead of you?*
"Because he came from the 'right side' of Point Hope?"

"I guess it's easy to judge that kind of ambition, too."

"I'm not *judging* it. I'm trying to understand it." But as
she made the denial, she knew that what he'd accused her of
was true. She had already made her judgment of Lorena Delacroix during this afternoon's interview. "So...if it was her
choice, why does she hate you?"

"I don't think she does," he said.

"She gives a pretty good impression of it."

A muscle tightened in the line of his jaw, knotting and
then releasing. Callie watched the movement, illuminated by
the glow from the neon sign.

"Lorena needs a lot of attention," he said finally. "Tom
didn't always provide it."

"So you did." The tone was flatter and harsher than she'd
intended. It sounded like an accusation.

He turned his head, looking at her in the semidarkness.
"*Not* after she was married. If that's what you're thinking."

It had been, of course. She had thought that's what they
were talking about. Small-town adultery. The kind of ordinary, everyday gossip someone like Virginia would probably
relish.

Phoebe had been right, she realized. This didn't have anything to do with the murder.

"And that's what Virginia wanted to tell me? The fact that
you and Lorena had once...been involved, and she married
Tom Delacroix instead?"

"I don't *know* what Virginia wanted to tell you."

She waited, the music again filling the silence between
them. "What does that mean?" she asked finally.

She was too tired to deal with this, she thought. She felt

empty, both physically and emotionally. And this whole story seemed to have been drawn out past the point of relevancy.

What the hell could it matter if Ben and Lorena Delacroix had once slept together? Especially if, as he claimed, that relationship had ended before she'd married Delacroix.

Ben took a breath, expelling it so that it was almost a sigh. And then he turned to face her again.

"I was stationed at Fort Polk. In Louisiana," he explained, probably aware from her expression that she wasn't following. "I hadn't been home in a couple of years. My mother was dead and my daddy wasn't the kind to write, so I didn't have any idea what was going on back here. Then, all of a sudden, Lorena shows up."

"At Fort Polk?"

"I didn't think anything about it at the time. It was exactly the kind of silly, thoughtless thing she'd do. The kind of thing she'd done all her life. A little wild. Not very smart. She'd ridden the damn Greyhound bus, all that way to Louisiana. Just to see me, she said. And I have to confess, I wasn't opposed to her being there. A little flattered, I guess. Homesick, maybe. I hadn't known that until I saw her."

"So you...renewed your acquaintance," she said, her voice still too flat, so that his mouth tightened in response.

"We had sex," he corrected, his tone matching the lack of expression in hers. "We spent most of that weekend in bed in a motel room. I put her on the bus back here on Sunday afternoon. And I didn't see her again for three years."

"Were you in love with her?"

It was a woman's question, the kind of thing that had seemed important to ask until she had. Then it seemed only ridiculous.

"No. And before you start judging *that*, I can tell you she wasn't in love with me either."

"She just needed some *attention*."

"I thought so. I found out later that there was a little more to it than that."

"Meaning?"

"Meaning she'd been sleeping with Tom Delacroix for several months before she made that visit."

"And you were supposed to be her last fling before the wedding?"

It made sense. According to him, he and Lorena had a history. Maybe she had been reluctant to give that relationship up. To give *him* up. And that was something which, as another woman strongly attracted to Ben Stanton, Callie could certainly understand.

And there had been a more than twenty-year gap between Tom Delacroix's age and that of his wife. The tabloids had speculated at the time of their daughter's murder that Lorena had married Tom for his money.

So none of what Ben was telling her should come as a surprise. Before she married Delacroix, Lorena had arranged one last meeting with a man she had probably found sexually attractive most of her life.

"Everything she'd ever wanted was right at her fingertips," Ben said, "and she couldn't get him to commit. She couldn't get him to marry her. Why should he? He was getting what he wanted. Lorena wasn't the kind of woman anyone could imagine Delacroix choosing for his wife. When he did, as hard as she tried, she never fit in. Never was accepted by his friends. Certainly not by his family."

"Then why did he marry her?" Callie asked, throwing the question out, not because she cared, but because it seemed called for. Expected.

"He married her because she turned up pregnant," Ben said. "Carrying the child Tom Delacroix had always wanted and his first wife hadn't been able to give him. A little girl," he added softly, as the slow chill of realization began to make its way up Callie's spine. "A little girl they named Katherine."

CHAPTER TWELVE

"SHE WAS YOURS." Callie whispered the words as the implication of what he had just said hit her. "Kay-Kay was *your* daughter."

It made sense of the years he'd spent trying to solve her murder. Not the devotion of a good cop, but a father's desire to bring to justice the murderer of his own child.

"I don't know," Ben said flatly.

"But given the timing…" She knew this was something he must have gone over again and again, trying to prove, if only to himself, whether Kay-Kay could have been his.

"By the time I got out of the army and came back here, Lorena was married. At some point I learned she had a child. I don't remember how or when because it didn't make any great impression on me.

"I even saw Kay-Kay occasionally. No bells went off. There was no instant recognition of kinship. No blood called to blood." His voice was still low, the tone almost mocking. "I didn't know how old she was. I hadn't been around enough kids to even make an educated guess about her age. And frankly, trying to do that never crossed my mind."

"You *never* suspected?"

"She looked like Lorena. Like she had when she was little. There was nothing about her that would make you think she might be anything other than what she was supposed to be. Tom Delacroix's heir. And the absolute light of his life."

Tom doted on that little girl, Virginia had said. And Doc Cooley's assessment had been much the same.

"Then how in the world could you believe he killed her?"

"Because Lorena told him."

It took a few seconds for her to comprehend what he meant because it seemed so bizarre. "She *told* him Kay-Kay wasn't his? Why would she do that?"

"I told you. She needs *lots* of attention."

Emotion, which had been carefully contained when he had talked about the possibility that Kay-Kay could be his child, was now in his voice. It was the same anger she had heard the day she confronted him with the similarities between the murder in North Carolina and the one in Point Hope.

"She told him Kay-Kay wasn't his daughter to get *attention?*"

"Maybe being married to Tom was getting dull. Or maybe Lorena had finally realized that the things she'd thought she wanted all her life hadn't made her happy and they weren't going to. I don't have any idea why she decided to tell either of us anything. And after all this time, I don't know that what she told us was the truth. All I know is that in my case—"

He stopped the words, cutting them off abruptly, and again she waited.

"For some reason, she had decided she wanted me back in her life. Maybe she thought that knowing Kay-Kay was mine would somehow…" He made that small negative motion with his head again, his eyes once more on the water. "Who knows what she thought. I've given up trying to figure Lorena out. All I can tell you is that she came out to my house one night and told me Kay-Kay was mine and that she'd finally told Tom the truth. Less than forty-eight hours later that little girl was dead."

"And you believed Tom had killed her…in *revenge?* Oh, Ben, that doesn't even make sense."

"None of it ever did," he said. And then, after a moment, "I don't suppose you still want something to eat?"

Without waiting for an answer, he turned the key in the ignition, the movement of those long fingers somehow conveying the same fury his voice had held. The engine of the pickup roared to life, and he gave it enough gas that the wheels sprayed dirt and gravel as he backed out and headed across the parking lot toward the road. He made no attempt to ease their passage over the potholes this time.

"Ben," she said, putting her hand on his arm.

It wasn't protest. It was, perhaps, more in the way of comfort. Or apology. Because she had finally recognized that she had brought about exactly what Doc Cooley feared for him.

Ben Stanton had put this pain behind him once. As much as it would be humanly possible for him to do. He had gotten on with his life. Living in the same town. Living among people who knew every detail of what they, and he, viewed as his failure. He had been able to do that because he didn't give a damn what they thought about him. Only for what he thought about himself.

And he had cared about bringing Kay-Kay's murderer to justice. He had cared desperately about the death of a little girl, who might have been his own daughter. Now, after the agony had faded to something bearable, Callie had convinced him that his failure had been even more damaging than he had once believed. And his guilt greater.

He understood now that he had been wrong in his original hypothesis about the cause of Kay-Kay's murder. Because of that error in judgment, he had gone after the wrong man. And in doing so, he had let the real murderer escape.

Cooley had warned her, but she hadn't listened. *I thought it would break him, strong as he is. That baby's murder changed him, but thank God, it didn't destroy him.*

Another failure might. If it did, that was a guilt *she* would have to live with. Just as she would have to live with the knowledge that her questions might have led to Virginia Wilton's death. And in spite of it, Kay-Kay Delacroix and Mary Cameron were still dead. Their killer still unpunished.

"I have to make that call to Doak," Ben said, turning his forearm so that her fingers slipped off.

His voice was again controlled. He wanted a record of the phone calls Virginia had made this morning. And he would have to rely on Doak to get it. It would take an official request to obtain that information. Despite the air of authority Ben Stanton carried, an authority Withers still willingly obeyed, he no longer had the power to demand its release.

"Did Virginia know?" Callie asked, trying to come to terms with the repercussions of what she had set in motion. "About Kay-Kay, I mean? About the possibility…?"

"Despite Lorena's peculiarities, I can't imagine that would be something she'd want to broadcast. Surely she wouldn't want to bastardize her own daughter."

"But if Delacroix had divorced her for that reason, the question of her daughter's paternity would have come out."

"You didn't know Tom Delacroix," Ben said. "The Delacroix always had more pride than money. And they had a hell of a lot of both. Tom would never have admitted someone else had fathered *his* daughter, not even to keep her from inheriting.

"Besides," he continued, "it wouldn't be that easy to disavow her, even if he took Lorena to court or demanded proof of paternity. His name was on her birth certificate. Kay-Kay was in his will and had been since her birth. He had *always* acknowledged her. I'm not sure he could have gotten out of paying child support, at the very least, even if tests proved she wasn't his. Knowing Lorena, I'd be willing to bet she had checked all that out before she dropped her bombshell."

"So…why tell him? What *did* she possibly hope to gain?"

"Freedom. With a guarantee that she'd always be provided for—as Kay-Kay's mother. Or maybe she believed it would give her power. Something to hold over Tom's head. Something to use against him if he didn't let her do whatever she wanted."

"I don't understand."

"Maybe she threatened to reveal his impotence. Or to reveal that she'd tricked him into marrying her. To reveal to the world that the child who would get at least some of the Delacroix money, no matter what he did, wasn't even a Delacroix."

"Would he have given in to that kind of blackmail?"

"Opt for an ongoing private humiliation rather than a public one? If you knew Delacroix, that would make sense. I'm not claiming to know what Lorena was thinking. I never have."

"But at the time of the murder you believed that instead of living with those threats, Delacroix just decided to kill Kay-Kay? Why not kill Lorena? That I *could* understand."

That would have been a far more normal reaction. Believing Delacroix would kill a little girl he adored made no sense. She couldn't believe it had to Ben. Not even back then, dealing with all he'd been dealing with. Of course, she didn't know these people, and he did. All his life.

"There would still be the problem of Kay-Kay," Ben said. "If Tom managed to get away with killing Lorena, he couldn't afford to announce to the world that her daughter hadn't been his child. That would have appeared to be a pretty powerful motive for him to be his wife's murderer."

"That seems convoluted," she said doubtfully.

"Look, I never claimed to be objective about this. At the time, I thought the idea that he'd put his whole heart into loving a little girl who wasn't his had gotten to Tom. He thought about it through those two days, and then, when he was drunk enough, he snapped. Killing Lorena wouldn't have been nearly so easy as getting rid of the bastard she had foisted on him was." The bitterness underlying that accusation was clear.

"And then they just stayed together? He didn't divorce her. She didn't leave him. That should have been some indication—"

"United front. The world thought one or both of them had killed their daughter. Those accusations necessitated that they stay married. Or maybe she really didn't know that he'd done it. At least…that's how I read it then. A few months later Tom had his first heart attack. Lorena played at being devoted wife, along with her continuing role as grieving mother. Eventually, when the second heart attack killed him, she got what she had wanted all along. Her freedom *and* the Delacroix money.''

''Except Delacroix didn't kill Kay-Kay,'' Callie reminded him. ''He couldn't have because he didn't kill Mary. And the two murders have too many elements in common, even if you discount the rose, for all of them to be coincidence.''

''The Bureau's profiler told me something I've never forgotten. At the time…'' His voice faded.

''Ben?'' she questioned as the silence went on and on.

''He said drawing that rose was a sign of love. Like murderers who arrange their victim's body so that they look comfortable and at peace. Posing them, so the pain they just put them through won't be so apparent.''

''A sign of *love?*''

Of all the motives she had imagined behind the drawing, that one had never crossed her mind. And she wasn't sure, at least in Mary's case, that she could ever accept it.

''A sign of his affection,'' Ben verified. ''He drew something beautiful. Delicate, small and tender. And he hid it underneath her hair, protecting it from anyone else's eyes. It was just for her. When they told me that, it all seemed to fit. I thought the rose meant that, in spite of everything, Tom loved her. He needed to tell her that he did, even as he killed her.''

As he talked, the words realigned themselves in her consciousness, shifting to form another kind of pattern. Not the one Ben had thought they formed ten years ago.

''Hidden,'' she said. ''Hidden under her hair because what he felt about her was a secret. A secret affection.''

He turned his head, looking toward her in the darkness. The speed of the pickup diminished, slowing as he thought about what she said. And then, without comment, he turned his eyes back toward the road, his foot again pressing down on the accelerator.

BEN STOPPED the truck in the exact spot where it had been parked the first time she'd come here. He cut off the engine and killed the lights, but neither of them made any move to get out.

After a few minutes, the noise of the tree frogs resumed in the thick woods around the clearing. There were no lights on inside the cabin, but a halogen lamp set high on a pole beside the pier provided some illumination, filtering outward to fight the darkness in the front. Enough that she could see his eyes when he turned toward her.

"Stay here," he ordered.

"Why?"

She didn't want to stay here. Not alone. It was finally hitting home to her what she had done. A murderer had lain unexposed for more than twenty-five years, and she was responsible for bringing him out of hiding to kill again.

"I want to take a look around," he said.

"No."

"Callie—"

"Nobody knows I'm with you. They couldn't. We just need to go inside and make that call. The sooner we have the information about who Virginia talked to…"

The sooner they would know the name of the murderer? Could it really be that simple? Maybe it would be. They wouldn't know unless they tried.

She put her fingers around the handle of the door. At the thought of stepping out into that unknown darkness, however, she hesitated. She heard the door on Ben's side open and then close, the sound loud in the nighttime stillness.

She watched him walk around the front of the pickup. He opened her door and offered his hand, waiting for her to put her fingers into his. That's all she had to do. Trust him to protect her. She had no reason not to. No reason except…

Secret affection. The troubling phrase echoed again in her head. An affection such as a man who had just discovered Kay-Kay was his daughter might have felt?

"What's wrong?" Ben asked.

She shook her head, forcing herself to place her hand in his as she slid off the high seat. His fingers closed strongly around hers. As they did, in the diffuse glow cast by the lamp over the pier, she saw his mouth move. He was smiling at her.

He used his hold on her hand to urge her away from the truck, and then he slammed the passenger-side door. She jumped at the sound, just as she had tonight when the phone rang in Virginia's kitchen. And as he had then, Ben put his arm around her shoulders, guiding her toward the front door of the cabin. His home. His territory.

Was this where he had brought Kay-Kay that night? Was this the crime scene that Ben Stanton, despite the thoroughness of his investigation, had never been able to discover. No neighbors to watch his comings and goings. No one living near enough to hear anything. The perfect place for a murder.

She shivered involuntarily, thinking, too late, how completely isolated they were. *Hidden. Hidden affection.*

"Cold?" he asked.

As death. The words formed in her head, and as they did, she pulled away from his hold. She turned toward the truck, trying to visualize, even as she began to run toward it, if he had left the keys in the ignition.

"Callie?"

The sound of her name was accompanied by a soft *phut*, which seemed to come from the woods to the right of the cabin. And then, just as it had out in the bay, something hit her from behind. Her knees buckled as she was thrown to the ground.

Stanton's arms were around her. He rolled, carrying her with him. And then she was again facedown on the ground, his body spread-eagled over hers. He held her down, the side of her face pressed into the dirt.

She was too shocked to offer any resistance. She opened her eyes and realized she was facing one of the tires of the truck. She was so close she could smell the rubber, still hot from its recent contact with the highway.

There was another of the strange, pneumatic noises, and dirt sprayed over them. She closed her eyes, putting up her and in an ineffectual attempt to protect her face. Another *hut,* and the tire she was facing deflated, sinking into the andy soil with a hiss.

"Under the truck," Ben demanded. "Get under the ruck."

At some time between the dirt hitting her hair and his ommand, she had finally realized someone was shooting at hem. Using her elbows and knees, she scrambled under the protection of the pickup, canted now at a slight angle because f the flat. She turned her head in time to watch Ben join er.

"What the hell is—" she began.

"Shh," he whispered.

They listened together. Her wildly beating heart sent blood oaring through her ears, so that she was afraid she wouldn't e able to hear anything but its pulse. In the stillness that had allen after those three quick shots, however, she clearly eard movement in the bushes.

And she heard Ben's instructions. He turned his head, his nouth near enough that his breath brushed the sweat-lampened hair at her temple.

"Crawl out on the other side," he whispered. "Just far nough to give me room to follow. Then lie there and wait. When I tell you to run, head for the boat. Keep low and keep noving."

The boat. The one at the end of the pier? Under the light?

"Now," Ben said.

Despite her confusion, she obeyed, dragging herself by her lbows toward the other side of the pickup and then, reluc-antly, out into the open on the other side. Ben was right behind her.

"Stay down," he ordered.

As soon as his body cleared the truck, he strained upward, ingers closing over the handle of the driver's-side door. He ased it open, but apparently the noise was enough that who-ver was in the woods figured out what was going on.

Three more bullets, fired through the same silencer as the

first had been, struck the pickup and whined away into the night. Ben had flinched from the sound, ducking automatically to protect his exposed head. Before the scream of the ricochets had faded, however, he was clambering up into the cab again. As he did, a bullet shattered the glass of the passenger-side window.

"Son of a *bitch.*"

She had time to wonder what had prompted that before he dropped to the ground beside her.

"Okay?"

She had nodded before she realized he wasn't looking at her. Nor was he waiting for an answer. Instead, he was pulling himself along the ground toward the front of the truck, using his elbows, knees and feet, just as she had, to propel the movement.

She lifted her head, trying to understand what he was doing. She could see the stock and then the barrel of a rifle moving back and forth as he shifted his weight from one side to the other as he crawled. He had gone back inside the cab to get the gun from the rack above the back window.

The fact that he was armed *should* make her feel better. Despite the adrenaline flooding her system, however, the initial shock was wearing off. She was becoming aware of the signals her body was sending to her brain. Her elbows were raw, and her breasts and knees ached from where Ben had thrown her to the ground. Her palms, abraded when she'd used them to try to break her fall, stung.

Another shot rang out, this one not muted by the silence and much closer than the previous ones had been. Ben's gun. His shot. And just as she arrived at that realization, he barked out the command he'd told her to expect.

"Go."

CHAPTER THIRTEEN

TO THE PIER. To the boat. Just as everyone else always did, Callie reacted automatically to the authority in Ben Stanton's voice. She scrambled to her feet. Crouching behind the projection of the truck, she raised her head in an attempt to spot the pole that marked the beginning of the pier.

It was gone. At least the light on top of it was. For a few seconds, she didn't know where to go, disoriented by the darkness and by the time she'd spent crawling along the ground without any visual references.

As she hesitated, Ben's fingers closed around her upper arm. He began to run, for the first few steps literally dragging her along behind him. Eventually, her feet began to move of their own accord. She was totally dependent on his guidance because she was running blind. Not only did she not know the terrain, but in the darkness she couldn't see a thing.

Suddenly the toe of her sandal caught on something—a root or a vine. It held her foot momentarily, pitching her forward. Ben's fingers dug into her flesh. The strength of his hand managed to keep her upright, despite her stumbling, off-balance stagger. After a few steps she regained her equilibrium.

She concentrated on maintaining it as he tried to pick up the momentum they had lost. He pulled her along as shots from that muted rifle followed them, destroying the sense of security she'd felt when Ben asked her to come home with him.

As they ran, her eyes began to adjust to the darkness, and their surroundings swam into focus. She could see the pole.

The long dock that extended out into the water. Even the boat at the end of it, gleaming white and beautiful in the faint moonlight.

As they approached the pier, a bullet hit one of the planks, sending up a shower of splinters. They sprinted through them, the sound of their feet hammering across the boards. She could hear her own breathing, seeming as loud as their footsteps.

Behind them, their assailant continued to fire. A few shots hit wood, their impact coming a split second before she heard the rifle's throaty *phut*. Several struck the surface of the water, the noise almost lost under the pounding of their feet. As soon as they reached the boat, Ben shoved her against its side.

"Climb," he ordered, turning to provide covering fire.

Her hands fumbled for the rungs of the ladder, and she pulled herself up and over the side as his rifle barked again. Once onboard, she stopped to catch her breath.

Almost immediately, she heard Ben storm up the ladder. Then he was beside her, pausing long enough to push her down into the bottom of the boat. He headed toward the bow, and after a few seconds, she heard the powerful engine come to life.

She wondered briefly about the mooring ropes, but apparently that's what he had been doing after he'd directed her to climb the ladder. Huddled on deck, she listened as the boat roared out of the boathouse and into the bay, leaving the steady cough of gunfire that followed it farther and farther behind.

"WE SHOULD BE safe here," Ben said.

He had returned from securing the line around a cypress knee to find Callie sitting on the deck, her head back, eyes closed. At the sound of his voice, she opened them, looking up. She would be able to see nothing more than his silhouette, a blacker shape against the dark, moss-draped branches arching over the slough where he'd hidden the boat.

When he'd left the boathouse, he hadn't had any destination in mind. His sole purpose in taking the cruiser had been to get them away from the shooter. With the truck disabled, the bay had offered their best chance to do that.

Once out on the water, he'd remembered this place. Secluded and remote, it would serve their purposes, at least for tonight. Although there were people in the area who knew these backwaters as well as he did, he hoped the murderer wouldn't be one of them.

"You okay?" he asked, concerned by her lack of response. He stooped beside her, balancing on the balls of his feet.

"I think so," she said. Her voice sounded remarkably steady, considering all she'd been through. She took a deep breath, audible in the stillness, before she added, "A little bruised and battered, but...nothing serious."

"You weren't hit, were you?"

She had probably never had to dodge bullets in her life, but he couldn't fault the way she'd handled herself. As he had from the beginning, he found himself admiring her ability to remain cool under fire. Literally under fire this time.

"No," she said. "You?"

It was a rhetorical question. A returned courtesy. Except he hadn't been as lucky.

"I caught a ricochet," he said. "A fragment of one, anyway."

In the sudden silence, he evaluated the sound of the water lapping against the boat. Their passage had caused those ripples. Eventually they would die away, and he'd be able to hear if anything else came up the slough. Not that he was expecting company, he reassured himself.

"You were hit by a ricochet?"

"Nothing serious," he said. "There's a first aid kit in the cabin. I thought maybe you might..." He hesitated, feeling awkward about the request.

"You want me to take a look at it," she said.

She didn't sound particularly eager. Of course, neither was

he. He didn't think the damage was enough to put him ou
of commission, but his shoulder hurt like hell. And the
wound had continued to bleed sluggishly, which wasn't a
good sign.

He was feeling pretty rough around the edges. Hunger
lack of sleep, maybe even a touch of shock from the loss o
blood had all taken their toll. As soon as they got below, he
could do something about a couple of those.

"Would you mind?"

As he asked, he wrapped his fingers around the top of the
railing, using it to pull himself to his feet. She didn't move
so he extended his hand to her.

He had done that before, he remembered. Offered to help
her down from the truck. She had put her hand in his, and
then, after they'd walked a few feet toward the house, she
had broken away from him and headed back to the pickup.

She must have heard something he hadn't. And her quick
reaction to it had probably saved her life, taking her out o
the path of that first bullet.

"I don't mind looking at it," she said, "but you should
understand that isn't my area of expertise."

She put her fingers in his, and he pulled her to her feet
This time he resisted the urge to put his arm around her
shoulders, realizing only belatedly that might have been wha
she had been reacting to back at the cabin. An unwanted
familiarity. If so, it was a mistake he wouldn't make again.

"So how does it look?" he asked.

"I told you I'm no expert," she said, cool fingers pressing
carefully along the torn flesh, "but I think it's just a gouge
There doesn't seem to be anything under the skin. It look
as if the fragment just tore some of the flesh away."

That should be good news, he thought. His nausea had
returned with a vengeance as soon as they'd exchanged the
fresh air above deck for the humid staleness below. And the
image she had just painted of a piece of metal scoring a
furrow across his back didn't help.

"Peroxide?" she asked.

"What are my other options?"

He listened as she rummaged through the contents of the first aid box. "Mercurochrome." The noise continued briefly. "I don't see any alcohol. Wouldn't that be better?"

"Beats me," he said. It would hurt more, but that hadn't been her question. "I've got bourbon. Too good for pouring over a scratch, but I wouldn't be averse to drinking it."

"Me, either," she said.

Before he could offer to fix those drinks, she poured the peroxide over his shoulder. He could hear it, sizzling against the raw flesh, before it rolled, cold and wet, down his back. His body jerked in reaction, more from the unpleasantness of the sensation than from any pain.

"That can be our reward when this is over," she said, putting her hand, almost comfortingly, on his spine. "A good stiff drink."

And I'll be out like a light. That idea was more appealing than it should be, considering someone had been lying in wait at his cabin with a rifle and a silencer. Someone who was still out there in the darkness, maybe searching for them right now.

And whoever that person was, he'd been a step ahead the whole way, Ben acknowledged bitterly. From the morning he had found Kay-Kay's body, that bastard had played him like a fish. Making him dance to his tune.

Except fish didn't dance. And he had. For ten long years, he had done exactly what he'd been expected to do. Even to bringing Callie home with him tonight. He had done exactly what that son of a bitch had known he would.

"Ben?" she questioned, squeezing the top of his shoulder.

Compared to the antiseptic, her fingers were warm. Warm and soft. Just as the rest of her would be. Which was a hell of a thought, he admitted, given what was happening around them.

"What's wrong?" he asked aloud.

"Nothing. Just checking. You swayed a little."

"I'm okay. Slap a bandage on top of that, and I'll fix u
both a shot."

"I'm not crazy about your word choice," she said. The
attempt to inject humor into the situation wasn't completely
successful, but he'd give her credit for trying. "A drink doe
sound good, however."

"Does anything ever rattle you?" he asked.

"What the hell does *that* mean?"

"It was supposed to be a compliment. I was thinking abou
all that's happened since you've been here. You haven't le
any of it shake you."

"*All* of it shakes me," she denied, pressing a gauze pac
over the wound on his back. He flinched from the pressure
which eased immediately. "Sorry," she said.

She taped down the sides of the bandage without touching
the injury again. He listened as she put the things she'd used
back in the box and closed the lid.

"Especially Virginia's death," she said, obviously a re
sponse to his earlier comment. "I feel responsible for that."

"Responsible?" he repeated, sliding off the edge of the
table and turning to face her. "Why the hell would you fee
responsible?"

"Because I stirred this up again. If I hadn't come here and
started asking questions—"

"He would have gotten away with murdering a child. Two
children," he amended. "He *had* gotten away with it."

"Maybe. But at least Virginia would be alive."

"And maybe another little girl would be dead. Did you
ever consider that? You had *nothing* to do with Virginia'
death," he lied. "She said something to the wrong person."

"She wouldn't have if I hadn't come to Point Hope."

"You can't know that."

She didn't argue, but he could tell by her face that she
didn't believe him. Her eyes revealed the same bone-weary
fatigue he was dealing with. The same near-shock.

He picked up his shirt and shrugged into it. The sticky
blood-soaked dampness was unpleasant against his heated

skin, but he couldn't risk running the air conditioner. Not the way sound carried across the water.

"How about that drink," he offered. At least there was plenty of ice.

She nodded, leaning tiredly against the wall. He walked over to the provisions cabinet and worked the combination lock. He took out the bourbon and two plastic cups from the overhead cupboard. He poured two fingers in each and, leaving the whiskey out, carried the drinks over to where she was standing.

He handed one of the cups to her and tossed back the contents of his as if it were a dose of medicine. When he lowered his head, she was watching him, her own drink untouched.

"Bottoms up," he ordered.

"Do you have any idea who it is?" she asked instead.

"Who was shooting at us?"

"Who killed Virginia and Kay-Kay. Who killed Mary."

He shook his head. "Disappointed?" She said nothing, so he answered his own question. "I don't know why you would be. I haven't had a clue about any of this from the start."

"What Virginia knew…"

He cocked his head at the pause, questioning it, but before she completed the thought, she raised her cup, taking a sip of the bourbon. She grimaced at the taste, rolling it around on her tongue before she swallowed.

"I think what she knew had something to do with the other murder," she said.

"Why?" He wanted to know what she was thinking. And since he needed to stay awake anyway…

"Because that's the only new element. What I told her this morning. If it was something she had known all along, then she might have let it slip before now. The fact that there was another murder was new information. Apparently it triggered some memory. Later on, she must have acted on that and…"

She paused again, drawing breath before she took another sip.

"What exactly did you tell her and Phoebe?"

She shook her head. "I don't remember word for word. I mentioned North Carolina, but not the town. I told them when. Not the exact date, but...I think said twenty-six years ago."

"And you didn't mention the rose."

There was a small hesitation, but eventually she shook her head. She took another swallow of the whiskey, her reaction to the taste less apparent this time.

"You're sure?" he prodded, following up on the hesitation.

Her eyes came up too quickly. Widened. "I'm sure," she said. And then she added, "I did mention it to Doc Cooley. I had assumed he already knew, but he claimed he hadn't seen it. I didn't see how he could have done the autopsy and not have found it, but...it didn't feel like he was lying."

"He *didn't* see it. That's why there were no pictures of it in the photographs that were stolen. When I finally made myself look at them a couple of days after the funeral, there weren't any of the rose. I should have mentioned it to him, but I assumed he'd find it. And by the time I realized he hadn't, it was too late. At that point, Lorena and Tom weren't going to give permission for an exhumation."

"It must have been hard for Doc," Callie said. "To do the autopsy, I mean. Maybe that's why... He told me he delivered Kay-Kay. She'd been his patient all her life. I could hear in his voice how much he cared."

"I know now I should have sent the body to Mobile or Birmingham. Gotten a forensic pathologist to do the autopsy. But...I wanted Doc to do it. I knew he'd treat her right. With dignity."

She nodded, and then her eyes dropped to the remains of her bourbon. She rolled the cup, watching the liquid tilt from side to side.

"How did you get interested in the first case?" he asked. "The Cameron girl's murder?"

Again, there was a slight hesitation before she answered. And she didn't look at him this time. "I knew the family."

"What made you put the two together? You couldn't have spotted the stem in that photograph. Not unless you were looking for it. And not unless you *knew* what you were looking for."

The silence expanded. As he waited through it, he could feel the effects of the alcohol. It had hit his empty stomach and was already racing through his bloodstream. Strangely, he felt more alert, but also slightly disoriented. He eased his hip onto the edge of the table and reached across it, fumbling for the box of saltines he kept there, handy for any customer with a bout of seasickness.

"She was my sister."

His fingers had already closed around the top of the box of crackers before the sense of what she had just said hit him. He turned to face her, moving slowly. Wondering if the bourbon had had more of an effect than he'd suspected.

"Mary Cameron was your *sister?* But...*Cameron?*"

"When my father died, we moved back to Charlotte. To live with my mother's family. She began to use her maiden name. She said it was easier for me to use it, too, because of school. I didn't understand then that was because of Mary's murder. Because of the notoriety. No one in that house ever talked about Mary. Maybe, because I was so young at the time, they thought I didn't remember her death."

"Did you?"

"Not consciously, although there were always the dreams... Maybe what I *think* I remember now is only what I've read. I can't be totally sure anymore."

"How old were you?"

"I was three. Mary was six," she said softly. "We slept in the same room."

The words were almost stark in their simplicity. *We slept*

in the same room. If Mary Cameron's murder had followed
the pattern of Katherine Delacroix's...

"You were there," he said, realization closing around his
heart like a cold hand. "My God, Callie, you were in that
room the night he came for her."

SHE REALIZED only as she talked that she had never before
told anyone all of it. Not like this. And as she had told him,
she had never been sure she would be able to distinguish
what she remembered and what her mind had reconstructed
from what she had read. She knew that if there was anyone
for whom she needed to make this attempt, it was Ben.

"There were no signs of forced entry," she said, her voice
still as low as when she'd begun.

"Yet somehow he got in," Ben said. "And he took her
out of her bed without waking anyone." It had not been a
question.

She looked up from the bourbon she was still toying with.
"Or he lured her out. Doc said that to me yesterday. He was
talking about Kay-Kay, of course. I'd never thought of that
possibility before, but...he might have done that with Mary."

"How?"

She shook her head. "I don't know. I can't imagine. We
slept in twin beds, one on each side of the room."

Nothing had changed about that bedroom, not even after
Mary's death. There had been too many other things for her
mother and father to worry about, perhaps, including their
own grief. And every night they had sent her to sleep in that
same dark room, lying across from the empty bed from which
her sister had disappeared.

"And he didn't kill her there," Ben said.

She knew by the way the comment had been framed that
he was comparing everything she told him to Kay-Kay's
murder. The one about which he already knew every detail.

"There was a basement..."

As soon as she pronounced the word, she could smell it.
The odor dark and cold, like some ancient evil.

GAYLE WILSON   173

A bare bulb had hung down between the floor joists on an
old-fashioned, fabric-wrapped cord, the kind you never saw
anymore. When the chain was pulled, it would set the bulb
into motion. It swung in slowly diminishing circles, dimly
illuminating different parts of the basement as it moved.

"He took her there?"

She couldn't remember ever going into the basement of
that house. After Mary's death, the door was always kept
locked. Yet despite how young she had been when Mary had
been killed, Callie knew she must have gone there at least
once. Because she had never forgotten that circling light or
the smell.

"Can you tell me...?"

The pause in Ben's question forced her to raise her eyes
to his. They were compassionate, just as they had been when
he had knelt beside her in the boat. And because they were,
she found the strength to tell him the rest.

"She was raped. And strangled. Then, maybe for good
measure, because she was almost certainly dead when he did
it, he cut her throat."

There was no sound in the cabin after those whispered
words. They both knew that was a major difference between
the manner of Mary's death and Katherine Delacroix's.

Callie had no idea of the significance of that difference,
but she had almost reached the end of Mary's story. Now
there were only two things she had to tell him. He knew
about the rose. She wouldn't have to tell him that, but the
others...

For some reason, they had always been the worst to her,
even though she had long ago recognized that her horror was
illogical. Far worse things than these had been done to her
sister.

"Mary's hair... She had long blond hair, so light it was
almost white. Like an angel's. Everybody commented on it."

There were pictures of her and Mary, identical towheads
bent over their dolls or playing with one of the kittens. As

Callie matured, her own hair had darkened. Mary's, however...

"After she was dead, he cut it all off," she said, the words harsh, abrupt, breathless. "He cut off her hair, and then he stuffed it into her mouth."

"To keep her quiet," Ben said softly.

Anyone with an understanding of abnormal psychology would have recognized the symbolism. Mary's killer had closed her mouth, filling it so that she could never reveal his secret.

"That was one reason everyone believed it must have been my father. That and the fact there was no forced entry. Even after they found her in the basement, even after he must have realized they thought *he'd* killed her, he swore the doors had all been locked when he went to bed. He swore he'd checked each one of them himself. My father couldn't *not* tell them the truth. Not even after he understood they might use it to convict him for his daughter's murder."

"They tried your father for Mary's murder?"

"They wanted to, I think, but...they never brought formal charges. My father was a minister, one of only two in town. His congregation believed he was incapable of doing what had been done, of course. Maybe the world was more innocent then, but the police never charged him. It didn't matter. People always wondered. You could see it in their eyes when they looked at him. And he knew what they were thinking."

There was only one more thing she had to tell Ben. And then she would never have to think about the smell or that slowly circling light again.

"There was a sink there. In the basement," she clarified, thinking that perhaps he had lost the thread of the narrative because it had taken her so long to get to this point. "It had been used for laundry, I think, long before there were washers and dryers. I don't know if my mother ever used it herself..."

Her voice faded. She turned her head, as if she were looking out to where the bay stretched toward the horizon. Out to the dark water in which Kay-Kay Delacroix's body had been ritualistically washed.

"He bathed her," she said. "He washed Mary's body in that sink, just like he did with Kay-Kay. But..." She took a breath before she told him, knowing how important this was. "That couldn't have been done for the same reasons everybody believed it was done in the Delacroix case. There *was* no DNA evidence twenty-six years ago. Even if he hadn't washed her body, there would still have been no way to connect him to Mary's murder."

CHAPTER FOURTEEN

BEN OPENED HIS EYES to a darkness that was almost total. Moisture-laden air pressed against his skin like a weight. And he had no idea what had awakened him.

He listened to the stillness, concentrating on finding within it any sound that might represent danger. Footsteps on the deck above his head. Water lapping too strongly against the hull. An unfamiliar creak or rattle.

There was nothing. Only the peaceful, late-summer insect noises from the surrounding woods. And gradually, as he listened to them, his wariness dissipated. Nothing but a bad dream, he told himself, willing the tension from his muscles. Of course, he had heard enough tonight to precipitate a nightmare or two.

He searched his consciousness, trying to remember what he'd been dreaming, but there were no images left in his brain. Only those from the nightmare he'd lived with the last ten years. And those that had formed as he had listened to Callie.

Callie, he thought, jolted again by the sense that something was wrong. He had intended to stand guard all night, despite his conviction that no one could find them out here.

Of course, only a fool would be looking, considering the vastness of the area in which they had to hide. With that comforting thought, he closed his eyes. He needed to sleep. He needed to be clearheaded tomorrow to decide what had to be done.

And then his eyes opened again, that nagging uneasiness too strong to deny. He pushed up on his elbow, wincing as the wound on the back of his shoulder protested, and looked toward the bunk where Callie was sleeping. Totally exhausted, she had been out almost before he'd laid the rifle across his lap and leaned back against the wall facing the companionway. He had listened as her breathing settled into a slow, steady—

Realizing finally what had nagged at him, he listened again, ears straining in the stillness. Then, gripping the rifle, he surged up off the floor. The flood of adrenaline was overwhelming, making his hands tremble and his mouth go dry.

Not again, he prayed. *Dear God, please not again.*

Soundlessly, he crossed the cabin. He had taken off his shoes because he'd gotten them wet securing the lines. His toes gripped the polished floor as he shifted the rifle in his hands, his finger wrapping around the trigger.

He couldn't see a damn thing, but he didn't need to. He knew every inch of the cruiser by heart. Every plank that would squeak under his weight. The location of every piece of equipment he might stumble over.

As he climbed the stairs, the darkness gradually lightened. And when he reached the top of them, he could see Callie at the stern, outlined against the faint moonlight. His eyes scanned the perimeter of the boat. Then he turned, examining the bridge, charcoal against the shadow of the overhanging trees. There was no one there, and his gaze came back to the figure at the stern.

"Callie?" he questioned, keeping his voice low. She turned toward him, but there wasn't enough light to read her expression. "What are you doing up here?"

"I couldn't sleep," she said, turning back to the water.

There were always the dreams... Had she had one tonight? Another nightmare about her sister?

Still watching her, he bent his knees and, reaching behind him, propped the rifle against the bulkhead. Then he crossed the deck, stopping beside her. Her eyes were focused on the entrance to the slough. Beyond it, dark and vast, stretched the waters of the river and the bay. And everything that had driven them here.

"What's wrong?" he asked.

She shook her head, still without looking at him.

"It might help if you talk about it," he suggested.

She laughed, the sound devoid of amusement. "No one *ever* talked about it. When my mother moved back with her family, it was as if it had never happened. We all conspired to pretend it hadn't. It wasn't until she died that I felt free to read about Mary's death. When I did, I realized that the person who had killed her had never been caught. Never been punished. And no one cared. It was over, it was done, and no one cared about what had happened to Mary *or* to my father."

"I know it was hard for him—"

"Four years to the day after Mary died," she broke in, "he took out the gun he kept in his desk drawer and he shot himself with it. It was his birthday. That's why he had gotten up so early the morning he found Mary was missing. We were going on a picnic. A special birthday celebration. And every year after that—"

Her voice broke, but after a moment she strengthened it and went on. "He left a note. I was never allowed to see it. I found it with my mother's things after she died. There was only one sentence. No message for her—or for me—although we were as much victims of what had happened as he was. He had to know that. He *had* to know. I think he just…lost his way. After so long, living with something like that, maybe you do."

Ben didn't want to hear this, and yet there was a terrible fascination in knowing about this man. Mary's father, who had so much in common with Delacroix. An innocent man *he* had pursued.

"What did it say?" he asked. "That one sentence."

"I didn't kill my daughter."

After years of ignoring those doubting eyes, which must have haunted him every minute of his life since his daughter's death, that was the only thing her father had had to say to his family. And to the world. *I didn't kill my daughter.*

"I didn't kill mine either," Ben said, "but...there were times after her death when I thought about doing what your father did. And that's something I've never told a living soul."

There was no response to that confession. And after a moment he turned away, sorry he'd told her.

He started toward the bridge. By the time they got back to civilization it would be daylight. And finally he would be able to take some action against this bastard. To make up for his failure ten years ago. This was still his town. His case. His watch. Maybe he no longer wore the badge that made all that official, but it always would be. At least until he had put the person who'd killed Kay-Kay behind bars.

Callie's hand closed over his forearm, stopping him. He looked down at it, her pale fingers such a contrast to the darkness of his skin. After a moment she removed them, but he didn't move, other than to raise his eyes to meet hers.

"I came here to find *you*," she said. "To enlist your help. I knew that if there was anyone who cared as much as I did about finding justice for the two of them..." Her lips trembled on the last, but the movement was quickly suppressed.

He knew she wasn't asking for his sympathy. Although she *had* been a victim of her sister's murder, Callie hadn't chosen that path. She had come here instead to clear her father's name and to find her sister's killer. A murderer that everyone else, including him, had stopped looking for years ago.

Unexpectedly, she leaned toward him and, holding his eyes, stretched upward until her lips were a fraction of an inch from his. He didn't move. Couldn't move.

She was again close enough that he could smell the fragrance of her hair. This time it mingled with the warm, woman-scent of her body, caught and held in the moisture the humid air left on her skin. Intensified by the heat.

She closed her eyes and leaned forward to press her lips

against the corner of his mouth. The kiss was insubstantial, obviously *not* an invitation or provocation. His body didn't respond in quite the way his intellect interpreted it, however.

She stepped back, opening her eyes to look up at him. As he watched, his eyes locked on her lips, they slanted upward. When he didn't answer it, the smile became tentative. Uncertain. As if he had rejected some tender of friendship.

Except, as he had admitted to himself at least, friendship wasn't what he wanted from Callie Evers. Maybe it was time to clarify what she wanted from him.

Almost of their own accord, his fingers reached out to touch her upper arm. His thumb trailed down to the soft fragile skin inside her elbow. Then, still holding her eyes, he ran the pad of it back up, following the muscle that underlay the pale, smooth skin. Definitely a caress.

Her eyes widened, but they held on his as if mesmerized. And she made no effort to pull away, not even when his fingers closed around her elbow to pull her toward him.

He put his other hand on her opposite arm, and then, holding her by the shoulders, he drew her close, lifting her a little so that her mouth was again millimeters from his. Her body rested against his, her toes barely maintaining contact with the deck.

He tilted his head, aligning his lips to fit over hers. He expected her to recoil or resist. Maybe he wanted her to, finally giving him a chance to control *something*.

Her body stiffened, but she didn't struggle. Not even when his mouth fastened over hers. Not even when his tongue probed, demanding entrance.

He hadn't thought about what he would do if she refused. This had been sheer impulse, fueled by his admiration of a woman who knew when to be afraid, but not when to quit. And by his growing sexual attraction, an unconscious seduction on her part, which had begun the day she stood at the foot of his front steps, challenging everything he believed.

By the time he had been forced to consider the possibility that she might refuse to respond, her mouth had opened. And then there was no pretense of reluctance. Their tongues met and melded as her lips clung to his. As hungry for this as he had been.

When her arms went around his neck, he released her shoulders. His palms cupped under her hips instead. He bent his knees, lifting her into his erection, which was hard and hot and uncomfortable, straining against the confines of his jeans.

Her body molded itself to his, two halves fitting together as they were intended to. Except there were too many barriers for them *really* to be together. And he wasn't thinking right now about psychological ones. He was thinking only of physical barriers. His jeans. Her slacks.

He wanted them off. He wanted to take her right here, the decking cool beneath her bare back as he drove again and again into her yielding softness. As their tongues continued to explore, he removed his right hand from her hips, bending his knees even more to maintain that elemental contact between them. He slipped his fingers, flattened, between their bodies, working by feel over the buttons of his fly.

His knuckles were moving against the most intimate part of her anatomy, so she had to know what he was doing. *And* what he intended. She made no protest. Not even when he succeeded, freeing his arousal from the constriction of both his jeans and his briefs.

He slipped his hand inside her waistband, the tips of his fingers tracing along the top, searching for the opening. When she realized what he was doing, her arms released their hold around his neck. Her hand fastened over his fingers, trying to pull them away. He ignored it, concentrating on her waistband.

Side opening, he discovered. Using only his thumb and forefinger, he slipped the button through the buttonhole and found the tab of the zipper.

Again protesting fingers got in his way. He pushed them aside, determination driven by need. By desire. By a hunger as hot and wet as the grass-clogged backwaters around them.

As soon as he'd lowered the zipper, he brought his other hand around, hooking his thumbs in the waistband of her slacks, one on either side of them. He pushed downward, forcing the waistband over the curve of her hips. Once past that slight resistance, they fell, pooling around her feet.

The panties she wore left most of her buttocks exposed. Her skin was cool, incredibly smooth under his palms as his hands again cupped under her hips. Despite her slenderness, there was a satisfying, womanly roundness to them.

He lifted her again, bending his knees and coming up strong and hard under her. He could feel the cleft between her legs, covered now by only that thin band of silk, damp and hot against his bare erection. The sensation was electrifying. He gasped, breath sucked inward as if he'd been plunged into ice water.

The sound was a louder than her answering moan, which seemed to originate from somewhere deep in her throat. Low, guttural and wordless, it didn't sound shocked, as his rasping inhalation had been. It had sounded... *Pleased?*

He wasn't sure of his assessment until she moved, intentionally deepening the contact between them. He pushed upward again, responding to that encouragement.

His hands still under her bottom, he lifted her, near enough that he could see the film of moisture above her parted lips. Near enough that he could feel her breath moving against his cheek. Near enough that the almost dazed look in her half-closed eyes made him remember all she'd been through the last two days.

And that was the last thing he wanted to do. He didn't *want* to think about how vulnerable she was. He didn't want to be noble or controlled. He didn't want to be any of the things he knew he should be. He just wanted to be inside her.

Inside her heat and wetness. The dampness of his skin sliding over hers. Hipbones impacting together as he drove into her again and again, burying everything bad that had ever happened to either one of them in the hot, mind-numbing sweetness of hard sex. Destroying evil with something that was as old and primitive. And just as powerful. Life-giving instead of life-taking. They both needed that affirmation right now.

"Ben?" she said.

Her voice was hoarse. Pleading. And the sound of his name, whispered in that particular tone, changed the dynamics of what was happening between them.

Maybe not enough to make him back off, but enough to let him know that with this woman it couldn't be *only* physical. Not just sex, as much as he needed the sheer mindlessness of that, the escape from thinking it would provide.

"If you're fixing to say no," he warned, the words clipped and demanding, fighting that emotion he hadn't want to feel for her, "then you damn well better do it quick."

"I'm not like this," she said, her voice almost plaintive.

"Like what?" he mocked, pulling her body into closer contact with his.

"Like someone who would...do something like this."

"It's called making love."

"I *know* what it's called," she said. For the first time, there was an edge to her denial. "What I don't know is why *we're* doing it."

Despite the ache in his groin, the trembling muscles, the too-rapid heart rate, he didn't laugh or get mad because, God help him, he understood exactly what she meant. They'd gone from being adversaries to physical intimacy in a matter of days. And despite the fact that he'd made love to a lot of women through the years, one-night stands had never been his style.

"Maybe we're 'doing it' because someone tried to kill us tonight," he said, "and we've just now figured out we aren't dead. And we know we could have been."

For some reason, her eyes, holding on his, filled with tears. She blinked, trying to control them, and he realized he'd never seen her cry. No matter what was happening. No matter what horrors, past or present, she was forced to confront.

"Don't you start crying," he said, his voice harsher than he'd intended. He hated it when women cried. He always had.

"I'm not *crying*," she said forcefully.

She put her hands on his chest, pushing him away. He took a deep breath, trying to think, but he refused to move.

Her objection had been only that. An objection. He knew from her first response that if he pressed her, if he just went on with what he was doing, she would eventually let him make love to her. She was as aroused as he was. And there was some part of her that needed this release as much as he did.

She said no, but I knew she really wanted it. And how many times, he wondered, had some guy with a hard-on used *that* justification? How many goddamn times?

Slowly he straightened, releasing her. She slid down his body, inadvertently moving against his arousal, sending a powerful aftershock shuddering through him. She held onto his shoulders until she'd regained her balance, and then she took a step back, trying to put some necessary distance between them.

As she did, her feet tangled in her slacks, which were still lying in a small, white puddle on the deck. She glanced down at them, reaching out with one hand to steady herself. The tips of her fingers encountered the ribbon of dark hair that arrowed down across his stomach.

She jerked her hand away as if it had been burned, but her eyes had risen to lock on the place where she'd touched him. Stubbornly, almost angrily, he made no attempt to cover himself.

She hadn't objected when he'd undone his fly. And she had played a major role in getting him this aroused. It didn't seem she had any right to be offended by the results.

Even as he thought that, her eyes came up. And what was in them didn't indicate she was offended. Instead...

"Callie?"

She said nothing, her eyes on his. Then her fingers, the

ones which had just brushed his body by accident, reached out again. Their touch was almost as tentative as her smile had been, but this time it was clearly no accident.

It was permission. Or invitation. And he needed no other.

He took the single step that closed the distance between them. Bending, he lifted her into his arms and started toward the stairs that led to the cabin below.

"Not there," she whispered.

Unsure what she'd said, he inclined his head, bringing their faces so close his nose touched her cheek. His steps slowed.

"Please," she begged. "Not down there in the dark."

With that request, a pain acknowledged but unspoken, moisture unexpectedly burned behind his eyes. He raised his chin so that she couldn't see his face, lips flattened against any expression of the emotion that welled up inside him.

And as he looked up, he realized the sky had lightened. The first hint of dawn. Without comment, he carried her back to the stern, kneeling to lay her on the cool, smooth decking.

Despite what he had thought before, despite their mutual hunger, this was no longer about release, however much that might be desired.

She had never asked for his pity. He knew that would be the last thing she would want from him, so he wouldn't sully the courage that had brought her to Point Hope by offering it. There was now, however, undeniably, an element of protectiveness in what he felt for her.

And a recognition of the fragility she hid so well. *Not down there in the dark.* Not in that place of endless nightmares. And as he lowered his body over hers, he vowed this was a shadow he would defeat and then erase from her life.

Her eyes opened, looking up at him in the subtle half-light. His palms shaped her face, thumbs caressing away the dampness at the corners of her eyes. And then, lowering his head, holding her eyes until the last possible second, he allowed his mouth to fasten over hers.

THE FIRST TIME Ben had taken her had been about need, both his and hers. Their lovemaking had been almost frenzied. And despite his obvious intent and her body's responsiveness, ultimately it had been mostly for him.

The second time, however, there was no sense of urgency at all. She had been aware of the difference from the moment his hands and his tongue had begun to move again over her body.

She couldn't remember when he had removed the rest of her clothing. She was aware of her nudity only because she could feel the roughness of his unshaven cheek and callused fingers against her breast, as well as the warmth of his tongue, laving with an unconscious authority over its hardened nipple.

Her body shifted, her back arching to create a closer contact with his lips. In reaction, his mouth closed around her breast, its hard suction creating a matching pull deep within her lower body. She shivered, feeling her responses build so that every touch, every flick of his tongue, every movement of his lips, brought her nearer the edge.

We've figured out that we aren't dead. And we could have been... Reason enough, had they needed one, for taking comfort in each other's arms. Taking comfort in still being alive, if nothing else. And after all, the need to procreate after danger was an ancient and potent biological urge.

For her, she had finally been forced to acknowledge, this was far more than that. More than a confirmation that they had survived the night. It had been, almost from the first time she'd studied those grainy newspaper images of this man.

Now he was flesh and blood. A physical reality. And to her, he was truly larger than life. Perhaps because he had saved hers on more than one occasion.

Or because, despite the effect it had, he'd been brave enough to do what she'd asked of him. To move beyond his circumstances and convictions to arrive at the truth about Kay-Kay's killer.

He had been strong enough to survive even that. And to

come through it to the other side, still capable of the gentleness with which his hands were moving over her body.

Without warning, his mouth abandoned her breast. His thumb replaced the warmth and dampness of his lips, moving back and forth across the sensitized nub as his tongue began to examine her ribs on its journey down her body.

Slowly and without any haste, he traced each individual arch of bone, leaving a trail of heat and moisture on her skin. Lower and lower, until finally his tongue began an equally unhurried exploration of her naval. And then lower still, until it moved with unquestioned skill against the very heart of her sensuality.

Her breath caught, the inhalation sharp enough to make him hesitate. In protest of that hesitation, her hand fastened in his hair, silken between her spread fingers. And when his tongue moved again, increasing the tempo of its strokes, her hand closed too tightly around the strands she'd captured.

With movements sure and powerful, his mouth continued to caress. Waves of sensation built within her body, radiating upward from its heated core. Traveling along nerve pathways that had been created for this one purpose, serving no other.

Her lips parted, her breath releasing in a low sigh as the spiraling vortex began to collapse around her. With an exactitude that demonstrated untold experience, his body moved on top of hers. With one hand, he guided his erection. The other slipped beneath her hips, lifting them. He drove against the most hidden and vulnerable part of her, so hard and deep that despite his painstaking preparation, she flinched.

"Shh," he whispered, breath warm against her temple, lips moving against the sweat-dampened hair. "Shh."

His hips rocked forward, the moisture of their first encounter easing his passage. When he moved again, it was little more than a shift of weight, and the soreness became something else. Something anticipated. Known. Desired.

The muscles that had tensed relaxed, her bones melting and then reforming around him. It was his inhalation this time, a softly indrawn breath that presaged the next, deeper thrust. And then deeper still, until finally he filled her completely. Beyond fullness. An intensity that was again almost frightening.

She was incapable of movement. Incapable of response. Incapable of anything but breathing in the salt-fragrance of his skin. She turned her face, feeling the rasp of his beard against her cheek. So dear. And dearly familiar.

Unconsciously, her muscles clenched around his erection, reacting to that surge of emotion. An emotion which had almost nothing to do with their physical intimacy. Far more to do with her growing feelings for the man who held her.

As he began to move above her again, she opened her eyes, looking over the dark, broad shoulder that strained against her breast. And only then did she realize it was morning.

Another night had passed. Another endless darkness to be lived through. And they had.

Slowly, the sensations that had spiraled away when he'd shifted over her returned. Like summer lightning, they flickered and roiled throughout her body. Building. Until they became a wave, overwhelming everything in its path as it rushed to crest, slowly and powerfully, against the beach.

Her hands found purchase in his. She held them, their fingers interlocked, as they rode that crest together. Sensation peaked and then retreated, leaving them spent and exhausted, muscles trembling in the aftermath.

He lifted his head, his breathing ragged and uneven, to look down into her eyes. "When this is over—"

"Over?" she interrupted, the pall of sadness almost inevitable at the reminder. "Will it *ever* be over?"

His mouth tightened, and then he brought their joined hands to his lips, brushing a kiss, as insubstantial as the one that had begun this, against her knuckles.

"Ben?"

He raised his head again, his eyes as clear as the sea. "I'll find him, Callie. I was wrong before, but…it's been long enough. No more victims. No more, I promise you."

And slowly, still holding his eyes, she nodded.

CHAPTER FIFTEEN

"GET A COPY of the calls Virginia made during the last forty-eight hours. If you have to, ask Judge Morehouse to subpoena the records," Ben said, his instructions rapid-fire.

He was speaking into the phone at Phoebe's. They had come straight here from the slough where they'd spent the night, tying the cruiser up at her pier. It made more sense than going back to Ben's, and Callie had a key. Besides, her car was still here.

Ben listened for maybe twenty seconds before he said, "I don't give a damn if it is Sunday. This is police business—" The sentence was cut off abruptly, obviously in response to what Withers was saying. "Son of a *bitch*," Ben exploded. "You *make* them get to it, Doak. This morning. And don't take any of their crap about what they can and can't do. Tell them you've got a murder on your hands. What about the fingerprints?"

The pause was longer this time, and his eyes found Callie's as he listened.

"Somebody was lying in wait out at my place last night," he said after a moment. "Somebody with a rifle and no qualms about using it. I can damn sure prove *that*."

She could tell by his expression, even before he spoke again, that he hadn't liked Withers' response.

"If the two *aren't* related, then why the hell would somebody be out there shooting at us?" As he listened this time, he shook his head, lips compressed. "Because she's right, damn it. Tom Delacroix *didn't* kill Kay-Kay. Somebody else did. Somebody in this town. Somebody with a connection with that other murder in North Carolina. And we have to figure out what it is."

Another pause.

"We need those phone records," Ben said, his voice calmer. "We have to know who Virginia talked to between..." He hesitated, brows raised in inquiry as he looked at Callie.

"Around seven," she supplied.

"Between seven and two yesterday. And we need the autopsy results as soon as possible." He listened once more, his mouth again tightening in frustration. "Okay," he said finally. "Do what you can. I'll call you back in a couple of hours."

He set the receiver on its cradle with more force than was necessary. When he turned back to Callie, his eyes were bleak.

"Nothing usable on the prints. Doak says it looked like the surfaces in the bedroom had been wiped. Even if he's right, it doesn't prove anything. Other than Virginia dusted."

"I can't believe there weren't prints on the screen door."

"Nothing clear enough to be read. And now Doak's trying to say that it could have happened like the paramedics thought."

"It didn't. You know that."

"But I'm not sure we'll be able to prove it, even with an autopsy. Judging from where that wound on her head was, it's going to be tough for the coroner to say with absolute certainty whether she fell and hit her head or whether somebody hit her."

He pulled out a chair at Phoebe's kitchen table and sat down. He leaned back, and then straightened, grimacing.

"You ought to have somebody take a look at that."

He nodded, but she knew the injury was the last thing on his mind right now. "I could fix us some breakfast," she offered.

"I had a charter scheduled for this morning," he said. "I never even thought about it until now."

"Can you call someone else to take them out for you?"

He nodded again, but didn't make any move toward the phone.

"How about some coffee at least?" she asked.

"Coffee sounds good."

"Buck Dolan's not a native, is he?"

The crease she had noticed before formed between the dark brows. And she supposed that *had* been a leap. Her mind had been making those all morning. Trying to find a way to get from where they were to what they needed to know.

"His accent's different," she explained.

"People retire here or they move down for the climate. Half the people in this town weren't born here."

"And were any of them born in North Carolina?" she asked. It had felt as if he were dismissing her idea out of hand.

"Maybe, but I'm not sure how we could go about finding out which ones," he said, his tone considering. "Maybe cross-reference the tax records. I think some of those require you to give your place of birth. Maybe voter registration. I can tell Doak to put Billy on it when the courthouse opens on Monday."

"But you think it's a long shot," she said, mollified by the seriousness with which he'd discussed the idea.

"No more than any of the other things we're looking at. After all, Virginia may not have made *any* phone calls yesterday."

"And if she didn't?"

"Then I'll go out to my place and take a look around. I need to do that anyway."

"Look for what?"

"Footprints. Tire tracks. Casings. Whatever he left. And he *will* have left something. Whether it leads us anywhere..."

He started to shrug and winced. He rolled the damaged shoulder in an attempt to loosen the muscles. When he realized she was watching him, he pushed up from the table, walking over to the counter to begin making the coffee.

Callie didn't offer to help. She didn't even want to move. She felt worse than she had last night. Too little sleep and too little food, combined with too much stress and adrenaline.

After watching Ben fill the carafe, she made herself get up and open the refrigerator door. She wasn't sure she could face scrambling eggs, if they both starved to death. Thankfully, there were several plastic containers, neatly covered with colored tops, on the shelf next to the eggs.

She would have been hesitant to open anything enclosed in plastic in her own refrigerator. Phoebe, of course, would never let food go bad, not even leftovers.

Callie took out the largest container, holding one edge of it against her stomach as she eased the lid up on the opposite side. The sensation of the cold plastic against her midriff was welcome. Almost refreshing.

And the contents, the remains of a peach cobbler left from dinner two nights ago, seemed surprisingly inviting. She walked back to the table and set it down in the center before she looked up. Ben was watching her.

"Peach cobbler," she said. "Not exactly breakfast food, but…it looks good to me."

He turned and opened the drawer beside the sink. He took out two spoons, holding one out to her with a small salute.

"Want it warmed?" she asked.

He shook his head and walked back to the table. He handed one spoon to her and then sat down, dipping the other into the cold pie. He had taken a couple of bites before she joined him.

She didn't bother to pull out a chair. She propped her hip on the side of the table, their spoons alternately dipping into the plastic bowl until the contents were gone. Ben picked up the dish and tilted it to scrape the juice out of the corner.

"I like the way you think," he said, putting his spoon and the container down before leaning back in his chair. As soon as his shoulder made contact with the cross bar at its top, he straightened. "Son of a bitch," he said under his breath.

"That's probably inflamed."

"Just sore."

"How long's it been since you had a tetanus booster?"

"How the hell do I know? Do *you* know how long it'
been since you had one?"

"Of course," she said truthfully.

He shook his head, avoiding her eyes by looking acros
the room toward the sink. "Coffee's ready," he observed.

"*I* fixed breakfast."

His eyes came back to her face, widened a little. After
moment, amusement replaced the surprise.

"You union or something?" he asked.

"Or something."

He pushed up again, sighing theatrically. He poured tw
cups, leaving it black, and brought them to the table. He se
hers down rather than handing it to her. Then he took a lon
swallow of his before he put his cup down on the table.

"In lieu of toothpaste," he said.

He cupped his hand behind her neck, drawing her towar
him. He didn't hurry the movement, giving her time to pu
away if she wanted to. She didn't. She wanted him to kis
her.

When he did, it was in marked contrast to last night's hea
and passion. His lips met hers, caressing, and then, after
moment, his tongue invaded. Her mouth opened willingly
She could taste the coffee, the flavor darkly rich and pleasan

He broke the kiss, his mouth hovering just above her
"How do you think Phoebe would feel about our taking
shower?"

"Individually or together?" she asked, a little breathless

He laughed, releasing his hold on her neck. His thum
brushed along her cheekbone and was then pressed brief
against her lips before he stepped back.

"I *know* how she'd feel about our showering together. An
I don't think that's a game we can afford to play right now.'

His eyes were serious. She had forgotten how very blu
they were, surrounded by that sun-darkened skin.

"You go first," she offered. "You want me to throw your clothes in the washing machine?"

She could tell from his expression that the idea was appealing. She knew how much she was looking forward to getting out of the clothes she'd been wearing for the last twenty-four hours and into something clean.

"I guess not," he said finally. "Take too long for them to dry. You don't suppose Phoebe's got something I could wear."

"I can look."

She wasn't hopeful. According to Phoebe, her husband had been dead for more than twenty years. Callie doubted there would be a single masculine garment in this house, especially something large enough to fit Ben.

"Double-check the back," he ordered. "I'll do the front."

He picked up the rifle he'd brought in from the boat and headed toward the front of the house. Obediently, she checked the lock on the backdoor and the night latch. Both were secure.

On her way to the hall, she picked the two cups of coffee up off the table. Ben was waiting at the foot of the stairs, and they climbed them together.

"Towels are in the cupboard with the bird decals," she said.

"What are my chances for a razor with a decent blade?"

"I'll bring you one of mine."

He nodded. They stood awkwardly in the hallway at the top of the stairs for a moment.

"Don't go back downstairs alone," he said finally.

"Nobody knows we're here."

"It won't be hard to figure out. Not with my cruiser and your car sitting out there in plain sight."

"You don't think he would try something in broad daylight."

"I don't want to take any chances. Just stay close. As a matter of fact," he said, holding the rifle out to her.

She looked down at it and then up at him. "I don't have

a clue how to use that. I think I'll be a whole lot safer if yo
just keep it with you. I'm going to look in Phoebe's roo
for something for you to wear, and then I'm going to grab
change of clothes from mine. I'll stay within screaming di
tance.''

"Scream loud. I'll have the shower going."

"Believe me, if I start screaming, you'll hear me."

THE FIRST COUPLE of drawers were the hardest. By the tim
she finished searching those, she had realized Phoebe ha
nothing to hide, except a propensity for hanging on to ga
ments long past their expiration dates. As someone had sai
last night, Phoebe's generation lived through the Great De
pression. The "waste not, want not" lessons they'd learne
then were hard to give up.

Callie closed the top drawer of the dresser and turne
Closet, she decided, walking over to it. There was a vertic
row of pictures hanging on the narrow wall beside its doo
She stopped to look at them, her hand already reaching fo
the knob.

A bride and groom, the occasion obvious only because c
the cake on the table and the bouquet in the young woman'
hand. She was dressed in street clothes, a style that Calli
guessed would be pre-war, late 1930s or early 1940s.

She leaned closer, trying to determine if this was Phoeb
The era was right, but it was hard to recognize the famili
wrinkled features in the glowing face of the bride. Her eye
moved to consider the groom, who looked even younger. H
was grinning at the camera, obviously pleased with his day'
work.

Above the black-and-white wedding photograph was
hand-tinted picture of a young man in uniform. Hobart? sh
wondered momentarily. The uniform he wore, especially th
beret, and the style of photography itself indicated this wa
from a different era. Her gaze moved back and forth betwee
the groom and the young soldier. Phoebe's son, she decide
the one who had been killed in Vietnam.

The third picture was a family grouping, taken when the children were much younger. Two sturdy little boys, dressed in matching cowboy outfits, smiled at the camera. The smaller held a broomstick onto which a cloth horse head had been attached.

She tried to remember the name of the son who lived in Mobile, the one who had picked Phoebe up last night. Older or younger? She didn't know and of course, it didn't really matter.

She opened the closet door and was struck immediately by the slightly musty smell of its contents, reminiscent of the odor she'd been aware of at Virginia's house yesterday. She fought the urge to slam the door. Instead, she willed her hand to reach up and push aside the dresses and knit pants suits hanging from the bar. After a few seconds it became obvious there was nothing here that had belonged to any of the men in Phoebe's life.

She had already stepped back, preparing to shut the door, when she noticed that someone had installed shelving down the right-hand side of the closet. She reached inside again, pushing the clothing all the way to the left, thinking these would be a more likely place to store unused clothing.

Her quick survey revealed there was none of that among their contents. Certainly no masculine garments. The top two held quilts, neatly folded, their bright patchwork patterns intricate enough that her fingers reached out to touch them, tracing over the thumbnail size pieces with their myriad tiny stitches. Then her hand moved downward, still caressing. The next shelf contained a mixture of items, including a crocheted afghan and a set of hand-embroidered sheets. And on the final shelf...

Her fingers hesitated. The most prominent item was the blue field and white stars of a folded American flag. She had certainly seen enough movies to know what it meant when the flag was folded in this tight, triangular shape. And beneath it was a scrapbook. Her grandmother had had one exactly like this—black pages, a thick cardboard front and back,

fastened together with laces that ran through the holes an
tied in front. Inside would be more photographs. Phoebe an
Hobart. The boys.

Her fingers stroked the cloth of the flag, moving almos
reverently over the shape of one of the stars. She raised he
head, listening to the distant sound of the shower. Then sh
pulled the scrapbook from under the triangle of cloth.

Still standing in the doorway, she opened the cover of th
album. Its size made it awkward to hold and turn pages a
the same time. She'd been right about the photographs, bu
it was too dark in the closet to see any details in them.

She closed the book, cradling it against her chest, to wal
over to the windows. Once there, she opened the albun
propping the top of it on the sill. As she turned the page
her eyes moving from one photograph to the next, she felt
pang of guilt. Looking for something to replace Ben's blood
stained shirt had given her a quasi-legitimate excuse to searc
Phoebe's bedroom. This, however, was sheer voyeurism.

Not that there was anything here that she thought Phoeb
would object to her seeing. There were more pictures of th
children—Christmas mornings and birthdays. The kind of in
nocuous family events of which everyone took photograph

"Callie?"

Ben's call startled her. She half-turned, thinking he migh
be in the doorway, watching her unwarranted invasion of he
hostess's privacy. As she did, the scrapbook slid off the sil
the top dipping downward before she could right it. A yel
lowed newspaper clipping fell out of the back, drifting to th
floor as Ben called again.

"I thought you were going to bring me a razor."

She closed the book and, holding it against her chest, ben
to retrieve the clipping. She tried to slip it inside withou
opening the album, wondering as she did if Phoebe woul
notice it wasn't in the right place. If it had had a "right"
place.

She hurried to the closet, trying to get the pages of th
scrapbook, still clutched against her chest, open enough t

llow her to slide the clipping inside. Finally it slipped down
etween two of them. One arm around the album, she
eached out with the other to open the closet door, and the
lipping fell out the bottom, again floating to the floor.

"I'm coming," she called, stooping.

This time the article had fluttered open on its way down.
As she leaned down over it, the headline caught her eyes.
Remains Of U.S. Servicemen Returned To States.

Phoebe's son? The date at the top was July 12, 1975. And
he would realize only later how strange it was that there was
o sense of recognition. No chill of premonition. Not until
er eyes dropped to the byline. *Fort Bragg, North Carolina.*

She sank to her knees, laying the scrapbook on the floor
eside her. She scanned the article, searching for names. And
here was one she recognized. James Hobart Robinson, age
wenty-one, of Point Hope, Alabama. *Phoebe's son.* Whose
emains had been returned to the United States in July of
975.

"What are you doing?"

She raised her eyes to find Ben standing in the doorway.
Wearing only jeans, he held a towel, with which he was
rying his hair. Seeing her face, the hand holding it stilled.

"Callie?" And when she didn't answer, "What's
wrong?"

Wordlessly, she held out the article. He hesitated a second
r two before he stepped into the room. Draping the towel
round his neck, he reached out to take the clipping, his eyes
xamining her face instead of looking at it.

"What's this?"

"Read it," she said, trying to think what this meant. It had
o mean something. It was too great a coincidence *not* to.
Too close to the time and the place of Mary's murder.

"Phoebe's son," Ben said. "He was killed in Vietnam."

"Look at the date."

He looked back down at the clipping. "He was on some
ind of covert mission. Special Forces. I don't remember the
etails, but there was a delay in bringing the bodies back to

the States. They had to negotiate for the remains after the war.''

"*July, 1975.*" Maybe it was only a coincidence. Maybe she had become obsessed with this, so that everything, every event, seemed to have a bearing on those two murders.

"Your sister," Ben said. And then he did exactly what she had done. He looked at the byline, and his eyes lifted to hers. "North Carolina. They brought the bodies back to Bragg.''

"Did Phoebe and Hobart go up there?"

"Damned if I know," Ben said.

"Who *would* know?"

"You aren't suggesting that Phoebe or Hobart..."

But she could tell he was thinking about it, even as he denied she could be suggesting it. And of course, Hobart Robinson had been dead by the time of the second murder. After a moment Ben shook his head.

"There's no way Phoebe could have been involved in either of those murders. You can get that out of your head.''

"A five-year-old and a six-year-old? You don't think a woman would be strong enough to strangle a child that small?"

"And rape her?"

"No semen was found on either body.''

"Maybe not, but there was physical evidence—"

"Of *penetration,*" she argued. "It didn't have to be rape. If you're a woman, what better way to divert suspicion.''

"That's insane.''

"So is murder. Especially the murder of a child.''

"And the murder of your best friend?"

"Virginia knew something. Something she promised to tell me. Phoebe's the only one we know for sure who knew that.''

"That's ridiculous, Callie. This whole...idea is absurd. We don't even know that they went there. The army may have shipped those bodies home. Jimmy's buried here. All we know is that the remains came back to North Carolina.''

"In the same month and year that Mary was murdered.''

"You can't think—" he began before she interrupted.

"Don't do what you did before. Don't make up your mind before you have evidence to prove or *disprove* a hypothesis."

His face changed, its features seeming to harden before her eyes. She wasn't sure whether that was in response to what she had just said or because he couldn't believe Phoebe might be involved. She didn't want to believe it either, but too many things fit together to completely ignore the possibility.

"I'm trying to gather that evidence," he said tightly.

"What if Virginia didn't make any phone calls? Will you consider this then?"

"I *am* considering it. I'm just finding it damn hard to believe. I've known Phoebe Robinson all my life. Hobart, too."

"But you *don't* know if they went to North Carolina to pick up their son's body?"

"I was...what? Fifteen? I wasn't keeping up with who went where. They buried him here. That's all I know."

"And Hobart was still alive?"

"In '75?" He thought about it, and then he nodded. "I'm pretty sure. We can check that easily enough."

"He *wasn't* alive when Kay-Kay was killed," she said.

Phoebe was. And Phoebe's son had to be the connection they had been looking for to North Carolina. Same month. Same year.

"What about last night?" Ben asked.

It took her a second to realize he was referring to whoever had shot at them. Phoebe hadn't even been here. They had watched her drive away with her son.

Her other son? Callie wondered. Was it possible—

"And do you really think it was Phoebe holding you under the water that night?"

"No," she admitted, remembering the feel of that hand pressed against her forehead. The hard, masculine strength of the arm around her throat. "Maybe Doak was right. Maybe that had nothing to do with what's happened since. Or with the murders. Just...someone trying to scare me away."

Phoebe had been the one who had been so insistent that she go out to the bay that night. And Phoebe had been the first one she'd told about the book she was supposedly writing.

Maybe Phoebe had put someone up to making that first attempt to scare her off. Burge or Buck Dolan? Both were there that night. And either one of them could probably have been convinced to pull that prank. *If* Phoebe told them to. Phoebe of the strong, dominant will.

"I'm not buying this," Ben said.

"She taught her in Sunday School." *Secret affection?*

"Did she know Mary?"

Her eyes lifted, focusing on his face.

"Phoebe's only connection to the area was that her son's body came through there," Ben reminded her. "*If* she even went to Bragg to collect it. You think she just stopped off at some house in the middle of the night to murder a kid? With Hobart's help? Or did he wait for her out in the car?" The last was coldly sarcastic. And it was a perfectly reasonable question.

"I don't know. That doesn't seem to make any sense..."

She shook her head, knowing there were too many unexplained elements to make the leap she had made. There *were* coincidences. Even of this magnitude.

But she didn't understand why Phoebe hadn't mentioned this link to North Carolina when Callie told her and Virginia about Mary's murder. Maybe she hadn't given them enough information. Or maybe it had been nothing but a coincidental convergence with a horrible, grief-stricken time in Phoebe's life. Maybe she had never made the connection between the dates and the location.

"When you're looking for suspects, you have to consider what people are capable of," Ben went on, hammering home his point. "Phoebe wouldn't be capable under *any* circumstances of doing what was done to those two little girls. Besides, you're leaving out something very important. *Why* would she kill them? There has to be a reason for those two deaths.''

''Is there *ever* a reason to murder a child?''

''Fear,'' Ben suggested.

''Fear?''

''Usually fear of discovery.''

''If...they were being sexually abused?''

''That's always been a possibility. And that's not a woman's crime, Callie. Neither is this kind of repeat pattern.''

''There have been women serial killers,'' she argued, but logic, reason or maybe just sheer humanity was already making her doubt the conclusion she had jumped to only minutes before.

''Not like this. Not that we know of.''

''So where does that leave us?''

''Right where we were before you found this,'' he said, lifting the clipping. Then he folded it and slipped it into the pocket of his jeans before he held his hand out to help her up.

CHAPTER SIXTEEN

SHE SHOULD HAVE KNOWN Ben wouldn't be able to leave it alone. Within an hour after their showers, he had been trying to touch base with Withers again. And having no success.

There were a dozen explanations for Doak not being home, including the possibility that he had gone to the airport to meet Virginia's daughter. It was also possible that he didn't want to talk to his former boss again, since they were having such a fundamental disagreement over the cause of Virginia's death.

"Maybe he's out at your place, doing all that stuff you said you were going to do," she had made the mistake of suggesting.

Ben's eyes had come up from the receiver he'd just slammed down in frustration. "Want to ride out there?"

They had, but that had turned out to be another wild-goose chase. The soil was too sandy for the smudged tracks they found to tell them anything. Based on a few broken twigs, Ben thought he'd located the spot where the sniper had hidden, but there was a disturbing lack of physical evidence. No casings. No footprints. Nothing that would lead them anywhere.

And to add insult to injury, the windshield of Ben's truck had been smashed in. It looked as if someone had taken a baseball bat to it, although they didn't find whatever had been used in the attack. Nor was there any logical explanation of why it had been carried out. Callie was beginning feel that while they were out chasing their tails, whoever had committed the two murders was sitting back, laughing at them.

"Now what?" she asked on the way back into town.

"Let's go by the police station. Doak might be there."

"On a Sunday morning? Besides, I thought you were convinced he wasn't taking this seriously. At least not the possibility that Virginia was murdered."

"But he can't deny what happened to us last night. And that says panic to me."

Doak's panic? Or the killer's? "I don't understand."

"That looks like an overreaction. All of this does. Everything that's happened since you arrived. You haven't come close to identifying the murderer. So why try to kill you?"

"Because he thinks I might," she suggested.

"But no one has. Not in a quarter of a century. Whoever this is has been safe for a long time. He has to have been thinking he'd gotten away with it. So why react so strongly to someone taking another look at Kay-Kay's murder? There have been other people down here during the past ten years, trying to do the same thing you said you were doing."

"Because no one's ever put the two murders together before."

"Exactly," Ben complimented. "Which means he thinks he *can* be tied in some way to the other murder. There's some thread that leads from there to here. And he knows it."

"But...we *don't*. We haven't found any connection, other than Phoebe's son's body being returned to Bragg that same month."

"He can't afford to give us time to find it. That's why things are happening so fast. So we won't make that connection."

"Then it must be something obvious."

"At least to him," Ben said. "What are you doing?"

She had slowed because they were approaching Dr. Cooley's house. "Cooley still sees patients. If he's here, he could look at your back."

"He'll be at church."

"Not unless he goes to Sunday school," she said.

As she turned into the drive, it was obvious she'd been right. Cooley's car was parked beside the veranda.

"We don't have time for this," Ben protested.

"Ten minutes. And if you don't get that checked out, you're going to end up with an infection that could put you in the hospital. Frankly, I don't think *I* can afford *that*."

She pulled to a stop behind Doc's car, shutting off the engine and turning to face him. "No one else is concerned about what's been going on. Doak is perfectly willing to believe Virginia's death was an accident. So are the paramedics. Everyone thinks what happened to me the night of the jubilee was a prank. They'll say the same thing about your windshield.

"You're the only person here who believes Kay-Kay's murderer is active again. And the only person who knows he's trying to kill me. Besides, it's not just me he's after now. That damage to your truck looked like an act of sheer rage. He...or she," she amended, "thinks *you're* a danger to him now. He didn't think that before, at least not for the last eight years. Now he thinks I've told you enough about Mary's murder that you could discover his connection to it, even if he gets rid of me. And apparently he knows you well enough to know that once you get your teeth into something..."

"I wasn't much of a threat to the bastard before."

"Well, you are now. Unless you go down with lockjaw," she said, opening her car door.

"Mighty early on a Sunday to come visiting," Cooley called.

Callie looked up to find the old man standing at the side of the porch, hands on the banister, looking down at them.

"Not that you ain't welcome," he said. "I told you before. I'm always hoping for a visit from a pretty girl."

He was dressed for church. His trousers were linen, the untreated, old-fashioned kind that wrinkled. With them, he was wearing a blue shirt with a wide white collar and a navy tie with small white polka dots.

He had probably been waiting until the last minute to put on his jacket. After all, he'd told her he had no air-conditioning. Callie could see the sheen of sweat at his temples, the thick hair damp with humidity or his recent shower.

"Business and not pleasure, Doc," Ben said, moving a little stiffly as he climbed out of the other side of her car.

"Business?" Cooley questioned. "What kind of business?"

"Your kind," Ben said, smiling up at the old man. "Got a scrape I want you to look at."

"You been fighting again? How many times I got to tell you that it's a gol-darn fool pair of legs that'll stand around and let their head get beat up."

Ben laughed, walking around the back of the car. Callie had started up the front walk as Cooley's laughter joined his.

"This wasn't a fight, Doc. Not unless you'd call something so one-sided that I didn't get in a single lick a fight."

"I'd like to see the man who could keep you from getting in your licks, boy."

Doc walked across the porch as he talked, meeting them at the top of the steps. He looked closely at Ben's face, clearly evaluating. Then he put the back of his hand against Ben's forehead. When he took his fingers away, he shook them as if they were hot, his lips pursing in a long, low whistle.

"What you got against modern medicine, boy? Or are you just trying to suffer in silence in front of this sweet young thing. What do they call that now? Being macho?"

Neither of them pointed out that no one had called anything by that term in more than twenty years.

"No lectures, Doc. She's given me enough of those. Just shoot me full of some expensive miracle drug, and we'll be on our way," Ben suggested. "Then you can get on to church."

Cooley turned, opening the screen door and ushering Callie into the front hall with a sweep of his hand. The inside walls were covered with a patterned paper, and the rooms she could see from the foyer were dominated by huge pieces of furniture.

The house was definitely Victorian, just as she'd originally surmised. And she'd bet the furniture was original to it, bought or made for the house when it had first been built, and lovingly maintained through all these years.

"I expect I've got a few sample miracles lying around," Doc said. "If you ain't picky about expiration dates."

Once inside, Callie had turned back toward the front door, not sure in which direction she should head. Cooley was waiting for Ben to precede him into the house.

"He doesn't know when he had a tetanus booster," she said as soon as they were both inside.

"I expect I've got a record of that, too," Doc said, directing her toward one of the doors on the right of the central hall.

The room had obviously been his office. There was a small anteroom, which had been created by the addition of a partition. A door in the middle of that was open, and Cooley led the way through it into his examination room. A paper-covered table, complete with metal stirrups, stood in its center. Around the walls were several tall cabinets, painted a glossy white, which held instruments and an array of dark bottles.

Callie could vaguely recall this same kind of home medical office in her own small hometown. Even the smell of it, slightly antiseptic and anxiety-producing, was familiar. Nostalgic. Apparently this kind of setup had been fairly widespread in the rural South, at least up until the '70s.

"Now where's this scrape you want me to look at?" Doc asked, motioning Ben onto the table.

Callie looked around, but there was no seating in the room except a metal stool. Its position at the head of the examination table left no doubt it wasn't intended for visitors. She had already leaned against the wall before she realized that, although she had seen a lot more of Ben than was about to be revealed, this examination should, by tradition, be private.

"Should I maybe...?" She hesitated, gesturing vaguely toward the door through which they'd entered.

"You ain't bothering me," Doc said, watching Ben shrug out of his shirt as he pulled on a pair of latex gloves he had taken from a box at the top of the table. "She bothering you?"

Ben shook his head. "She's already seen this. Poured peroxide over it. I don't know how the hell it got infected."

"Let's take a look at what's going on," Doc said, lifting his chin to view the wound through the bottom of his bifocals.

Apparently the gauze square Callie had taped over it last night had loosened during Ben's shower. There was nothing covering the gouge now, and looking at it, she understood why he had been unwilling to lean back against anything. The wound was ugly, the flesh around it swollen and discolored.

"How in the world did you do this?" Doc asked, gloved fingers feeling gently along the gash.

"Ricochet," Ben said. "Somebody was lying in wait for us out at the house last night. Somebody with a rifle."

The big fingers hovered just above the injury, as Doc lowered his head, looking at Ben through the top of the glasses.

"Are you telling me somebody shot at y'all?"

"More than once. Shot out a couple of tires, too. We made it to the boat, but when we went back out there this morning, we found whoever it was had bashed in the windshield of my pickup."

"Good Lord," Cooley said, his hands suspended in midair. "Over what she's fixing to write about?" He tilted his head toward Callie, but he didn't turn to look at her.

"Over Kay-Kay's murder," Ben said.

"'Cause they don't want all that mess stirred up."

"'Cause they don't want it *solved*."

"There ain't but one person who don't want that baby's killing solved, boy. And that's whoever killed her."

"Then I guess that's who we're talking about," Ben said.

There were several beats of silence before Doc said, "So you finally come around to her way of thinking." His hands began to press around the wound again.

"I didn't have any choice. Two different murders. Two little girls. Two towns, hundreds of miles apart. And Tom Delacroix couldn't possibly have committed the first."

"You sound mighty sure."

"He was under lock and key at the time. One drunk driving incident too many for even his daddy to stomach."

"You know as well as I do how slipshod those rehab places are. Who's to say he didn't sneak out?"

"He was there that night. I checked the patient logs."

Callie hadn't realized he'd done that, but then, knowing his thoroughness, she shouldn't be surprised. He must have made that call the morning after she'd shown him the information she'd accumulated on Mary's murder.

"And what day would that be?" Cooley asked.

He walked over to one of the cabinets and returned with something long and slender, encased in cellophane. He stopped in front of Ben to tear it open, extracting a pair of surgical tweezers. He used the foot pedal to open the metal garbage can under the table, dropping the wrapping he'd removed inside it.

"July 9, 1975," Callie said.

Doc's eyes focused on her briefly before they came back to Ben. "And you're sure he was locked up on that day."

"I checked it when Callie told me about the first murder."

Doc nodded, his lips pursed. "So what does that mean?"

"That someone besides Tom Delacroix killed both of them. That other little girl in North Carolina *and* Kay-Kay."

"And you're thinking it was somebody from around here? From Point Hope?" Doc asked, stepping around to the side on the table.

"Based on what's been happening," Ben agreed.

"And he was out there shooting at you last night."

"*And* in Virginia's bedroom the morning she was killed."

"*Killed?* That sounds like... Hell, you ain't thinking somebody murdered Virginia? I told you what happened. Paramedics told you the same thing. She fell and hit her head and bled out because of the medication she was on.''

''Except I don't believe that's what happened. I think she knew something, Doc. Something the killer couldn't take a chance on her telling Callie.''

''Something...like what?''

''You remember when Jimmy's remains were returned?''

''You talking about Jimmy Robinson?'' Doc asked. He focused his bifocals on Ben's back. ''You want a shot 'fore I do this?''

''Do what?''

''I think there's some trash in here. Fleck of metal maybe. I'm gonna be digging around a little bit, but it probably won't be any worse than a needle. Up to you, though.''

''Just do it,'' Ben ordered.

Although Callie couldn't see Cooley's hands, she could tell from Ben's face when the doctor began probing for the debris. Ben didn't make a sound, but his lips compressed. After a moment, the crease formed between his brows and the muscle in his jaw knotted. His eyes met hers briefly before they fell to concentrate on his hands, which were resting flat on his thighs.

Suddenly she decided this was a procedure she preferred not to watch. She turned her back to the examination table, taking a breath and focusing on the row of certificates on the wall behind her, determinedly ignoring what was going on across the room.

The nearest frame held Everett Cooley's diploma, which had been issued by a university she wasn't familiar with. Probably regional, she decided, her gaze moving on to the one beside it.

''So what about Jimmy Robinson?'' Doc asked.

Callie took a step to her left, physically moving down the line. The next three frames held documents concerning Cooley's medical degrees and certifications. While she studied

them, she listened with half an ear to the conversation behind
her.

"You know how his body got home from Fort Bragg?"

"I didn't even know it came from Bragg," Doc said.

"Apparently all the remains from Jimmy's unit were originally transported there. Maybe because they were Special
Forces. Or maybe that was standard procedure after the war."

"Beats me," Doc said. And then, in an entirely different
tone, "Gotcha." There was a ping as if he had dropped
something metallic into an equally metallic container.

Callie didn't turn around, but her neck and shoulders ached
with sympathetic tension over what he was doing to Ben.

"If Phoebe went up there, either for some kind of me-
morial service or to bring Jimmy's body home, would Hobart
have gone with her?" Ben went on. "Would he have been
able to, I mean?"

"Tell me when this was again."

"July '75."

Then there was a prolonged silence, broken finally by a
gasp. Callie half-turned at the sound. Ben's head was down,
however, the hands that had been flat on his thighs clenched
into fists as Cooley continued to dig around in the wound.

After a few seconds Callie made herself return to the wall
display. There was nothing she could do to make this any
easier for Ben, and she knew what Doc was doing was necessary.

She had run out of diplomas and degrees, though. She
turned her attention to a grouping of photographs. Most were
black-and-white, scenes and people she recognized from the
time she'd spent in Point Hope. More interesting than the
documents.

"I doubt Hobart would have been able to travel any distance by car that summer," Doc said, "Neither him nor
Phoebe would fly. Can't think how they would have got up
there. *If* they went."

"Then I guess the army flew Jimmy's remains home,"

Ben said, his voice sounding strained. "The other was a long shot."

"You aren't trying to put Hobart Robinson at the scene of that other murder, are you? That one in the Carolinas."

"Callie found a clipping about Jimmy's body being returned to Bragg. Same month and year. It seemed worth following up."

"I doubt Hobart ever killed a rat, much less a child."

"Like I said," Ben agreed. "It was a long shot. The dates are probably just coincidence."

"This is gonna sting," Doc warned.

Callie took another step to the left to study a photograph of a group of men, all in uniform, standing in front of a Quonset hut. A few wore sunglasses, but most were squinting into what appeared to be strong sunlight. She leaned forward to read the tiny, precisely printed line of white lettering in the bottom right-hand corner. *Free Clinic July 1973.*

She looked back at the row of faces, maybe eight or nine of them. The word clinic had a medical ring. Despite the unexplained uniforms, she tried to find Everett Cooley's features in one of the faces. Just as it had been with that smiling pride, whom she had known must be Phoebe Robinson, it was impossible. The passage of nearly thirty years, the sunglasses, dark hair—all served to disguise Cooley, if he were here.

She looked at the picture above the first, which contained a similar grouping. Fewer soldiers this time, and there were several children lined up in front, looking shyly at the camera. Most of them were barefoot, and there was a telltale thinness to both their bodies and their garments that bespoke real poverty. At least it did to someone who had grown up in Appalachia.

The neat lettering on this photograph was no more enlightening than the other. *Our patients July 1974.* Again she searched the faces of the men. Most of them seemed to be in the prime of life. Late thirties or early forties. There was a scattering of younger faces—leaner and harder.

"Were you in the military, Dr. Cooley?" she asked, look-ing over her shoulder. "Is that where these pictures were made?"

"Reserves," Cooley said, his eyes still on Ben's back.

"Who are the children?"

There was a small silence, and it was Ben who answered her.

"Doc doesn't like to toot his own horn, but instead of going to summer camp, he and some of the other reservists who had medical training used to run free clinics during those two weeks. Doctors, dentists, whoever had medical expertise they were willing to share. Y'all did that for years, didn't you, Doc?"

"A while," the old man agreed. "We enjoyed it, and it got us out of drilling. Okay, looks like that's everything that was in there. A shot of antibiotics and a bandage, and this ought to heal up nicely. I'll check about that tetanus booster."

As Callie listened to his footsteps cross the room, her eyes returned to the wall, studying the next photograph. In this one the photographer had arranged the people so that behind them in the distance was a series of mountain peaks. There was something tantalizingly familiar about them, evoking a sense of near-recognition. The same kind of mountains where she had grown up, old and heavily wooded, weathered by time and the elements.

"I know the Army kept your shots up to date," Doc said, "but I can't find any record of you having a booster since you came home. You been treated by anyone since I re-tired?"

"Haven't had any call to be," Ben said.

"Everybody needs an annual. Even you." Cooley noisily slammed the file drawer which had contained the records he'd consulted, and his footsteps recrossed the room.

Callie's eyes dropped to the precise white letters at the bottom of the third picture. *My last clinic, summer of 1975.* And then her eyes found the mountains again.

Aware of Doc moving behind her, opening cabinet doors and shifting their contents around, she looked back at the dates on the first two pictures. July 1973. July 1974. And then on the last. Summer of 1975.

That summer. The summer Mary had been murdered. Moving almost frantically now, her eyes skimmed the faces of the men again, trying to find something familiar in any of them. Something that would tell her—

And when she found it, her heart stopped, her breath literally freezing in her lungs. There was no mistaking the long, silver-gilt hair she remembered only from the photographs her mother had kept of the two of them. Identical fair heads bent together over a book.

She turned in time to see Everett Cooley push down the plunger of the needle whose point he had injected into Ben's upper arm. And then Doc's eyes rose, meeting hers. In his was a malevolence of such incredible force, she couldn't imagine how he had kept it hidden so well. And for so long.

"It's Mary," she said, pulling her gaze from Cooley's to focus on Ben, who had been watching the fluid from the needle go into his arm. "She's in one of these. I think he knew her."

She was afraid none of that made sense. Despite her near-incoherence, however, Ben immediately surged up from the table, trying to push the old man away from him. Cooley didn't release the needle, holding onto it and Ben's arm with a strength that seemed unnatural for a man of his age. Of course, he was a big man, his body bulkier than Ben's muscled leanness. And she had always thought of him as being older than he really was.

Ben shoved him again, reaching out at the same time for the needle, trying to pull it out. This time, Doc released his arm, stepping back and taking the needle with him. He backed away as far as he could, still watching Ben, his eyes almost feral.

"Tell me you didn't kill her, Doc," Ben demanded, his

hands curling into fists. "Tell me you didn't butcher my daughter."

"She wasn't *your* daughter, no matter what Lorena told you."

"How the hell do *you* know what Lorena told me?" Ben asked, taking a step toward the old man.

Cooley pressed against the wall, but his voice showed no sign of fear. "Tom always told me everything. Including what that slut said about the two of you. She played us all for fools, boy. You ought to have figured that out by now."

Ben shook his head, the movement strangely uncoordinated, as if he were trying to clear his vision. Involuntarily Callie started toward him, drawing the old man's eyes. Again, she was struck by the raw hatred within them. Then as Ben took a staggering step toward Cooley, they shifted back to him.

"What'd you give me, you bastard?" Ben demanded, the words thick, as if he had been drinking.

Cooley didn't answer, his eyes still watchful. Ben shook his head once more, and then he lunged forward, aiming a roundhouse punch at the old man, who dodged instinctively.

The blow didn't even come close. All it did was unbalance Ben so that he was carried forward by its momentum, his body crashing into a wheeled instrument cart. He slid down the side of it, trying to stay upright by grabbing hold of its edge.

The cart shifted under his weight, turning over to land with a crash beside the examination table. Ben rolled onto his back, closing his eyes tightly and then opening them, trying to get them to focus.

"Get out," he commanded, the words slurred, distorted by the effects of whatever Cooley had given him.

Instead, Callie ran to him. She wasn't sure whether her intent was to get him to his feet or to defend him from Cooley. She stooped down, pulling on Ben's arm. "Get up," she begged.

His eyes were open, but he didn't move. The movement

came at her peripherally instead. From Cooley, who was running toward them. She looked around, searching for something she could use against him.

The only thing within reach was the metal garbage can. It was heavier than she'd expected, but somehow she managed to lift it. And despite the awkwardness of her semi-kneeling position, she heaved it toward the doctor.

Cooley warded it off, and the can landed on the floor with a distracting clamor. Left off balance by the throw, Callie tried to right herself by putting her palm on Ben's chest, aware that she hadn't even slowed Cooley down.

And then suddenly he was there, right beside them. She realized belatedly that she would have to get to her feet if either of them was going to have any chance against him. Because there was no doubt in her mind that he intended to kill them. Just as he had killed Mary and Kay-Kay.

Cooley's sudden lunge had a purpose that she hadn't been aware of, however. As she tried to stand, he bent, gripping the leg of the metal stool that stood at the head of the table. With one fluid, powerful motion, he swung it at her.

She had time to get her left arm up. She heard a bone snap as the metal seat hit her wrist. And then, virtually unchecked, the stool continued its upward arc, slamming viciously into the side of her head.

CHAPTER SEVENTEEN

EVEN BEFORE she opened her eyes, Callie knew where she was. The smell that lingered in her nightmares was all around her. A wave of terror washed over her, so strong it left her weak. She fought back the sob that ached in her throat.

If she cried out, he would hear her. He would find her, despite the darkness. And then he would do to her what he had done to Mary.

She wanted to clamp her hands over her mouth. She had done that before, stifling any sound that might betray her. Huddled in the darkest corner under the stairs, palms crossed over her lips, she had watched him. And she hadn't cried. If she could only do that now...

Despite her instinct not to move and draw his attention, the impulse to put her hands over her mouth was irresistible. When she tried, however, a shard of agony lanced through her left arm.

There was something wrong with it. Something wrong with both her arms, she realized, because she couldn't move them.

Panic bubbled upward in her chest, demanding a verbal release. Instead, she pressed her lips together as tightly as she could, rolling them inward and clamping her teeth over them to keep from crying out.

As she did, she opened her eyes and slowly turned her head to the side, trying to locate him in the dimness. Pain roared through her skull, its intensity making her sick.

She swallowed the building bile and closed her eyes against the onslaught. Willing the agony to fade. Willing her-

elf to silence. After a moment the pain in her head dulled
o something bearable, a level that allowed her to think. She
:ouldn't remember how she had hurt her head. She didn't
emember…

And then, like an image from a dream, there was a flash
)f something silver impacting against her temple. She had
)ut up her arm to ward off the blow—

That must be what was wrong with it. Whatever he had
iit her with had made contact with her forearm before it had
iit the side of her head.

But that hadn't happened here. That had been somewhere
n the light. Somewhere with a different smell. Somewhere…

Another image floated up through the fog that obscured
ier brain. She had been bending over someone.

Ben. The name was in her consciousness before she really
emembered him. But Ben hadn't been there the night the
nan had taken Mary, so she was confused again. She hadn't
(nown Ben when she was a little girl. Which meant…

She raised her head, trying to see her surroundings. The
igony in her skull, which had eased, came back with a vengeance, pounding through the bones until she thought they
vould break apart.

And suddenly, in the midst of it, she remembered some-
hing else. The flash of silver had been a stool. That's what
ie had hit her with. Because she had been trying to get Ben
ip, so they could get away. So they could get out of there.

There. Which was…Doc Cooley's office.

The thoughts formed in her brain, as if an unseen hand
vere pushing pieces of some scattered jigsaw puzzle back
nto place. Making sense of what had been, seconds before,
)nly chaos.

The dark figure from her nightmares had a face, but it was
iot the one she had seen that night, bending over Mary as
:hat bare bulb had circled, illuminating and then hiding what
ie was doing. This face was different, but still she knew it.
Everett Cooley. Beloved doctor. Brutal murderer. And he

would kill her and then he would kill Ben if she didn't get them out of here.

The resulting rush of adrenaline energized her. She struggled to sit up. And failed. All she could do was lift her aching head a few inches. Far enough that she could now see the thick leather straps which tied her to the table. One stretched across her hips, pinning her hands to her sides. The other was just below her breasts.

The sob she had fought escaped then, echoing off the walls. It was followed by another, slipping out before she could gather control. *Too loud. Too loud.*

Despite the sickening jolt of pain, she turned her head, her eyes searching for him on the other side of the room and then as far behind her as she could. They scanned over glass-fronted cabinets that seemed replicas of the ones in his office upstairs. These, too, were full of instruments and bottles.

There was no one else here. Not unless he was hiding in the shadows. Watching her. Enjoying her panic.

She worked to calm her breathing, which, like the sobs, seemed to echo too loudly in the stillness. As she did, she heard a noise, something that had been there for a while, hovering on the rim of her awareness.

It was coming from above her head. Her eyes focused on the ceiling over the table. It was too dark to distinguish anything beyond the straight, even lines of exposed beams and the patches of shadow between them.

Beyond them, from the house above, she could hear what she had now identified as footsteps. They would move, the rhythm plodding and regular, and then they would stop. Then, after a moment or two, they would start again, repeating the pattern. Back and forth across the room over her head.

She listened for endless seconds, her breathing suspended as she strained to make sense of what was going on. That was not Ben, of course. The image of his lifeless body, stretched out on the floor of Cooley's office, eyes staring upward unseeingly, negated that possibility. He might even be dead, she admitted, fighting another building sob. She had no idea what had been in the needle Cooley had shoved into his arm.

All she knew for sure was that she was in the basement alone. And whatever Cooley was doing upstairs, he wouldn't leave her alone long. At least, he wouldn't leave her here alive.

Frantically, she began to struggle against the unyielding restraints, setting off every screaming torment in her battered body. After a moment she was forced to stop in order to control the growing nausea.

Obviously she was suffering from the effects of a concussion. The blow to her head had caused a period of unconsciousness deep and prolonged enough that Cooley had been able to drag or carry her down the stairs without her being aware of it. And she knew enough to know that her loss of consciousness was not a good sign. Nor were the nausea and disorientation she had experienced when she'd awakened.

She desperately needed to think. She had to do *something*, or she and Ben were both dead. And then Cooley would slide their bodies into the dark waters of the bay, and no one would ever know what a monster he was.

Slowly, closing her eyes and forming a wordless prayer, she began to try to work her right wrist, the one that wasn't broken, out from under the strap. The leather was tight enough that it bit cruelly into the flesh of her forearm. She pressed her hand into her thigh, trying to create enough space between it and the strap that she could pull it free.

There wasn't much room to maneuver. The top strap held her upper arms against her body so that she could barely bend her elbows. She twisted and turned that arm, trying to slide her hand from under the stiff leather.

As she worked, she realized that the pattern of footsteps over her head had changed. They had headed off in a different direction now, seeming to move away from her. Efforts to escape suspended, she tracked them until they faded away.

Was he coming here? Would the next sound she heard be those plodding footsteps on the stairs that led down to the basement where she lay, strapped to a metal table like a lab animal in some medical experiment? *Like a lab animal...*

Slowly, she turned her head again and surveyed the instruments behind the glass-fronted cabinet doors with a new and terrifying understanding. She had just remembered that Doc Cooley had not only been Point Hope's beloved doctor through the years. He had also at one time been this rural county's coroner.

And finally, she knew where she was. She even understood the purpose of the table where she lay. She was in what once had been Doc Cooley's morgue. In his home, just as his office was.

IT WAS THE VIBRATION that woke him. And the effort it took to force his eyelids up far enough to create even a slit of light in the swirling darkness was enormous.

At first, he didn't understand what he was seeing. It was only after it had moved away that he realized the object that had literally been in front of his nose was a shoe. *Doc's shoe.* He made the identification without much interest in it, his eyes slowly closing again. *Doc's summer, church-going white bucks.*

As he listened to the sound of those retreating footsteps, he gradually became aware of sensations other than the slight vibration they communicated through the old wooden floor. The coolness of its surface beneath his cheek and temple. The cotton-like dryness of his mouth. The dull ache in his head.

And underlying all of those was again that nagging sense that something was wrong. There was something he should be doing. Something important. Whatever it was, however, it seemed too difficult to think about.

His mind began to drift, retreating into the peaceful world it had occupied before Cooley came into the room and woke him up. He wondered, the thought floating almost idly through his consciousness, what Doc had wanted. And then, the question only slightly more troubling, he wondered why e was lying on the floor. That seemed...wrong. Yet Doc adn't even asked him why he was here.

He heard a door open somewhere, unoiled hinges creaking. He put his tongue out to lick his lips, trying to gather enough moisture in his parched mouth to swallow. He needed water.

Water. The word reverberated in his head. Maybe he was out on the water. There was that same feeling of undulation, as if the waves were moving beneath the hull. Except he knew he was in Doc's office. On the floor. And a second ago Doc's Sunday shoes had been right beside his face.

He tried to lift his head, pushing onto his forearm. The room spiraled sickeningly around him. He put his hand out to steady it, touching an object on the floor beside him that he hadn't been aware of before.

It was the wheeled cart he'd overturned when he'd fallen. And he had fallen because...

He shook his head, trying to clear the mist that not only blurred his vision, but his ability to think. And to remember. Callie had been looking at some pictures while Doc had created that gouge on his back. And then...

Tetanus, he remembered, pleased by that small success. Doc had been going to give him a booster. Or maybe it was already too late. Maybe that's what was wrong. Maybe that's why he felt like this—so thickheaded and lifeless.

He managed to get the other hand under him, putting it flat on the floor and using it to push his upper body up. He still had to get to his knees, he discovered. Once he had, he rested, swaying slightly. Head hanging, he tried to find some reserve of strength that would allow him to climb to his feet.

Maybe Doc could give him something. Something to stop the fever. There was too much to do for him to be out of commission. Callie had told him that. It's why they'd stopped by Doc's in the first place. And he couldn't imagine why they had both left him alone, so sick and lying on the floor.

Maybe Doc would do that, if he thought he was drunk. Doc might just let him sleep it off. But not Callie. She'd be in here trying to make him get up. She'd be trying to make him—

She had been.

He could remember looking up at her. And then... And then something had hit her, hard enough that he had heard the blow. Hard enough to knock her backward and onto the floor. He searched his memory, but there was nothing else there. Nothing until Doc's footsteps had awakened him.

He turned his head, looking at the place where Callie had knelt beside him. There was nothing but a dark smear on Doc's heart-pine floor. It looked like something had been spilled. Had he done that when he'd knocked over the cart?

He reached out with his left had to touch the smear. His right elbow gave way, his body collapsing, almost gently, onto the floor. His reaching hand fell short, inches from it. target.

His cheek was again flattened against the cool, smooth wood, the feeling too pleasant to resist. His eyes closed, and then, nagged by the thought of that something he needed to remember, he forced them open. In spite of how hard he tried, however, whatever it was that was so important wouldn't come to him.

It would, he told himself. Eventually. He just needed a minute. If he could just close his eyes and rest, he knew it would all come back to him.

DESPITE THE FACT that she had recognized the seriousness of her predicament from the time she'd awakened, the cold horror of this new discovery made her efforts to escape even more frenzied. Frantically, she twisted and turned her wrist, fighting to slip her hand beneath the leather band that held it.

It wasn't until she slid her arm at an angle across her body that she succeeded. Sucking in her stomach as much as she could, she was able to work her hand from under the strap. Elation roared through her, creating a renewed determination.

She knew she would never be able to do what she had just

one with the wrist Doc had broken. Incredibly sensitive to movement, it was probably swollen as well. She would have unfasten the strap that held it, working blind and one-anded.

Her fingers skimmed over the leather, searching for a uckle or a fastening. She started on the right-hand side, orking her way across the strap by feel. She was able to ouch the far side with only the tips of her outstretched, raining fingers.

And there had been nothing along the entire length of the ather. No release. No buckle. Which meant...

She started back on the right side again, feeling carefully ong the edge of the table. The strap came from underneath, ut, even stretching her arm as far as she could below the lge, she could feel nothing that would release it.

The urge to scream out her frustration was so strong she ad to stop the movement of her hand to concentrate on de-eating it. She forced herself to remember what was at stake. ot only her life, but Ben's. And to remember what this astard had gotten away with through the long years. Mary nd her father. Kay-Kay. If she gave up now...

Breathing in small, sobbing inhalations, she made her fin-ers search again, reaching as far as she could toward the ft side of the table. No matter how much she strained, she ould go no farther than the edge. She closed her eyes, again enying the urge to panic, as she tried to think.

All she had to do was to turn her upper body a little under le band across her chest. The leather must have some give. fter all, she had gotten her hand out by working against it.

She began to push her right shoulder against the strap's nyielding strength. *Fraction of an inch. Fraction of an inch.*

Aching fingers, their tendons stretched beyond endurance, ouched the metal of a buckle. Straining with every ounce of ill she possessed, she got her fingernails under the side lges of the tongue. She began to pull it slowly upward, rawing it out of the buckle. Away from the tooth that held

As she worked, inching the tongue upward with her nail, millimeter by millimeter, the footsteps came back into the room above. Moving back and forth again directly above her head.

Despite the fact that she had thought she couldn't extend her reach any farther, now she did, tugging desperately at the leather. When the tongue finally came free, she repositioned her fingertips, drawing it toward the table so that the hole pulled away from the point of the prong. She threw the strap to her right and, without pausing to celebrate, immediately went back to work on the one across her chest.

The reach was easier this time. Confidence growing, she stretched her arm across her body, fingers searching under the table for the buckle. And, although she was able to reach farther underneath the edge this time, it wasn't there.

Either the fastening was literally under the table or the upper strap had been buckled on the other side. And since the pieces of leather were obviously not original to the table, given its purpose, it was entirely possible Cooley had done exactly that. Diabolically clever in thwarting any attempt to escape? Or simply a chance occurrence that had had the same effect?

After only a few seconds spent trying to make her good arm bend backward into a position only a contortionist could assume, she knew she was going to have to unfasten the buckle with her left hand. The one attached to that damaged wrist.

It isn't broken, she told herself fiercely, dragging the arm across her body. *Bruised. It's only bruised. Ignore the pain. It's only pain. All it means is that you're still alive....*

With the first stretch she knew the truth that litany couldn't hide. At least she could move her fingers, which meant there was hope. Forcing her eyes to focus on the instruments that waited behind the glass doors of the cabinets, she extended her fingers until her vision blurred with tears.

It felt as if she were literally tearing the bones in her wrist

part. She envisioned a crack in them, spreading and then
splintering, but despite the pain, she couldn't quit.

Above her head the footsteps retraced their path, fading
away once more. She was panting now, her terror that he
would come down here before she'd succeeded almost destroying her ability to stay calm and think rationally.

Finally, her desperate fingertips touched the tongue, the
nails of her thumb and forefinger gripping the edge of the
leather and beginning to draw it upward. She tried to count
the seconds between the disappearance of the footsteps and
the time it took to free the hole from the prong. The numbers
wouldn't stay in her head, and so she had no idea of the
passage of time.

At last it released. She closed her eyes, allowing the
strained muscles and tendons to relax, trying to will away
the excruciating pain. After a few seconds, she pushed the
strap off her body with her right hand.

Then, using that arm to lift herself, she sat up on the edge
of the table. Her right leg reached for the floor. As she prepared to jump down from the table, she cradled her damaged
forearm against her stomach.

It was farther than she had anticipated. Weak-kneed, she
staggered when her feet hit the floor. The air thinned and
then blackened around her head. She leaned against the table,
panting again, waiting for the vertigo to subside.

When it had, she pushed away from the table, her eyes
searching for an exit. There had to be some other way out.
Other than the stairs which led to the house above, which
were clearly illuminated by the light that came from the top.
It seemed to lure her toward them. *Some other way,* she told
herself, eyes examining the shadowed corners.

Apparently, the basement had been only partially finished.
Most of it was only a darkly yawning crawl space. She considered hiding there, but eventually he would find her. Or, if
there was no other exit, he might lock the door at the top of
the stairs, leaving her here to die. Alone. And in the dark.

She drew a long, deep breath, fighting that lifelong fear,

as she continued to examine her surroundings. Beyond th
last of the cabinets, far from the bulb at the top of the stair
a fainter light filtered into the dimness.

Still cradling her arm against her body, she ran toward i
There was a narrow passage between the last cabinet and th
wall, which led into the other half of the basement.

High on the opposite wall was a window. It had bee
morning when they'd entered Cooley's house, and yet ther
was only a smudged grayness coming through the glass. Sh
hurried toward it, wondering again how long she had bee
unconscious.

When she was close enough, however, she realized th
sunlight was blocked by a decades-long accumulation c
grime. Given the pristine conditions of the rest of the hous
she knew that had to be deliberate. Someone might questic
why a basement window was boarded, but who would que:
tion why it wasn't clean.

She looked for something to climb up on. And when sh
found it, she struggled to drag a wooden crate, one-hande
across the concrete floor. It made too much noise, but sh
couldn't help that. She had to get out of the house and g
help. It was their only hope.

She pushed the box against the wall and stepped up on i
With her right hand, she scrubbed at the dirt, exposing
small area of glass that looked out on the driveway.

Cooley's car was still there, the trunk standing open. Sh
couldn't see hers. She enlarged the area she was looking o
of, allowing her to see more of the drive, but her car wa
definitely gone. It had been moved from where she'd parke
it. He had hidden her car, just as he would hide their bodie
And then no one would ever know.

She straightened, running her fingers around the edge c
the window, looking for the latch. When she found it, sh
pushed it upward, relieved that it moved as smoothly as if
were kept well-oiled and frequently used. Then she shove
at the sash, trying to slide it up.

Unlike the lock, however, it resisted. Dreading the pai

he forced her other hand up, adding its feeble strength to the effort. Still the window wouldn't budge.

Too many coats of paint, she thought. All that meticulously painted trim. She ran her fingers along the edge of the frame, encountering not the multiple layers of paint as she'd expected, but a line of small, round depressions. Despairing, she traced their pattern, reinforcing what she had known instantly. The bastard had nailed the window shut, countersinking the nails, so there was no way they could be removed.

She sagged against the wall in defeat, leaning her forehead against the window. The glass was cool, temptingly soothing against her throbbing head, but she couldn't stay here. She had to do something. She had no choice but to keep trying until he came for her.

As if on cue, she heard the sound she had been dreading—and expecting—since she had awakened and realized where she was. The door at the top of the stairs opened with a small, revealing creak. And then the plodding, deliberate footsteps she had listened to crossing back and forth above her head started down the basement steps.

CHAPTER EIGHTEEN

SHE MADE A QUICK, despairing survey of her surrounding, looking for some kind of weapon. There was nothing in th part of the basement but the crate she had shoved under th window. And it was too heavy to pick up. Besides, othe than throwing it at Cooley, she couldn't imagine how sh could use it.

Hide, her mind screamed. She had done that before, an she had survived. *She* had survived, but he had gone on t kill another child, another little girl, exactly as he had kille Mary. And now there was no one else left to stop him. N one else who knew what a monster he was.

And so, instead of cowering in another nightmare corne she ran back toward the section of the basement where Coo ley had set up his morgue. There would be something i those glass-fronted cabinets she could use against him.

Just before she rounded the corner formed by those cab nets, the measured footsteps stopped. Either Cooley ha reached the bottom of the stairs or he had come down ther far enough to see she was no longer strapped to the table.

Or maybe he had heard *her* footsteps, running back towar the room where he'd left her. Maybe he was waiting in ther for her.

She didn't care if he was. She had only one thought in he mind. One goal. She was going to do now what she had bee incapable of doing twenty-six years ago.

As she came through the narrow opening, she glanced to ward the stairs and then around the perimeter of the room There was no sign of Cooley.

Which doesn't mean he isn't here, she thought, trembling ngers opening the first of the glass doors.

Her eyes traced over the array of implements, a confusing ssortment of saws and scalpels and plier-like instruments he didn't recognize, all laid out in neat rows on metal trays. Ier hand hovered over them, hesitating. And then it darted orward, her fingers closing over one of them. Clutching her hoice, she had begun to turn when he hit her.

It was that aborted motion which saved her. The downward hop of his hand, aimed at her neck, landed on her shoulder nstead. The shock was so great that for a second or two she vas almost paralyzed. Then, completing the movement she'd egun, she drew her elbow as far back as she could, until it anged hard against the cabinet behind her.

She drove her hand forward again, plunging the scalpel he held into the soft, yielding belly of Everett Cooley. He agged against her, and she fought the urge to pull the blade ree in order to get away from him. Instead, she used every unce of willpower and a lifelong rage to push it deeper.

He moaned, and she felt a rush of exhilaration. She had urt him. She had hurt the bastard. Vindication, however mall, for all the years of fear and survivor's guilt she'd suf-ered.

Then, like a wounded animal, Cooley roared an inarticulate xpression of his own rage. He threw up his arms and stag-ered backward. She didn't have time to release her hold on ae handle of the scalpel. When he moved back, it slid out f his stomach.

Almost reflexively, Callie looked down at the blade. There vas no blood on its shining surface. It seemed as clean as vhen she had selected it from the metal tray.

Despair welled, replacing that momentary exhilaration. It vas as if he truly were a creature from some nightmare. In-incible and indestructible.

With an infuriated scream, she rushed at him, the scalpel eld low, her fingers wrapped around its handle, positioned

exactly as they had been when she'd first picked it up. Sh
drove the blade into his stomach again.

As she did, she finally realized that his bulk made that are
less vulnerable than many others. She should have repos
tioned the weapon, driving it downward, into his neck or hi
chest instead.

It was too late now. She drew back her hand, determine
to strike again. He raised his arm to ward her off, and the
the intent of the gesture changed, becoming a blow. Awk
wardly aimed, the back of his hand struck the side of he
head, knocking her away as if he were swatting aside a
annoying insect.

The force of it was powerful enough to send her stumblin
into the cabinets behind her. She careened off them, and h
hit her again, using his fist this time, the blow coming fror
the opposite direction.

It struck her temple, almost exactly where he had hit he
with the stool. Her head snapped back, recoiling with enoug
force to crack the glass in the door behind her.

His fingers closed around the wrist of the hand in whic
she held the scalpel, banging it again and again against th
thin pane of glass in the other door until it shattered. As he
fist broke through, one of the shards that had remained in th
frame sliced open the skin on the back of her hand, and th
blade fell from her fingers.

Holding her wrist with one hand, Cooley reached behin
her, driving his other through the panel her head had starre
Glass fell noisily over the metal trays and the instrumen
they held. And suddenly, with that sound, she understoo
what he was doing.

The image of that grisly array of blades behind her flashe
through her mind. She surged forward, pushing the old ma
back, trying to drive him away from them. Trying to pu
those deadly instruments out of his reach.

The element of surprise succeeded, at least briefly. Sh
managed to get her forearm up, positioning it under his chi

In spite of the near-electric shock from the impact on the broken bone in her wrist, she shoved his head back.

And then, as he had before, he roared, charging forward and driving her back into the tall cabinet, which teetered dangerously. Again his hand reached behind her, grabbing for something on its shelves.

She could see his face, lips drawn back from yellowed teeth, a sheen of sweat on his smoothly shaven cheeks. She could even smell him. Soap. Aftershave. Toothpaste. A murderer on his way to church.

Fury at the success of his long deception gave her renewed strength. Once more, she managed to push him back an inch or two, but he was better prepared this time.

He rushed forward, his bulk overpowering her. He slammed her body against the cabinet behind her. There was a loud report, as it tilted and then went over, carried backward by their combined weights.

It landed on the concrete floor with a crash. The glass doors at her back shattered completely. And as the cabinet collapsed, she fell into it, with Cooley on top of her.

Stunned, she lay unmoving for a second or two, held immobile by his weight. She opened her eyes—face-to-face with the horror from her nightmares. Her forearm was still beneath his chin, holding his head up, his face only inches from hers.

His eyes were glazed. Staring. Even in the dim light it was obvious that the pupils were dilated and fixed.

She waited for him to move, adrenaline-driven blood rushing and throbbing in her ears. There was no other sound. The only smell was the scent of mildew. And as they lay together in a bizarre lovers' tableau, the dust from the cabinet's landing swirled and drifted and finally began to settle around them.

"YOU'RE OKAY," Ben said again, while he held her, rocking her back and forth as if she were a child.

They were huddled together on the basement stairs. Shell-shocked. Unable to move. Unable to do anything other than struggle to comprehend that they were still alive. And that the enemy who had haunted both their lives was finally dead.

She hadn't even heard Ben's shot. Or if she had, she hadn't recognized it for what it was. And only now was she beginning to understand the near impossibility of what he had done.

Just as the cabinet had begun to topple, Ben had fired the hunting rifle he'd taken from Doc's collection. And despite the effects of whatever drug Doc had injected into his arm, he had managed to hit a moving target in the dimly lit basement.

He had been afraid that he might hit her. That was the first thing he'd told her after he'd pulled the old man's body off, freeing her physically from its burden.

Cooley's death had freed her from the rest. She had been three years old when Mary was murdered. Although she had blocked the memory in order to survive, apparently she had never forgotten the events of that night. They had colored almost every aspect of her life since.

"We have to call Doak," Ben said.

"I know," she whispered.

She didn't want to move from his arms, and yet she wanted out of here. Out of the darkness. Away from the smell. Away from Cooley's stiffening body. Away from his private morgue where, she now believed, he had brought Kay-Kay that night.

"Come on," Ben said, using the stair railing to pull himself up. He reached down, taking her elbow, but she gasped as he touched her arm. He released it immediately. "What's wrong?"

"My wrist. I put it up when he swung that stool at my head. Reflex action. I think it cracked a bone."

"Probably saved your life," Ben said, stooping beside her to put his arm around her waist instead.

He was right. The stool had still hit hard enough to cause a concussion. And if she hadn't partially deflected it...

"Worth a broken bone," she said, glancing up at him.

He looked as bad as she felt. The pupils of his eyes were wide and dark. The light shining down on them from the top of the stairs illuminated his face, gray under the tan.

"I can't believe it's finally over," she said.

She couldn't. Although the pace at which events had unfolded since she'd arrived in Point Hope had been frenetic, it seemed she had lived with this nightmare forever.

Ben used his thumb to wipe something off her cheek. She wasn't sure if it was blood or tears, or maybe a smear of dirt. And she didn't care. She did care very much, she had found, about what that gesture conveyed.

"What now?" she asked, fighting the ache in her throat.

"We get the authorities in here. And then—" He shook his head, his eyes moving to the room at the foot of the stairs. "This is going to devastate this town."

It would. Everett Cooley had been more than a respected member of his community. He had been venerated. Worshipped.

"At least it's closure," she said. "For you. For Kay-Kay. Even for Lorena. Her husband's been exonerated. And so has she, I suppose. There were always people who thought she had something to do with her daughter's death."

"Maybe she did," Ben said, his eyes still focused below. "Just not in the way they thought."

"What does that mean?"

"Doc said she played us *all* for fools."

"I don't understand."

Perhaps it was the trauma they had been through, but there was too much of this she still didn't understand. Maybe, with Cooley dead, they would never know all the details.

"I've been trying to figure out what he meant," Ben said. "And now, I guess there's only one person left who can tell us."

LORENA DELACROIX'S eyes widened when she opened the front door and saw him standing on her porch. Ben knew

Doak had called her early this afternoon to give her the news about Doc, but it had taken him all day to get a chance to come over here.

By the time he had taken Callie to the hospital in Baldwin County and had waited for the results from the CT, the morning had been gone. Because of the severity of her concussion, the doctors had decided to keep her overnight for observation.

Knowing she was in good hands, Ben had spent the afternoon helping with the search of Doc's house and doing some of the paperwork on what had happened. He had lost track of time, but it must be pretty late because Lorena was already undressed.

The robe she was wearing was nothing like the ones his mother used to wear, Ben acknowledged bitterly. The material of this one was thin and silky. Obviously expensive. And it managed to cling in all the right places.

Despite the hour, Lorena's hair and makeup were still carefully in place. He shouldn't be surprised at that attention to her appearance, even given the news she'd received today. Since she'd married Tom Delacroix, Lorena had taken pains to live up to that image of old money. At least, to her version of it.

The shock in her eyes when she recognized him lasted only a few seconds before it changed into something that looked suspiciously like satisfaction.

"I guess somebody warned you," she said.

Ben had come to demand an explanation for Doc's comment. He couldn't make sense of what she'd just said or of that smirk, not in context with the events of today. "Warned me about what?"

His head still ached from whatever Doc had given him. He couldn't remember the last time he'd gotten more than a couple of hours of uninterrupted sleep or had anything to eat. And when he did—remembering also the way Callie's mouth had tasted, sweet and cold from the peach cobbler—that memory didn't make him any more willing to put up with Lorena's poisonous tongue.

"I've already told the media how you sat on information you knew would exonerate us," she said. "And that it wasn't until Callie Evers came down here and called your hand that you did anything about it. That's gonna be included in every headline trumpeting the news that you finally caught Kay-Kay's murderer. So don't think you're going to come out of this with anything to your credit, Ben Stanton."

"I was wrong about Tom. I've admitted that publicly," he said, feeling his anger build. He didn't know yet how much of that was justified and how much was the result of the stresses of the last twenty-four hours. "But maybe if you'd told me the truth from the beginning, I might not have come to the wrong conclusion about your husband."

There was something in her eyes, a flicker of surprise or of fear. It was quickly controlled. And then they were again hard. And very cold.

"I don't know what the hell you're talking about," she said, "but I'm not interested in hearing your excuses. It's over, Ben. This is a done deal. There's nothing you can do to stop it."

She began to close the door, but at the gloating expression on her face, something snapped inside him. He put his hand flat against one of the imported leaded-glass panels and shoved it inward, hard enough that she was forced to step back, her eyes widening once more.

"You told me Kay-Kay was my daughter, but that was a lie, wasn't it?" he demanded. "You lied to me, just like you lied to Tom. I'm here to find out what lie you told Doc."

The blood drained from her face, leaving two spots of color on her cheeks. And the emotion this time wasn't hard to read.

"I don't know what you're talking about."

"Before he died, Doc said you played us *all* for fools. I got to thinking about what he might have meant. And that made me remember a couple of nights when I saw Doc's car

in your driveway. Him and Tom being friends, I didn't think
too much about it. But his car was here at least one night
when I knew Tom was out of town. I remember thinking at
the time that was strange. Wondering what Doc was doing
here so late."

"Everett Cooley was my personal *physician.*"

"And he was also your lover," Ben said, the words distinct. He couldn't prove that, but given what they had found
at Doc's—

"How dare you?" Lorena said. Her breasts heaved under
the thin robe.

"I've got the pictures." Seeing her face as that registered
was almost satisfaction enough to make up for what she had
done to them all, Ben thought. Almost enough. "They're
evidence now," he went on, "but when it's all over, you
may be able to get them back. Or maybe your lawyer can."

She swallowed, the movement strong enough that he could
trace it down the smooth line of her throat. "Evidence?"

"The thing is those aren't the only pictures Doc took," he
said, showing her no mercy. He wasn't feeling merciful right
now. Not with Callie in the hospital, and Lorena calling the
media to do all she could to blacken his name. "Did you
know about the others? Quite a hobby old Doc had."

"I don't have any idea what you're talking about," she
said, pushing the door toward him. His hand on the glass
stopped it.

"I'm talking about the pictures he took of your daughter."

There was again that telltale flicker in her eyes before she
said, "Kay-Kay was very photogenic. A *lot* of people took
pictures of her. People loved her."

"Except Doc loved her a little too much. And he had kind
of a strange way of showing it. By the way, the pictures he
took of Kay-Kay are a lot more revealing than the ones he
took of you."

She hadn't known. That, too, was obvious in her eyes. She
looked like he'd felt when they found them. And of course
the ones of Kay-Kay weren't the only ones they'd found.

That's what Doc had been doing while Ben had been lying unconscious on his office floor. He'd emptied everything from those secret files into his battered black medical bag, the one he carried with him wherever he went. They had found it sitting on the front seat of his car.

They would never know what he intended to do after he'd backed up all that pornography. *And* after he had taken care of him and Callie. Was he going to leave town this time? "Retire" somewhere. Or was he just destroying the evidence of his hobby in case anyone got suspicious when they found the bodies.

"Every time I took her in to see him I stayed in the room," Lorena said. "He never asked me to leave. There's no way—"

"And when she went on those hunting trips with him and Tom? To the beach. Or how about the time they took her to Disney World? There are pictures of all those, too. Daddy's little darling, invited along everywhere the two of them went."

"If you're trying to suggest that Tom—"

"I'm *suggesting* that Tom was dead drunk almost every night. You *knew* that. And that's when that sick old man—"

"Stop it," she demanded, turning away. "Just...stop it."

"You told Doc she was his daughter, too, didn't you? And then when he found out from Tom that you'd told me the same thing, he figured out that you'd not only been two-timing Tom, but you'd been two-timing him as well."

She looked back at him then, a sickness to match his own in her eyes. "Tom told him?" She shook her head, her eyes distant, unfocused. "You'd think a man wouldn't want *any-body* to know something like that. I never dreamed Tom would—"

"What the hell kind of game were you playing, Lorena?"

Her chin almost quivered, but at the last second, she lifted it, her lips tightening before she opened them to spit the words at him. "I was tired of being married to a drunk."

"Then you get a divorce," he said coldly. "You don't

play with people's lives." And finally it hit him—why she hadn't done that. The piece of the puzzle that had been missing. "Except you couldn't get a divorce. If you did, you'd have to give all this up. Tom's lawyers made you sign a prenup. You divorce him, you get nothing. You leave Tom, and you're screwed.

"*Unless,* of course," he went on, realizing some of it only as he talked, "you can find somebody who's able to support you in the style to which Tom's money had made you accustomed. And Doc and I were the logical candidates. You'd slept with both of us, near enough to the right time. You figured your daughter was a pretty good bargaining chip. And we both had money. In my case, the possibility of it, at least. Only something went wrong. It didn't quite work out the way you planned."

Ben hadn't bitten on the bait. He would have done right by his daughter, but he would never have married Lorena.

"I must have been the backup. Doc was obviously the one you were really after. Richer than me. And older. Not as long to live. Only he didn't bite either. So…what went wrong, Lorena? You can tell me or you can tell a grand jury. I think one will probably be convened to look into your role in your daughter's death."

"You wouldn't do that," she said.

He couldn't, but he could tell she wasn't completely sure of it. And having any of this come out would destroy the social position she wanted so desperately to maintain here in Point Hope. She was too stupid to know there wasn't one.

"You just try me, Lorena. Believe me, I'd love to drag you through the same cesspool Doc dragged this town through."

There was a long silence before she said, "He wanted a paternity test."

"And you couldn't afford that," he said, "because it might prove the very thing you didn't want it to. That Kay-Kay *wasn't* Doc's. So instead, you told me, and then you told Tom, that *I* was Kay-Kay's father, hoping I'd offer to marry you when he asked for a divorce. Only that didn't work out quite the way you planned it either. And two days later, she was dead."

"It wasn't my fault," she said. "Kay-Kay's death had nothing to do with—"

"You broke his heart, Lorena. Tom loved that little girl more than his own life, and you told him she wasn't his. So Tom got drunk and cried on his best friend's shoulder, and then Doc knew you'd been lying to him, too."

"It doesn't mean that that's why—"

"No, it doesn't," he agreed before she could finish. "Maybe Kay-Kay was getting old enough that he knew what he'd been doing was dangerous. Or maybe he'd reached a point were he couldn't stop. I suspect we'll find some others who'll come forward once this comes out. Or maybe," he added softly, "maybe Everett Cooley just knew you better than the rest of us."

Her eyes came up at that. Filled with moisture, they were starkly revealing.

"Maybe he knew the best way to get back at you for lying to him. You were playing us all for fools," Ben said, repeating the old man's words. "And if there was anything Doc didn't like, it was being played for a fool. He wouldn't like it at all that somebody like you had tried to put something over on him.

"So he figured out how to get back at you and to protect himself at the same time. He killed the only thing, besides yourself, that you've ever loved. He killed your little girl because of what you did to him. And that's something you're going to have to live with, Lorena, for the rest of your life."

EPILOGUE

SHE HAD ASKED the nurse to leave the light on, but when she opened her eyes, there was only darkness. She turned her head, locating the closed door by its thin rim of light.

By that time, she was awake enough to realize she wasn't alone in the bed. And to know who was lying beside her.

She laid her cheek against Ben's chest, breathing in the scent of his body. The clean, laundry-starched fragrance of his shirt was such a pleasant contrast to the medicinal smell of the hospital, which had been too reminiscent of Cooley's office.

Afraid she'd wake him, she resisted the urge to put her fingers over the muscle that rose and fell with reassuring regularity. Her lips lifted, wondering how he'd managed this. Wondering, too, about the reaction of the nurses who would be coming by for those hourly observations.

And then, deciding she didn't care about either, she settled more closely against his chest, curling her hand beneath her chin. She had already closed her eyes when she felt him stir.

"You okay?" he asked, his voice rumbling under her ear.

"What are you doing here?" she asked.

She allowed her fingers to touch his chin. It was obvious he'd recently shaved. Bathed. Changed clothes. And then he had driven all the way back to the hospital to lie down beside her.

"Couldn't sleep," he said.

She thought about the possibility that that was really why he was here, at least briefly, before she challenged it.

"Seriously," she demanded, and felt the depth of the breath he took before he answered her.

"I knew I'd feel better if I were with you."

She examined the words, deciding she liked the sound of them, whatever they meant. They lay without speaking for a few minutes, only the faint nighttime noises from the corridor beyond that closed door intruding on the relaxed silence.

"Did you talk to Lorena?"

"Yeah, and before you ask, you really *don't* want to know."

"I want to know why he killed them," she said reasonably. "I need to know that before... Maybe before I can let it all go. It shouldn't matter, I know, but..."

"He was a sick old man," Ben said, the words clipped and harsh. "Leave it at that, Callie."

"He *wasn't* an old man when he killed my sister."

More silence, less comfortable this time. She understood why Ben didn't want to talk about this, but it was there between them. It always would be. At least until she understood.

"He liked adulation," Ben said, his voice flat as if he were reciting a lesson. "Adoring patients, like Phoebe and Virginia. Kids like me who had grown up looking up to him. He liked doing the pro bono stuff, those free summer clinics he organized within the reserves. He especially liked it if it got him recognition. And it did. Community leader. Church deacon. The wise and benevolent physician, who also had a fondness for white-haired, angelic-looking little girls. The younger the better."

"There were others," Callie whispered, sickness moving into her throat at the thought.

"Dozens, but none that he murdered, as far as we know."

"Then...why? Why them? Why the two of them?"

"Kay-Kay to get back at Lorena, although..."

"Although what?"

He shook his head, the small familiar motion that didn't denote denial. "We'll probably never know why he killed

Mary. Maybe he couldn't resist touching her. Maybe she threatened to tell what he'd done. And he would know your father was someone who couldn't be bought off or intimidated into keeping quiet.''

An uncannily accurate assessment. Based, she supposed, on what she had told him about her father's insistence that the doors to the house had all been locked that night.

And her father would have been thrilled to be involved in something like the clinics Cooley had organized. He would have seen them as a wonderful boon for his poorest parishioners. He might very well have taken Mary with him when he carried the other children from his church to see the visiting doctors.

He loved to show off his girls. With that memory, the first she had allowed herself in a very long time about that sweet, gentle man, her eyes filled with tears.

"I don't know how Doc got into your house that night. Maybe Mary let him in. Maybe he told her he was going to bring by a special gift for your father's birthday. I know Kay-Kay opened the door to him. He might have thrown a pebble against her window, and seeing Doc outside, she would have gone down and let him in. And then he could have taken her wherever he wanted. She loved him, and he was always good to her," he said, his voice bitter with the knowledge of the price Katherine Delacroix had ultimately paid for Cooley's favors. "With Mary…"

His voice faded, and Callie waited through the stillness, seeing that circling bulb again. Enclosed in his arms, and with Cooley dead, the power it had over her had lessened.

"Maybe he never intended to kill Mary," Ben went on. "I don't know what went wrong. Maybe she cried out, and he thought he had to make her stop…"

The halting words touched a chord of memory buried so deeply in her mind no clear image surfaced to accompany it, not like her father's face had done. That explanation *felt* right.

Mary *had* cried out. She had struggled and fought. Then

he had gone very still. And when the light circled again, hat man had been bending over her.

"And then he never did it again? Not in all those years? s that possible?"

"Doc was all about control. When they opened the new outpatient clinic, he moved his practice there. They wanted him. Enticed him. It didn't last more than a couple of months because he couldn't stand not being in charge. He couldn't run things the way he wanted them run. Eventually he retired, raised his garden and kept his parents' house exactly as it was when he was a boy."

"It doesn't make sense, not that he could kill two little girls, and then…nothing."

"He valued the community's good opinion of him. He couldn't bear to lose that. Besides, he probably viewed what he had done to Mary as an accident. Maybe it was. At least her death. Maybe he never intended to kill her."

"And Kay-Kay? Are you suggesting that was an accident, too? And what he tried to do to me?"

"You endangered everything he'd worked for his whole life."

"Because I could tie him to Mary."

Ben had told her that was the key. She had been a threat because she had a connection to the murder in North Carolina.

"How did he know?" she asked. "The first time, out in the bay, he hadn't even seen me yet. And I hadn't told Virginia and Phoebe about Mary. I hadn't told anyone but you. How could he possibly *know* I was that threat?"

"Callie," Ben said softly.

For a second or two, she thought he was giving her a warning that he didn't want to talk about this anymore. And then…

"He recognized my name."

"Phoebe would have told him all about her new guest and where she was from. She always told him everything. Your name was unusual enough that he put two and two together.

He'd been waiting, all these years, for something like that to happen. Waiting for someone to show up who could connect him to Mary.''

"Then why follow the same pattern with Kay-Kay's murder? Why draw the rose on her neck? Why bathe her?"

"The same reasons he did those things in the first place. Because there are compulsions that are stronger than logic. Or the intellect. And remember, if I hadn't seen that rose..."

Cooley hadn't included it in the autopsy report or the pictures, of course. He didn't know Ben had seen it. And if Ben hadn't, no one would ever have known it was there.

"Virginia knew about the clinic," she guessed.

"A lot of people knew. She called Doc that morning, by the way. I don't know that she'd really put it all together, or if she just said something that made him afraid she might. It might not even have been the clinic. Phoebe and Hobart may have asked Doc to go to Bragg. He was there, in the same state. It would have been reasonable. Maybe that's what Virginia remembered."

And what Phoebe had thought of? Callie wondered, remembering those trembling hands clasped beneath the old woman's breasts as she had talked about never being sure about the right thing to do. Was it possible Phoebe had been trying to decide whether she should implicate an old friend in something so terrible she must surely have believed he couldn't have had any role in it?

"Poor Phoebe," she whispered.

"A lot of people aren't going to be able to believe it was Doc, no matter what we turn up. Cooley was a hero to the people of this town. Somebody they looked up to. Somebody they loved."

The word seemed to echo in the darkness. *It's called making love.* Ben had said that last night. Making love.

"So...what now?" she asked.

He didn't answer for a long time. Long enough that she turned her head, looking up at him for the first time. His eyes were focused on the ceiling.

"There'll be a lot of media interest. That's already started. Lorena's been helping it along, but...I suspect she'll back off now. Things will eventually die down again. An unsolved murder is always more interesting than a solved one."

"They'll want to know about Mary," she said, beginning to realize the implications of the media's interest for her.

"And about your father's suicide. About you."

"God," she said, the word low.

There was another silence.

"I've got a boat," he reminded her.

Despite the things they had talked about tonight, there was something in his tone that made her smile. He turned his head, leaning back a little in the narrow bed so he could see her face.

"Are you offering me an escape?" she asked.

"I'm offering..." He hesitated, and she felt the breath he took before he said, "I'm offering whatever you're willing to accept."

Whatever you're willing to accept. "That's a pretty open-ended invitation," she said, smiling at him.

"Yes, it is."

He hadn't answered the smile. His eyes seemed very blue in the dimness. After a moment, she shook her head.

"I'm not exactly sure..."

Suddenly, in the face of that steady regard, she ran out of words. If they were monitoring her heart rate, someone from the nurse's station would probably be in here fairly soon.

"You don't have to be," Ben said. "I'm not *sure* either, but...I want us to try. Maybe we'll find out that we don't even like each other—"

"No," she said. "No, we won't."

"There's been nothing even slightly normal about our relationship. Almost nothing normal," he amended, the stern line of his mouth relaxing.

"Yes," she said.

"Yes?"

"Yes. Whatever."

"Dammit," he said. "You're crying again."

"No, I'm not," she denied. "I'm just tired. Concussed. [
have a cracked ulna. But I'm *not* crying."

"A cracked what?"

"Ulna. It's the smaller bone in—" She stopped, becau
even in this light she could read the laughter in his eyes.

"Just checking," he said. "I didn't want there to be an
nasty surprises once I get you onboard."

"I think we've had our share of nasty surprises."

"Enough to last a lifetime," Ben agreed.

In a way, this had been far harder on him than on her. Be
had freely admitted his lifelong admiration of the old man

She, on the other hand, had succeeded in what she ha
come here to do, although the effects had been more fa
reaching than she could have imagined. The only thing th
had happened like she'd imagined it...

"So where are we going on this boat of yours?" she aske

"Some extremely secluded beach. Despite all the deve
opment, there are still plenty of them along the coast. (
maybe an inlet on the bay."

"Like the one where we were last night."

"Maybe," he said. He leaned forward and put his li
against her forehead. "Or maybe we need to stay closer
civilization for a day or two. Until we're sure you're okay.

"I'm okay. At least I will be..." She hesitated, the con
mitment too new, almost too tenuous for that confession.

"Me, too," he said. "Maybe that inlet's a pretty goc
idea. We lie low there until this dies down again...."

She waited a long time before she asked, "And the
what?"

"I don't know how you feel about Point Hope, but.
despite everything, it really isn't a bad place to live." H
throat closed against the promise of that, so that she couldr
answer him for a moment. "Unless there's something
someone waiting for you in North Carolina?" he added whe
she didn't respond.

Only memories. All of them ones she didn't want. She wanted new ones. And the best possibility of making those...

"Nobody's waiting for me. Not back there."

"Footloose and fancy-free," he said, lips nuzzling her hair.

She smiled a little at the nice, old-fashioned sound of that phrase. And then she told him the final secret she had kept. Because she thought he needed to know.

"There *was* a man once..." she began, but her throat closed again as she thought how near this reality had come to her expectations. Not many people in this world could say that.

"A man?" he repeated. He had gone very still, even his breathing suspended. "Somebody I should know about?"

"I knew him only from his pictures. From some newspaper clippings. Stories about how long he had tried to find the murderer of a little girl. How much he cared. And I think I knew even then, that if there was anybody in the world... I came here to find *you*," she said, "because I knew you were the one person who would help me find Mary's killer, but...I think I also knew, even then..."

"Callie," he said, and this time she knew what he meant.

She turned her head, looking up to smile at him again. Instead, his mouth closed over hers, his tongue invading with the sweet mastery she remembered. Far more powerful than any of her expectations.

SILHOUETTE® INTRIGUE™

AVAILABLE FROM 15TH NOVEMBER 2002

LASSITER'S LAW Rebecca York

Mine To Keep from *43 Light St*

Private eye Sam Lassiter easily found Laurel Coleman, the errant nanny who'd allegedly kidnapped her young charge. But she seemed far from dangerous and the innocence of her kiss pulled Sam into a vortex of emotion. Events forced him to take her on the run—but this time he faced his deadliest enemy…

HOWLING IN THE DARKNESS BJ Daniels

Moriah's Landing

Undercover agent Jonah Ries knew that someone was trying to harm vulnerable beauty Katherine Ridgemont. And even if she turned away from him when he revealed his dark secret, he would still fight to save the woman he loved from the unknown enemy, hiding in the night…

GUARDING JANE DOE Harper Allen

The Avengers

Burned out soldier-for-hire Quinn McGuire agreed to protect Jane Doe from a madman who claimed she'd committed cold-blooded murder. Which would be his greatest challenge—convincing her that she was innocent or finding the courage to confess his love?

ANOTHER WOMAN'S BABY Joanna Wayne

Lawman Lovers

Surrogate mother Megan Lancaster hadn't expected pregnancy to bring an FBI hunk stringing lights on her Christmas tree! Still her life was in danger, and agent Bart Cromwell's job was to protect her and her unborn child. Was there any hope that she and Bart could welcome the newborn as a family…for Christmas and forever?

1102/46a

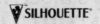

SILHOUETTE® INTRIGUE™

and

HARPER ALLEN

present

THE AVENGERS

**BOUND BY THE TIES THEY FORGED AS SOLDIERS
OF FORTUNE, THESE AGENTS FEARLESSLY PUT
THEIR LIVES ON THE LINE FOR A WORTHY
CAUSE. BUT NOW THEY'RE ABOUT TO FACE
THEIR GREATEST CHALLENGE—LOVE!**

December 2002
GUARDING JANE DOE

February 2003
SULLIVAN'S LAST STAND

April 2003
THE BRIDE AND THE MERCENARY

1202/SH/LC48

FREE!

2 Books
and a surprise gift!

We would like to take this opportunity to thank you for reading this Silhouette® book by offering you the chance to take TWO more specially selected titles from the Intrigue™ series absolutely FREE! We're also making this offer to introduce you to the benefits of the Reader Service™—

- ★ FREE home delivery
- ★ FREE gifts and competitions
- ★ FREE monthly Newsletter
- ★ Books available before they're in the shops
- ★ Exclusive Reader Service discount

Accepting these FREE books and gift places you under no obligation to buy; you may cancel at any time, even after receiving your free shipment. Simply complete your details below and return the entire page to the address below. **You don't even need a stamp!**

YES! Please send me 2 free Intrigue books and a surprise gift. I understand that unless you hear from me, I will receive 4 superb new titles every month for just £2.85 each, postage and packing free. I am under no obligation to purchase any books and may cancel my subscription at any time. The free books and gift will be mine to keep in any case.

I2ZEB

Ms/Mrs/Miss/Mr ....Initials ....
BLOCK CAPITALS PLEASE

Surname...

Address...

....

....Postcode ....

Send this whole page to:
UK: The Reader Service, FREEPOST CN81, Croydon, CR9 3WZ
EIRE: The Reader Service, PO Box 4546, Kilcock, County Kildare (stamp required)